BEING ALEXANDER

BEING ALEXANDER

Diarmuid Ó Conghaile

NEW ISLAND

BEING ALEXANDER
First published 2013
by New Island
2 Brookside
Dundrum Road
Dublin 14

www.newisland.ie

PRINT ISBN: 978-1-84840-281-2
EPUB ISBN: 978-1-84840-282-9
MOBI ISBN: 978-1-84840-283-6

Typeset by JM InfoTech India
Cover design by Andrew Brown
Printed by Bell & Bain Ltd, Glasgow

New Island received financial assistance from
The Arts Council (An Chomhairle Ealaíon), Dublin, Ireland.

10 9 8 7 6 5 4 3 2 1

Do mo mháthair

Dublin 2003/2004

I

May

Alexander Vespucci notices the texture of being.

He first had this sensation when he was three or so, in wellies and short pants, standing in the oil-stained driveway of their housing-estate house, picking peeling paint off the fence. Peeling paint was a point of entry. And what the boy experienced – but could not then articulate – was that the surface of reality was curved.

The woman next door didn't like him to peel paint off the fence. In fact, she didn't like him at all. You're a gawker, she told him, and she was right. He stared at people, fascinated by their strangeness, inquiring into it; until life taught him that people do not wish to be penetrated in this way, and he learned to tone himself down.

He had this same perception of *existence* on the morning his father was disfigured by death. A phone call at dawn summoned them: Jim was struggling. Alexander – aged eleven – and his mother and sister were driven to the cancer hospital by a kind neighbour. Travelling across town in that man's Citroën, buoyed up by the synthetic spongy upholstery and the space-age plastics, all in beige, Alexander knew already from the heaviness of the atmosphere, from the immanence of the fact in the beige interior itself, that his diseased dad had finally expired, killed gradually over many years through lack of love.

Later, as a disturbed teenager, Alexander struggled to reconcile the reality of infinity with the mousetrap quality of his life. At this stage, he was beginning – in verbal thought – to grope his way toward a description of his despair. Smoking upstairs on the 42 bus from Malahide into Dublin city centre, he pondered the improbability of his ill fortune. Of all the possibilities in time and space, how and why had he ended up in *this* specific body, *this* thick-boned skull, *this* particular configuration of identity and circumstance?

Even now, as a practised adult, an office creature, sitting at the weekly team meeting – which mercifully takes place only every couple of months – *being* affects his concentration. He finds it difficult to listen to the proceedings. People talk and the words shoot past him, their meaning lost. Worse, he sometimes cannot even maintain forms. The humans disappear. He registers arms and torsos, woven fabrics, hair, teeth, chatterings, wheezings, ha ha ha, glinting eyes, heat, grease, scent, the shedding of dead skin cells.

The smooth tabletop narrows as it flees from him, surfing over the assembly of lower limbs, some still, others agitated – jigging, crossing and uncrossing – each pair guarding the contained energy at the associated crotch.

He registers sexual identity, and this brings him back: the exuberance of Luke's zipper; the heavy under-curve of Imelda's breast – so close he could cup it in his palm without having to stretch.

'Is broadband on the agenda?' asks Evil Neville.

Alexander thinks of him as evil because Neville rhymes with devil.

'Could somebody please tell me what broadband means?' asks Imelda, in her thick Mayo accent, following the question with two shots of laughter like a donkey's bray.

Alexander nods to Neville, and Neville does the explaining. Neville likes to talk. He is a small, thin man, well proportioned, with pointy hair and diamond eyes. He was recently recruited as a Graduate Trainee. Imelda is also a Graduate Trainee, but from the previous year. Though she has been longer in the job than Neville, she knows less than he does on every given subject. Imelda is dim.

She came in at the height of the labour shortages, the only candidate for the job, and even then she failed the interview, but was hired through an administrative error.

'We've just completed a survey on broadband availability for small businesses,' Alexander adds wearily when Neville has completed his exposition. 'Myself, Neville and Luke worked on it.'

'It stretches it a bit to suggest there was any effort on our part,' says Luke with a chuckle. 'The consultants designed the survey and carried it out. We just wrote a letter telling them what to do.'

Luke is one of two Analysts.

'It took three of you to write a letter?' asks Dympna, the other Analyst.

This then is the full team: Alexander; two Analysts; two Graduate Trainees.

Before he was promoted to his current lofty position, Alexander imagined it would be a fine thing to be the boss. Now that he actually has staff, he realises that being the boss is just as tedious as not being the boss, but in different ways. In the end, the people he manages mostly just want stuff from him: attention; approval; meaningful work, but not too much of it; development opportunities; days off; tolerance of their mood swings. In return, he is responsible for the shit they turn out and the deadlines they don't care about; plus they constitute an extra set of people he has to avoid if he is late, or hung over, or wishes to disappear early.

'You have to get your letters spot on,' Luke answers Dympna. 'You know yourself how much value-added can be got in five or six rewrites.'

Alexander's attention attaches itself to the stubble on Luke's neck. There is remarkable uniformity in the length and blackness of the emergent bristles, but they change direction where the corner of his jaw meets the slopes of his neck, like a turn in a flock of birds. Alexander has observed that Luke washes and shaves only every second day, which isn't enough.

'We had to conduct a tender procedure,' Alexander says formally, trying to talk up the work. 'Anyhow, yes, broadband is on the Council agenda. The Chairman will take it as the first item on Thursday.'

'Am I ever going to get to a Council meeting?' Neville asks plaintively.

'Not in this life,' Luke snorts.

'I bet they don't even know I exist. It's not very motivating.'

The Council in question is the National Economic Advisory Council, their employer. Its members are eminences from business, government, public life, appointed by the Taoiseach on the basis of the sectional interests they represent, as well as easy cronyism. Alexander and his team are not members of the Council. They form the Council Secretariat. Alexander's boss, George Lucey, is the Secretary to the Council. Alexander is the Senior Economist. They are the only two of the staff who attend the Council meetings. The others are considered too junior. The Chairman doesn't like to have too many minions at the table, because they lower the tone.

'As part of your training, it might be appropriate at some stage in the future for you to have some exposure to a Council meeting,' Alexander says automatically, emptily. 'There would have to be a suitable opportunity. The Chairman is cautious about who attends.'

'You see,' Luke says to Neville. 'I told you so. It's never going to happen.'

'That's not what I said,' Alexander insists. 'Please don't interpret what I say.'

'Somebody has to.'

'I think the point is a valid one,' says Dympna. 'None of us has ever been to a Council meeting.'

'I met the Chairman once,' Imelda says. 'In the lift. Maybe at the next meeting we could all hide under a table and have a peek.'

'OK, that's enough,' Alexander intervenes. 'I know it's Friday afternoon, but let's keep it together for another few minutes. There's one more thing to discuss before we finish. The Accommodation Unit has been on to me to say that we're running up extremely high phone bills. Someone is using the phones – *our* phones – to call astrology lines.'

'Sex lines?' asks Neville, perking up.

'No. Astrology lines. You ring up and they tell you your horo-scope. Or so I'm told. The calls are made mostly at lunchtime, and the cost has now run into hundreds of euro.'

'It could be anybody in the building,' says Dympna, defensively. Alexander thinks she is blushing slightly.

Dympna is in the same age range as Alexander and Luke, which is ten years or so older than Imelda and Neville. She has a baby son at home, whom she adores loudly, and an unemployed husband, whom she likes to boss, in so far as can be discerned from overheard phone calls.

'It's a free-for-all out there, Alexander,' Dympna continues defiantly. 'Anybody can come along and use one of the phones, par- · ticularly if there is no one here at lunchtime.'

What Dympna says is true. Although the Council Secretariat is a little world unto itself, the Department of Finance accommodates the team in a large open-plan area. The Department also provides all their support requirements, such as IT and personnel services.

'Well, I'm not making any allegations,' Alexander says. He avoids looking at Dympna, whom he now suspects. 'Let's just keep our eyes open for any unusual behaviour. It's only *our* phones that are being used, which seems a bit odd.'

After the meeting, Alexander repairs to the long glass window in the corner of his office. It opens like a book, floor to ceiling, swinging inward on vertical hinges on the left-hand side. A cold breeze pushes into the room, sweeping with it the outside wildness of the space beyond. A couple of steps forward and he would drop like a stone to the courtyard five storeys below. A quick death. But how would he feel as he accelerated downward through the air? He is sometimes slightly tempted to jump, but knows that he won't.

Generally these windows cannot be opened. A few weeks ago, the last time the window cleaners came around, a cheerful guy in white overalls forgot to relock it when he had finished wiping the outside pane. Since then, in the late afternoons mostly, Alexander has used this new availability of openness to sneak a smoke, which is otherwise impossible in the smoke-free building. This delicious pleasure reminds him of his youth. He and his elder sister, Helena, his only sibling and his partner in crime, used to smoke out of the windows of her bedroom late at night, looking out onto their suburban rear garden and the backs of the boxy houses opposite, gossiping, joking, slagging off all the things they didn't like, proclaiming the coolness of whatever they admired.

Helena was a rebel then, always getting into fixes. Now she is a lawyer, with a golf-playing husband, two loathsome children, and a house-with-mortgage in Malahide, where she and Alexander grew up. He, by his comparison, is a loser: unmarried, renting, stuck in a job that doesn't pay particularly well and that offers no ready path for advancement.

For years, he thought houses and mortgages were boring, irrelevant; then at some point the subject became very interesting indeed, but by that time he was priced out of the market. Taking together his and his girlfriend's salaries, they could probably just about afford a hovel in some part of the city they would ordinarily find repellent, or a badly built semi-d in a housing estate in a field somewhere, thirty or forty miles from Dublin, with a deadening commute into work, and probably a car-trip even to the nearest village. This is his Housing Problem.

In his trouser pocket his mobile phone vibrates against his thigh. His hand races to answer it before the ring-tone sounds, and almost succeeds. *Paul M M*, reads the screen, which stands for Paul Mooney mobile.

'What are you up to?' Paul asks.

'Reflecting on my good fortune.'

'You've had a change of circumstance then?'

'Not really. I'm just enjoying a cigarette. I'm focusing on the small pleasures.'

'You can tell me all about it later on. Are you guys still OK for tonight?'

'Yes, barring any unforeseen obstacles.'

'See you around eight so. Danny and Aoife are confirmed as well. There's trouble in the camp there, so we could be in for some entertainment.'

Leaving the office on Friday evening is a release to freedom.

With summer newly arrived, fresh and young, Alexander still feels gratitude for the brightness and the comparative warmth. The grass along the canal banks is lush, growing strongly, and the trees – though not yet in full overflow of foliage – are brimming with life. Even the craggy-barked trunks seem infused with potentiality.

The women of the city have shed their winter coats. Their bodies are discernible again in all their splendour: arms and legs, long necks, cleavage – a startling eruption of breasts at every turn. The Great Breast Giveaway, he sometimes internally labels it. The Amazing Breast Extravaganza. And each woman who passes within the scope of his vision is automatically evaluated. The sexual reptile is primitive, tireless, discriminating in its own essentially binary way: fuck; blank; fuck; fuck; blank. The socialised human is cautious, well-behaved, seeking nothing more as it marches homeward than a second glance, an affirmative look.

The canal banks are a breeding ground and social space for all sorts. Alexander passes a group of winos at their ease: three men and a woman, sitting on the grass, drinking cider from sallow two-litre bottles. He can pick out the lord among them, around whom the others have arranged themselves in conscious and unconscious deference. This one is stretched out, propped up on an elbow, enjoying the sunshine on his worn face as he directs the conversation, languidly, but with much swearing.

A hundred yards further, another of their number, or one nearly like them, is screaming into a mobile phone, his body being pushed through contortions by his rage.

'Where are ya? Tell me where are ya! I'll fuckin' burst ya, ya scumbag shitface! Where are ya? Because of you, my bud was nabbed by the pigs. Now he's banged up in Pearse Street. Where the fuck are ya?'

Alexander is afraid to get too close to this event. Before he is within ten yards, he steps with outward calmness onto the road and crosses over to the opposite pavement. The screamer has come upon a galvanised steel lamp-post and is smashing the phone against it. Within a few bangs there are pieces of plastic flying in different directions. Moving out of range, knowing that he is safe, unnoticed, Alexander allows himself to gloat a little at this self-harm: That's not very clever, he thinks.

His own phone rings. It's his sister.

'I'm suddenly highly popular,' he says. 'You're my second call this month.'

'Where are you now?'

'Walking home, reflecting on winos and their mobile phones.'

'Winos have mobile phones?'

'So it seems; though not for long. . . . Hey, that's not very politically correct of you: winos need connectivity just like everybody else.'

'Listen, I'm ringing about Maisie. She fell down a steep stairs in the nursing home. She has severe concussion. She's comatose. It happened this afternoon, and they've moved her to the hospital. Mum rang me about ten minutes ago.'

'Is she going to die?'

'The doctors say she's stable, but that they can't give any assurances, blah, blah, at her age.'

'We should probably go down.'

'Mum and Uncle Mick are already on their way by train. But I don't think it makes sense for me, with the kids and everything. We've got a few things happening this weekend. I mean, if she's not conscious, what's the point?'

On his mother's side, Alexander is one hundred per cent Irish peasant. Maisie is his maternal grand-aunt. She was born Maisie Ryan in 1908 on a forty-acre farm in the townland of Ballyryan, County Galway, about twenty miles outside Galway city. Maisie is now ninety-five and has been living in a nursing home in Galway for the last fifteen years, following an accident in which she slipped on ice in the farmyard and broke her leg.

Maisie is the youngest of six children, three boys and three girls, who were born in that order. The eldest boy died from wounds after the battle of the Somme. There is a half-told family story about the circumstances in which he enlisted. Alexander is vaguely aware that he was a hothead who got into trouble. The next brother was shot dead by the Free State army in the Civil War. The youngest brother lived into his seventies in a regional mental institution, having been committed in the 1950s by Maisie – with the assistance of the local doctor and parish priest – on the grounds of his refusing to go to Mass and not wanting to do any work around the farm.

The girls made a more lasting impression on human affairs. The eldest two emigrated to the States in the mid-1920s and returned in the 1930s, married to Galway men whom they had met in Detroit. The children and grandchildren of the eldest girl are collectively – tribally – known to Alexander as the Gradys. The second girl was Alexander's maternal grandmother, and the clan to which she gave first issue is his own, the Murphys.

Maisie stayed on the farm all her life. She married a local man, whom Alexander knew as Uncle Johnny. They remained childless. Of that generation, everyone is dead now except Maisie; and she being without natural heirs, the state of her health and the condition of her will are matters of keen interest to the Gradys and the Murphys. Forty acres of good land in Ballyryan were always valuable. Back in previous decades, when nearly everyone was still poor, the relatives would have bloodily murdered each other for that land. Nowadays, the need is less urgent, but the appetite is whetted. Greed is up. In monetary terms, the value of the land has surely multiplied in the boom, but it would be difficult to guess a figure, so much being dependent on the right planning permission.

Alexander rings his mother, Brigid. Given the circumstances, he expects her to have her mobile phone switched on, which is not always the case. She answers immediately.

9

'I'm on the train,' she says, her voice loud and the intonation already sliding back into the Galway accent.

'Helena told me about Maisie's fall.'

'Did she fall or was she pushed?' Brigid asks rashly, before switching to a quieter tone. 'I'd better watch what I'm saying. You never know who might be listening. Did I ever tell you the story about the two girls speaking Irish in the lift in the Empire State Building?'

'Why would anybody push her down the stairs?'

'Why do you think? And who do you think? Sure, they've been waiting for that woman to die for twenty years. I always thought it was very suspicious the way Tommy Óg Grady was there the time she fell and broke her leg.'

'He drove her to the hospital!'

'Yes, he did, but maybe he assisted her in falling as well.'

'But wouldn't he know that she would hold such a thing against him?'

'If she knew what happened. There are ways to trip a person.'

'I bow to your greater knowledge of these matters.... How long will you stay in Galway?'

'Two or three days anyway, till I see how she is. Are you going to come down?'

'Not straight away ... if she's stable. I'm busy tonight and tomorrow, and I've a lot on in work over the next few days. I might go down next weekend. I'd like to see her.'

'Why are you so busy at work?'

He can hear the gear shift in his mother's voice. She doesn't really have any interest in his work, or in the other details of his life, but makes inquiries as a matter of course. Sometimes she compensates for her lack of interest by conducting an exaggerated interrogation, question after question, with a minimum of attention to the answers sandwiched in between.

'The Council is meeting next week.'

'What Council?'

'The National Economic Advisory Council. Remember: that's who I work for.'

10

'I always forget. My children have such complicated jobs. Remind me again what you do. I'm sure somebody will ask me in Galway. They'll think I'm an eejit if I don't know.'

'I *do* economics. I advise the government on economic policy.'

'But surely the government would have experts for that sort of thing.'

'Yes, I'm one of the experts.'

'But, sure, what would you know about it?'

'About what?'

'About running the country.'

'Very little.'

'That's my point.'

'I'm agreeing with your point. . . . Listen, I'd better go. Call me if anything happens.'

Alexander and Julia live in a large dingy basement flat in Rathmines. When they first moved in, which – astonishingly – is eight years ago now, Julia thought it was cool and alternative. She had just broken up with her playwright boyfriend – an interim affair – and it was important to her to maintain some artistic credibility. She baulked at the idea of the small modern apartment that Alexander suggested at the time. In the years that followed, her views have gradually changed. Recently she has professed a hatred for the flat.

'We live in a hole,' she declared a few months ago when they were out with friends of hers.

At the time, Alexander winced at this observation because it made a hole of their home. Later he was angry, believing that she was criticising him for not being able to provide them with better accommodation. In truth, he is fairly sick of the place himself. What before was a den of spaciousness, a lovers' private palace, has become simply ugly.

The house itself is a fine Victorian redbrick on a quiet tree-lined road. The entrance to the basement is through a creaky wrought-iron gate and down a set of steps into a little yard that he and Julia populated with a few potted plants in the early days of their domestic enthusiasm. Most of the plants are unkempt and thirsty-looking now,

11

competing with weeds for whatever is available in the dry cracked soil. It is a cheerless assembly, apart from the resilient gorse bush, which is still in good bloom, though past its peak.

He opens the door, enters the dark low-ceilinged hallway and performs his routine of taking off his shoes and dropping them into the cupboard, along with his briefcase, from which he first removes the newspaper. Having switched to summer mode, he is wearing no overcoat. He takes off his suit jacket and carries it with him into the main room of the flat, where Julia is sitting on the sofa under the front window, flicking through a fashion magazine.

He hates her magazines, thinks they are akin to pornography, and has never been able to get used to them.

The overhead light is on. The front of the house faces north, so this room always requires artificial illumination, although there is a point on a clear summer afternoon when dazzling sunlight bounces in from an upper-storey window of a house across the road.

He flings the newspaper onto the table and sits into the armchair, provisionally – because he still has his suit trousers on and his jacket over his arm.

'What's up?' he asks.

'Nothing is up,' she answers, without diverting attention from her magazine.

She leafs quickly through the glossy pages, eyeing the pictures. This is nearly always how she reads, as if she were searching for some particular article, although in fact she is not. Beside her lies a pile of magazines, along with a tin ashtray in which a neglected cigarette is burning away, smoke streaming up toward the yellowed ceiling. Nearby, on the brown-carpet floor, stands a glass of white wine, its belly shining with condensation. In the very first moment in which he apprehends it, Alexander finds in this thin-stemmed object, this container enclosing pale liquid, a certain beauty, a vividness – the fact of being, and of being perfectly still. And then it is gone, disappearing into the fabric of ordinariness.

Julia's best feature is her hair. She has a thick long flood of it, in tight little curls, dark brown with a natural undertone of auburn, which glistens when freshly washed. Apart from her hair, Julia is not especially pretty. Her lips and nose are nicely formed, but her brown eyes are too big for her pale, round face. Nevertheless, she has always been an attractive woman, quick witted, confident in her own sexiness, which resides in her small curved body rather than her face. She is slow and graceful in movement. She enjoys the shapes of herself.

Seeing her now, sitting on the sofa in a cream blouse and white knickers, her pale naked legs folded beneath her, emphasising her thighs, her hair tied loosely behind her head, Alexander feels the possibility of arousal.

'You do realise that we haven't had sex for a couple of months,' he says.

Julia pauses in her flicking through the pages. She reaches down to pick up her cigarette, takes a drag, makes a round with her lips and blows out the smoke.

'Is this a new seduction technique, or are you just making conversation?'

Alexander shrugs. They both know that he has never had any seduction technique. If their bodies gravitate to each other – naturally, fortuitously, deliberately – he knows what to do. But if he is coming at it cold, he has only two standard gambits. If they are not in bed, he says: 'Do you want to go to bed?' If they are already in bed, he says, jokily: 'Will we have some kissing?' In this respect, he has gotten worse over time, rather than better.

When they first got together in college, they had sex all the time, as often as possible, automatically, urgently. They never wondered whether or not to have sex, because both of them always wanted to. Even after college, when they got back together following the breakup and moved into the flat, they had sex every night, until the point when Julia said: 'You know, we don't have to have sex every night.'

That was the beginning of their domesticity, of their drifting away from each other physically.

'There's a bottle of wine open in the fridge, if you want a glass,' she says, returning to her magazine.

'Maisie fell down the stairs.'

'Is she alright?'

'She's in a coma. I might have to go down to Galway ... if she dies ... or if she comes out of it.'

'That's a pity,' she says, clearly indifferent.

Alexander gets up with a sigh and walks through to the bedroom. This is the one room in the flat that he likes, because it has the bed in it (his favourite zone), because it looks out onto the back garden and gets great light (if the curtains are open), and because their books are kept here in a tall stack of wooden shelves that take up most of one wall. These shelves, purchased in Habitat shortly after they moved in, are the only piece of furniture they actually own. Everything else belongs to the landlord and reeks of bedsit. For instance, the wardrobe, which Alexander now opens, is a big dark square-shouldered thing that no one has ever loved.

Alexander slips off his trousers and folds them onto a hanger, careful to ensure that the creases are perfectly parallel. He fits his jacket onto the same hanger and slips it onto the crowded wardrobe rail. When he first started work, he ignored such matters, but now he is fully programmed to office life and is careful to hang up the suit of the day every evening when he comes home, keeping it neat, stretching out the time between visits to the dry-cleaner.

He unbuttons his shirt, removes it in two practised movements, gathers it into a ball and fires it toward the waiting wicker basket at the end of the bed, where it disappears successfully into the round dark aperture. The accuracy of the throw gives him a moment of satisfaction.

Down to his socks and jocks, Alexander closes the wardrobe door and turns to face himself in the mirror on the opposite wall. Certain features attract his immediate attention: the signs of flab and sag around his belly and nipples, the sun-damage redness of his lower neck, the blurring chin line, the sad-bastard green eyes that remind him increasingly of his father.

'Fuck you,' he says to his reflection and turns away in anger and disgust.

He wanders back out into the hall and sticks his head into the living room.

'Do you want to go to bed?' he asks, trying to maintain a casual tone.

She looks up.

'Oh, so you *were* seducing me,' she says, lightly enough, watching him, pausing for thought, or for effect. 'I have to wash my hair.'

'There's loads of time to wash your hair.'

'Off out for a few beers?' asks the taxi driver, glancing at Alexander in the rear-view mirror.

'We're going to a dinner party,' Julia interjects complacently before Alexander can respond.

'It amounts to the same thing,' Alexander says. The term *dinner party* is not one he would use. 'We'll all be well plastered before midnight.'

'Speak for yourself,' Julia says.

'Well, why didn't you volunteer to drive then?'

'Because I'm not your chauffeur.'

The trip to Sandymount, where Paul and Karina live, is a short one, fifteen minutes, although there is enough time for a moderately diverting monologue from the taxi driver about how Britain will have to join the euro because they are losing too much revenue from Irish Manchester United fans, who are no longer prepared to journey across to Old Trafford because of (a) the hassle of changing money, and (b) the crap exchange rate.

Alexander is generally happy enough to engage with taxi drivers, once the driver is of the friendly cheerful know-it-all variety, rather than the odious foul-mouthed know-it-all variety. When Julia is with him, he plays up his man-of-the-people aspect just to annoy her. Julia doesn't like her taxi drivers to be too familiar. She prefers the silent morose strain, newly released from Mountjoy Jail.

'I'd be surprised if Irish Man U fans were the decisive factor in a decision by Britain to join the euro,' says Alexander, unable to remove entirely the note of condescension in his voice. 'But who knows?

15

You could be right. Gordon Brown has these five tests that have to be passed. Maybe he should add another one based on Ryanair traffic volumes between Manchester and Dublin.'

'I'm telling you. They'd be mad to ignore it. The Irish punters are staying away in droves.'

Tall Paul opens the door and greets them with a big smile.

Paul played basketball in school (though not in college, owing to a back problem). That was how he met his wife, Karina, who is also tall. They were together for their final years in school, but then broke up when Paul went to Trinity and Karina to catering college. In the year after college, when Paul, Danny and Alexander set off for London, Paul was already planning to get back together with her. 'I need some-one now who'll shift my arse into gear. She has the measure of me.'

This was said on one or more of the many boozy nights they had that first year in London. It was a doss year. The following summer, Paul returned to Dublin to do a round of interviews for investment banks. He landed a job with Citibank and was posted immediately back to London, moving into a (relatively) swanky flat with another Citibank recruit and drastically reducing his consumption of drink and drugs. The paths of the three college friends diverged at this point. Alexander came home and got a job as a researcher with an economic consultancy firm. His career never recovered. Danny stayed on drinking in London for another year, getting annoyed with Paul for not coming out to play any more, then returned to Dublin to take up a post as a trainee journalist with *Irish Investor* magazine, and seriously stepped up his alcohol intake. Karina joined Paul in London after her final hotel placement ended.

'You guys are late,' Paul says, cheerfully, ushering them into the ample hall. 'But you're not as late as the other two.'

'Julia had to wash her hair.'

'We're still putting the finishing touches to the first course. Go ahead into the dining room. I'll bring you gins and tonic. Or would you prefer something else? Julia? ... I don't care about this muppet. He'll drink what he's given.'

Paul slaps Alexander on the back and thinks he's being funny. Unable to generate a quick riposte, Alexander wants to say, 'Fuck you, asshole,' but he lets it pass.

'A gin and tonic would be perfect,' Julia says. She slips off her silk wrap with an almost-twirl as she greedily takes in the expensive decor, also glancing up the stairs to the first landing, to spy out further riches.

'Do you want me to hang that up for you?' Paul asks. 'You look great, by the way. I forgot to kiss you.'

He reaches down (it's quite a distance), his hands encompassing her bare shoulders, and places his lips on her cheek. Alexander is discomfited by the audible mechanics of the kiss.

'Roy Keane is the hero of our time,' Alexander asserts as he swallows another prawn, washing it down with a good gulp of the tasty white wine. He is already enjoying himself. 'So what if he's a bit of a prima donna? Just *manage* it. McCarthy's job as a *manager* was to make sure that his best team was out on the field.'

'I'm outraged at that attitude,' says Paul. 'Keane was petulant. How many people would give their right arm to play for their country?'

'Not so loud,' says Karina. 'You'll wake the neighbours' children.'

'He betrayed his country,' Paul continues at a slightly lower volume.

'No. His country betrayed him.'

This has been one of their favourite conversations since the World Cup the previous year. Now that the heat has gone out of the Northern Ireland situation, it is the only thing to get worked up about. Their positions are always the same: Alexander is pro-Roy; Paul is anti-Roy; and Danny is too philosophical to have a straightforward opinion. Julia and Aoife don't care. Karina, still an active sportswoman herself, falls into the Roy camp, though she feels there was wrong on both sides.

Alexander likes Karina. He met her first on a night out in The Stag's Head, a favoured watering hole in their Trinity years. It was a big Christmas reunion: the place was packed with their pals from college. Paul and Karina were back from London. Alexander knew her only through Paul having mentioned her. When introduced, he felt something pass between them for an instant: a quickening of the air; a light punch to his belly. Inside his mouth, his tongue pushed forward infinitesimally, involuntarily, and with a very specific and (in the circumstances) unusual intention: to lick her nipples. Not that her nipples were on view. He was struck at the time by her height, her obvious fit-and-healthy condition, her short-cut, ash-blonde hair, and her natural modesty, which was rare in their Trinity circles. She is a bit heavier now, bigger in her breasts, and has started to look tired or strained around the eyes.

'Roy is a cartoon character,' says Danny mildly. Danny and Aoife have been subdued since their arrival. Danny looks psychologically bashed, which probably means one of two things, or both: he's been on a bender; or he and Aoife have been knocking each other around the place. 'He's a media invention. . . . I'll tell you who's a real hero of our times: Hugo Strongboy.'

'Hugo is rich, not heroic,' Julia says.

Hugo is a friend of theirs who made a serious fortune when the dot-com madness was at its height. NASDAQ was soaring. You felt like an idiot not to be making millions from stock in some heavily loss-making internet initiative. Hugo was an investment broker, then an investor, then a divestor. He got out at exactly the right time, emerging with his personal wealth in the tens of millions.

'What's the difference?' Danny asks. 'He's done it himself.'

'His old man is loaded,' Paul points out.

'Your old man is loaded,' Alexander says to Paul, then scans the table to recall who else has a loaded father. 'Let me see. I don't know about Karina's dad or Aoife's dad, but you're both Southsiders, so your folks must be reasonably well off. And Danny comes from landed fucking gentry.' Alexander pauses here, slightly prolonging the eye contact with Danny. The Carters were big landlords in County Galway. Danny's parents still live in the ancestral home, though the estate is only a small fraction of what it once was. Alexander refrains

18

on this occasion from mentioning that his own Ballyryan ancestors lived in a cottage within a few miles of Danny's folks' place. Danny doesn't like him to talk about this. 'My parents were civil servants. That rules me out. Julia is a Belfast Catholic, which rules her out, on the balance of probabilities, as well as in fact.'

'Excuse me,' says Julia in mock hauteur. 'My dad is a business-man.'

'A small businessman,' Alexander retorts. 'He's practically a tradesman.'

'He makes more money than you do.'

'That wouldn't be hard.'

'What's wrong with being a tradesman?' Karina asks sharply.

'Absolutely nothing. Tradesmen are magnificent creatures. But in socio-economic terms, while they might do well, they're never going to be really rich.'

'The last plumber who came to us owned three houses,' drawls Aoife. 'He was just back from a fortnight in the Caribbean.'

'If he owns three houses, he's a landlord, not a plumber.'

'That explains why the toilet still doesn't work,' quips Danny.

'My dad is a tradesman,' says Karina. 'We're a working-class family and proud of it.'

'He's a builder,' Paul almost shouts. 'There's a bit of a difference.'

'Getting back to Hugo,' Danny interjects. 'Even if his father has a few bob, it doesn't matter. He's living the Celtic dream. The guy was in college with us, went drinking with us, and now he's a multi-millionaire.'

'He didn't go drinking with us that often,' Julia points out.

In college, Julia hung around in the same circles as Alexander, Danny and Paul. It was actually through Danny that Alexander first got to know her. She and Danny had some sort of fling in first year, though Alexander has never been able to work out exactly *what* sort. It is not a subject he would ever raise with Danny, and Julia has always been sketchy about it. Whatever it was, it ended quickly. By the time Alexander met her, she and Danny had apparently agreed that their relationship was – as she put it then – platonic.

'Maybe that's why he's so successful,' says Aoife hoarsely. 'He steered clear of pissheads like you guys.'

'And he never took any drugs,' Alexander says. 'He was fairly straight that way.'

'He wasn't straight,' says Danny. 'Hugo was above straight. The man was perfectly balanced: captain of the rugby firsts, honours student, well able to hold his liquor, never veered from the lovely Emma, who is now herself a high-flying marketeer. He's a hero, I tell you. A role model.'

'Why don't you suck his dick if you're so keen?' says Aoife in abrupt, raw irritation, tipping the dinner table into sudden embarrassment, like a plane dipping unexpectedly into a steep turn.

'Tell us about your junket to Africa,' Danny says to Paul.

A little bit pissed, enjoying his food, an ideal conversation opening before him, Paul relaxes back into his seat, a grin of pleasure spilling onto his lips. He is chubbier now than he was in college, but still boyish, good-looking. He has let his fair-brown hair grow this past year. It is longer than bankers usually allow themselves, and this contributes to the air he has of being perfectly satisfied with life, with himself.

It is just the three lads talking now. Karina is down in the kitchen frying venison steak, having told Paul to stay put, that she would do it herself. At the other end of the table, Julia, after a few attempts, has drawn the reluctant Aoife into a civil conversation. They are talking about Dermot, Aoife's cousin, a journalist who used to work with Danny in *Irish Investor*. Now he is a political reporter with the *Irish Times*, a rising star. Alexander and Julia met him only once, a couple of years ago. It irritates Alexander – although he gives the appearance of not attending to this conversation – that Julia always asks after Dermot.

'It wasn't a junket, man. I was doing business there. We were putting together the finance for an electricity plant. I met the entire government. You have to laugh at these places. The stuff is straight out of a comic book. The President flew in from out of town to help

20

close the deal. They hailed his coming like he was the Son of God. Some flunkey burst into the meeting room. "The President's plane has landed." Then the man himself arrives in a fucking armour-plated Rolls-Royce that is so fucking heavy it's leaving ruts in the dust-track. I kid you not. He has this big army escort with him, all these fat generals with swagger sticks. Everybody laughs like they're Idi Amin. Actually, the President himself was impressive – a small thin dude, intelligent.'

'Is there much corruption?' Alexander asks ingratiatingly. 'Does it affect business?'

'You factor it in at ten per cent of cost.... They have a great attitude to corruption. In a neighbouring country, recently – I heard this from a guy at dinner, he could have been the Chief Justice for all I know. Anyhow, this neighbouring regime got something like one hundred million dollars in aid from the EU for a big capital project. The King embezzled the money and spent it on a Learjet for himself.... So I'm saying to the guy who is telling me this: "That's a terrible state of affairs. How did he get away with that?" And he says to me: "It takes great balls." He's full of admiration for this King, big wide smile on his mug. And then I twig it. Corruption isn't bad. It's good. It's initiative.'

Paul speaks with animation and flourish.

'Sure it was the same here,' says Danny. 'The boys topping the polls even after all the dirt came out, actually getting *more* votes. It goes to show that we're a Third World country that's been fast-forwarded to Richville. To begin with, the peasants don't believe that they're good enough to make money the straight way.'

'Food's up,' says Karina, coming through the doorway, expertly carrying three large plates – waiter style – with juicy bloody medallions of venison. She passes them to Paul, Alexander and Danny, who are the nearest.

'I'm not going to have one after all,' says Aoife, reaching for the box of Marlboro in front of her. 'I'm sure no one minds if I smoke. I'm a bit off my food. I'm up the pole in fact.' She lights her cigarette, inhales, grimaces, exhales, begins to speak again while the smoke is still flooding out through her mouth and nostrils. 'Danny's not very virile, but he's fertile.'

Alexander has always regarded Aoife as a bit mad, appropriately mad, since you would have to be fairly unbalanced to stay shacked up with Danny for the guts of ten years, given his record of alcoholism and financial irresponsibility. He has thought this from the first time he met her, in Hailey's Comet.

Alexander and Julia were together in Trinity from around the time of their first Trinity Ball till just after the final exams. Their relationship disintegrated at that point, with Alexander going to London (and not wanting her to come with him), and Julia getting ever friendlier with her aspiring playwright, and deciding that she wanted to go into acting. Four years later, Alexander, long since back in Dublin, was firmly, if not very excitingly, established. By this time Julia had tired of her acting career, which had mostly consisted of waitressing and teaching English as a foreign language. She had done a Higher Diploma in Education, and was teaching Drama in a girls' secondary school in Dún Laoghaire. They fell into bed one drunken night (having met by happy coincidence at a party) and suddenly everything was back on. Within a few months, they had moved into the flat in Rathmines.

Around this time, Danny and Aoife were similarly beginning to cohere into a couple-like arrangement. Danny called Alexander on the phone one night:

'Come down to Hailey's to meet the missus. Bring Julia if she's on for it.'

It was already fairly late. Julia wasn't in the mood. She was drifting toward bed for an early night as Alexander hopped into the taxi.

Hailey's Comet is a tough working-class pub off the south quays, near to where Danny was living at the time. As a counterpoint to his comparatively aristocratic roots, Danny is attracted to roughness and unpretentious wit. He made Hailey's his local.

The night in question was Children's Allowance night and the pub was having a karaoke special. Everyone was drinking cans. Alexander didn't inquire as to the reason for *cans* precisely, but guessed it had something to do with sub-legal imports.

Aoife has a tall hatchet face with an imposing nose and big electric-red hair. Her brow is noble. Sometimes she looks beautiful, sometimes ugly. She is a woman in whom Alexander has zero sexual interest, regardless of how drunk he is. But Aoife that night appeared to find *him* attractive. She and Danny, together with a group from the house, were heavily intoxicated, bleary-eyed.

'So this is your famous friend Alexander? You never told me he was so handsome.'

With some local tarts singing *Stand By Your Man* on the karaoke, Aoife sat heavily on Alexander's lap, kissed his mouth with her beery lips, and ran her clumsy fingers through his newly cropped hair. Alexander was sober and too far behind them to be interested in catching up; besides, the next day was a working day. He bore her intrusions with embarrassment, trying to be a good sport. Danny looked on and laughed, glad that the two were having a good time. Later, Aoife was so drunk that she pissed herself. Thankfully, she was back in her own seat at this point. (The seating in Hailey's Comet was upholstered in vinyl rather than cloth, perhaps as a result of previous similar occurrences.) Alexander noticed a streak of liquid running under his stool. With his eyes he followed it upstream across the tiled-lino floor till he came to the point where it was spilling vertically, splashing, from the nearest bank of seating, falling in parallel with a pair of legs in jeans and boots. She was sitting in a little pool. He looked up at her. She was drawing on a joint that was doing a round; and shitfaced though she was, in the moment when their eyes met, she was watching him shrewdly as he observed her. Nobody else had yet noticed the spillage.

'I don't give a shit,' she said to him in a low angry voice. 'They can go and fuck themselves.'

'Maybe you shouldn't smoke if you're pregnant,' Karina snaps.

'I don't give a shit,' says Aoife.

'Well you should.' Karina is surprisingly irritable.

'Jesus, spare me. . . . Doesn't anybody have any Class A drugs?'

'If you don't like what's on offer, you can leave,' Karina replies, but in retort rather than as an ultimatum.

The others are grinning discreetly at Aoife's heartfelt plea for cocaine.

Alexander guesses in this moment that Karina and Paul don't have any children yet because they haven't been able to conceive, or Karina hasn't been able to hold the conception.

Karina appears to be debating with herself whether or not to take the argument further. She stands at the far end of the table from Aoife, arms hanging long by her sides. Her lips twitch. Her eyes are shining with additional moisture, but she has it mostly in control, whatever it is that is bothering her.

'Sit down,' says Paul soothingly, rising from his seat. 'I'll dish up.'

'I'm fine.'

'I have a good anecdote,' offers Alexander.

'Come on so, out with it,' says Danny with a laugh.

Alexander is known in this group for his occasional stories, which are often nothing more than quirky details that have caught his attention and been subjected to the magnifying glass. When he relates these things, the laugh – if there is one – is usually focused more on him than on the subject-matter itself. He doesn't mind Danny laughing at him for being odd. The pecking order between them has always been evident. Condescension from Paul used to enrage him, but gradually – as Paul's greater success in life has unfolded – he has become more resigned to the slights.

Karina allows herself to sit. She and Aoife face each other from opposite ends of the table, Karina angry, Aoife indifferent, poker-faced.

'I'll help you serve dinner,' Julia says to Paul, getting up. 'It'll give me a chance to nose around the kitchen.'

'It'll also give you a chance to escape Alexander's anecdote,' says Danny, which causes a ripple of amusement. Karina smiles slightly.

Paul and Julia leave the room. They can be heard laughing as they pass through the hall.

'You know how my office is near the canal. There's a big courtyard that's surrounded on three sides by literally hundreds of windows. Anyhow, a few weeks ago a duck comes flying into the courtyard and lands on my outside windowsill, which is a pretty big coincidence.'

'It's not a coincidence at all,' Danny says. 'The duck had to land somewhere. I hope that's not the punchline.'

'There is no punchline. It's not that kind of story.... The duck has an egg in his mouth. I sense that it's a male duck. Anyhow, he has an egg in his mouth which I would say is a duck's egg, judging by the size. He looks around to the left and the right, like somebody about to commit a crime. He lays the egg on the sill.... The coincidence here is that I spot him and see the whole thing. I would say that with ninety-nine per cent of the windows, there wouldn't be anybody there, looking out, at that precise moment. They'd be on a call, looking at the PC, whatever.... He lays it down on the sill. He spears the shell with his beak, lifts the egg up into the air and opens his throat to swallow the contents. He could be drinking his own young here. And one of the striking things about it is how inefficient he is. Most of the yolk spills down onto his breast.'

Alexander demonstrates with his hands on his own breast how the contents got distributed.

'Four out of ten,' says Danny.

'Five,' says Karina, returning to herself.

'It's better than that,' says Aoife, directing a line of smoke away from the table. This is already a gesture of conciliation.

'Think *Silence of the Lambs*,' says Evil Neville to Alexander, his diamond eyes twinkling.

Alexander is conducting the first of a set of individual interviews with his team members to get to the bottom of the astrology calls mystery. He now has additional information available to him: print-outs of the call records for each person's phone, including his own, over the last three months. The records show an even distribution of calls to premium numbers, mostly at lunchtime.

'I have no idea what you're talking about. Are you saying that the person who is making the calls is also a serial killer, or a cannibal, or a cannibalistic serial killer?'

'Boy, you should know your classics better. The villain in the movie isn't Hannibal Lecter. It's the guy who is killing the girls and skinning them in order to make a girl suit. What's the pattern with his victims?'

'Get to the point.'

'The geographical distribution of the victims was random, deliberately random, to disguise the fact that the killer lived really close to his first victim. He coveted first what he saw every day, and later diversified geographically in order to confuse the authorities.'

'You're confusing the authorities,' Alexander says.

'From which phone was the first call made?'

Alexander leafs through the records in front of him. It strikes him for the first time that the calls began about a month or so after Neville himself took up the job. But the lists of calls show that the first call, in fact the first five or six, were made from Imelda O'Brien's phone.

'Are you saying that Imelda is making the calls?'

Neville smiles.

'I wouldn't want to incriminate a colleague.'

'Have you seen her make the calls?'

'I can't say.'

George Lucey, Alexander's boss, brusquely enters the room without knocking. He strides right up to the desk, standing so close to it – next to where Neville is sitting – that the wooden overlap at the edge presses into his thighs. George is not very good with personal space. When he comes up to people, he stands right next to them. Now, with the desk in the way, he is standing right next to that.

Alexander nods to Neville to leave.

'Everything OK for today, Mr Vespucci?' George asks Alexander. He means whether or not everything is in order for the Council overnight meeting that will begin later in Ashdale House in County Wicklow. The Council has an overnight session once or twice a year. The members arrive in the late afternoon, discuss matters of state for a couple of hours, break; then reconvene for a long dinner, followed by drinks in the bar well into the night. The next morning, they meet again for a plodding, hung over strategic think-in.

'I don't like that fellow,' George adds in a confidential whisper once Neville has closed the door. George scrunches up his face and shakes his head as though he has just tasted something bitter, this to underline his dislike for Neville. The facial expression is so ridiculous that Alexander has to bite his inner cheek to keep himself from laughing.

'He was helping me with my inquiries into the phone calls.'

'Ah yes, the obscene phone calls. It doesn't surprise me.'

'They weren't obscene phone calls. It's an astrology service.'

'Astrology?' George raises his bushy golden eyebrows in puzzlement. Alexander suspects that he doesn't know what astrology means, that he thinks it's astrophysics. 'Then what's all the fuss about?'

'It's a waste of public money.'

'Oh yes, public money. Actually I wanted to speak to you about public money. But listen, I'm glad you're making progress on the phone call business. These things have a habit of biting you on the arse if you're not careful. We should nail somebody for it.'

George Lucey is a career civil servant who was transferred from the Department of Finance to the National Economic Advisory Council, probably to limit the amount of damage he could do. He is in his mid-fifties and will never be promoted again because he is a buffoon.

George must have been very good-looking in his youth, with his golden hair and blue eyes, his broad-shouldered physical assurance and swaggering gait. Even now he retains a definite leonine magnificence. He dresses well, in the sense that his suits, shirts, and shoes are well made, well chosen, and this adds to the impression of substance; but he is also messy and neglectful about his appearance. This morning he is tie-less and unshaven, and wearing the same shirt that he wore yesterday, an expensive-looking double-cuffed bright pink article that is now marked down the front with a bird-shit-shaped coffee stain. Since the Council is meeting this afternoon, Alexander presumes that George will be freshening up later, but this cannot be taken for granted.

There are a number of things that Alexander likes about George. The main one is that he leaves Alexander alone to run the Council's business. Alexander works directly with the Council Chairman, Stephen Banner, on all matters of policy. George takes no interest in anything other than what he terms housekeeping matters, which include protocol and procedure, personnel issues, finance, et cetera.

'Spending is very slow on the consultancy budget,' George explains. 'Is there anything that needs to be done – something the Council wants to look into for around two hundred k?'

'There's broadband,' Alexander says to him. 'They're very keen on it; some of them at least. Grace Sharkey rang me earlier this morning to check on the outcome of the survey. You remember that I'm giving a presentation on it at this afternoon's meeting. We could—'

George has narrowed his sky-blue eyes in slow reaction.

'That's a bit pushy of her. Would it not be more appropriate for her to route any queries through the Chairman? And why couldn't it wait till the meeting? I don't trust that one, I tell you. She's trouble.'

Grace is young and smart and ignores George because he talks shit and has no influence in the Council. George doesn't like people to ignore him. He wants to talk shit all day long but still be regarded as a man of consequence.

Grace is by far the youngest Council member. Alexander reckons that she is thirty-five or thirty-six, while most of the others are in their fifties. He thinks her appointment last year was a good one. Back in 2000, at the height of the madness, she made a fortune on the IPO of an internet company providing online training facilities for employers who do not want to spend money on human instructors. She now retains only a small holding in this company, New Paradigm e-Training Solutions, but is known as an important mover in a number of other hi-tech e-society initiatives. Alexander finds that she brings to the Council important perspectives on things the rest of them don't understand. Plus, she is cool and sexy.

'Well, her point was that it is not enough for us simply to diagnose the problem; we should recommend a solution. If broadband connectivity is bad, what should the state do about it?'

George is unconvinced.

'If you're looking for something to spend a couple of hundred grand on, this would be ideal,' Alexander says.

'I had in mind a review of entrepreneurial capability.'

'We did one of those last year.'

'Yes,' says George, smiling expansively, revealing the golden dental work in his large teeth, 'but I'm proposing to focus on *attitudes* to entrepreneurial capability. It's an entirely new field.'

George is deeply pleased with this idea, as though it were akin to a major scientific breakthrough. He sees that Alexander is not impressed.

'Talk it over with Banner,' George says, quickly ceding the point. 'The important thing is to get moving on the budget.'

Before lunch, Alexander summons Innocent Imelda to his office.

'You know that I'm conducting an investigation into the misuse of our phone lines over a period of months,' he tells her pompously. 'Multiple calls have been made to astrology services, including from your phone.'

Imelda titters like a donkey trying to cough up a morsel of grass that has gone down the wrong way: Hee-hee.

'You sound like a cop on the telly,' she says, clearly amused rather than anxious.

'This is a serious matter, Imelda.' Imelda dutifully drops the grin from her mouth. 'Have you been making these calls?' Alexander asks in a deeper voice, leaning forward over the desk, his forehead concentrated into a frown, his eyes fixed on her in what is supposed to be an unavoidable piercing challenge.

'Heee, hee-hee,' giggles Imelda, which pushes Alexander right back into his seat, mission aborted. 'It wasn't me. Sure, I wouldn't know anything about that sort of carry-on. Who would I ring? And anyway, I don't believe in horoscopes. Sure, that's all rubbish.'

'So who *is* making the calls?'

'Neville,' she says with authority, serious now.

'How do you know?'

'I saw him.'

Blup-blop chimes Alexander's mobile phone from where it is lying on the desk, plugged into the charger cable. He picks it up and examines the screen: a text from Danny, which he opens with a click. *Meet me stags head at 1. Need ur help.* Alexander's heart stops. His stomach drops. A flash of heat passes to the surface of his skin. Danny looking for help can mean only one thing: money.

'And why did he start off making the calls from *your* phone?'

Imelda reflects on this question. She examines Alexander's countenance first, then looks over his shoulder and out the window, as though the answer is hanging there in the fresh air like a magical fruit.

'I'm not sure,' she says in an honest tone. 'I think he did it to get me into trouble.'

'Here's the thing,' Danny says. However, before proceeding to present the thing, he raises to his lips his newly settled creamy pint of Guinness and takes a first slurp. Alexander finds this a bit ostentatious, since he, having the drive to Wicklow and the Council meeting ahead of him, has nothing for comfort but a fizzy orange juice that is too sweet.

Drinking Guinness in The Stag's Head is one of the great perennial pleasures in their common life. Through all the turns and crashes of friendship, family and career, through the acrobatics of sexual relations, through the relentless rapid expenditure of time, from New Year to Paddy's Day, from Easter to summer, from October to Christmas, knocking back pints at the round marble tables in this Edwardian pub has remained a splendid refuge.

'Things have been pretty chaotic this last while,' Danny says.

'You mean these last fifteen years.'

'Well, yes, but I'm thinking of the last six months or so. Aoife and I have really been kicking the shit out of each other. It's not good. So we decided to split up. It was a fairly amicable thing. But then along comes this business with ... eh ....' Danny clicks his fingers to indicate what he is talking about. He is looking studiously at the floor. He always avoids eye contact when asking for money. On the last occasion, when he touched Alexander for a fifty, he waited till they were having a parallel piss in the urinals before broaching the subject.

'We're going to London for an abortion. I have to borrow a couple of grand.' Finally now he faces Alexander, his eyes displaying vulnerability. He is uncertain how Alexander will respond.

There is a story here.

In their first and second years in college, Alexander was as penniless as he was socially talentless. It is fine to be socially talentless if you are resigned to hanging out with others who are similarly challenged. Once you know your place in the world, it is possible to have fun, to have friends. But Alexander had ambitions. He wanted to be cool and beautiful, popular. He wanted to hang out with cool, beautiful, popular people.

Danny was a prince in those days of their late teens, lean and good-looking, with remarkable reserves of experience and confidence, and buckets of disposable cash. For some reason that Alexander never understood, Danny had adopted him by Christmas in first year; and piggy-backing on Danny's promiscuous sociability and reckless spending, Alexander gained entry into networks that would otherwise have been denied to him. He faked cool. He found that popularity was more circumstantial than ingrained and could be arrived at approximately without great difficulty, although it was frighteningly superficial.

One night in the Buttery bar toward the end of first year, they and many of their friends were tripping on acid. It was everyone's first trip. Danny was being hassled by an English girl with marvellous straight long hair, freshly washed, the kind of hair that features in shampoo ads. She was one of the few who weren't tripping. She had missed her period (following a lacklustre tryst with Danny, so the bitchy gossip went) and was shrieking at him outside one of the toilets, trying to get him involved in her crisis. Danny's focus was elsewhere, a dim-witted smile on his lips. She pushed and tugged at his unresponsive, unbalanced figure.

Alexander, meanwhile, was seeing sparks. The walls were breathing. He was filled with child-like playfulness. He concocted a plan to rescue his friend. He saw it as *Escape from Colditz*. They talked it through in a moment of respite: they would wait for another lull; they would leave the bar by different exits, depart the campus by separate gates; they would meet in The Stag's Head for pints and cigarettes, and maybe they could get some hash to see them through the night while they were coming down.

Danny's money funded the evening: the acid, the pints, the cigarettes, the sandwiches. After their acid trajectory had peaked, when they were on the downward slope back to everyday ordinary, starting to feel a little disappointed, a shift occurred in their relationship. Alexander remembers the moment exactly: after the pubs had closed, walking back along a particular part of the perimeter of Trinity College, the tall railing-topped wall, how it curves at that point in the street, the direction they were headed, his being on the inside, the degree of darkness in the city sky.

'I'll get you back for the money sometime,' he said awkwardly, looking at the pavement ahead.

The communication came to fill the emptiness that was opening up in the wake of their high. Innocuous though the words seemed, he had uttered them against his own deeper judgement, knowing as he spoke that this was somehow wrong, a sin against their trip and their friendship.

'I can't believe you said that, man. You've killed my buzz.'

Danny exuded subdued resentment for the remainder of the night. He always had money, but never discussed the ownership of it, never openly calculated.

In the long time since, Alexander has paid and repaid a dozen times the debts he felt himself to have incurred in those first years. Not that he enjoys splashing out money or giving loans that he knows will never be returned. Quite the reverse. But whatever he has paid has never been enough to quash his own demon. Until now. After this – so he tells himself – the beast is slain.

'When you say a couple of grand, I take it you mean two grand,' he says.

'Two grand would be good. Two and a half would be better,' says Danny with a smile. He has jumped over his own embarrassment, and is negotiating now.

Danny's face is red and puffy from years of excessive boozing. His dark hair is thinning rapidly. Physically, he is in poor shape, overweight, easily breathless, but he can still – with an effort – switch on the winning charm.

'Remind me again why you have no money,' Alexander says. 'With all your radio gigs and newspaper columns. Don't they pay you at all?'

'I hardly need to explain it. As you well know, I'm an alcoholic and a compulsive gambler. I never pretend otherwise.'

'And why should I fund your habits? I'm the wage slave with the dull job, scrimping and saving to make a deposit on a house. Why don't you ask Paul or hero-of-our-time Hugo Strongboy?'

'You know I can't.... I didn't know you were saving up for a house. That'll be a long save, though I suppose I'm not helping my cause by saying that.'

Danny allows himself a snigger.

Alexander drinks some of his fizzy orange and glances at the bar, wondering if his steak-burger-and-chips is on the way. Danny has declined to eat, saying he is not hungry.

'From an economic point of view,' Alexander begins in a different vein, 'there's a distributional failure here. I don't mean money. Look at Paul and Karina. They need a baby; or she does. You've got one you don't want. Doesn't that point to a solution? Now that I think of it, even Julia wants a baby. Or at least she did last year. She hasn't mentioned it recently.'

Danny bears this digression with good-humoured if obvious patience.

'You guys *should* have a baby,' he says, causing Alexander to jerk sharply on his stool.

'Why the hell would you say that?'

'Why not? What else are you doing? It's not like you go out that much.'

'I go out plenty,' Alexander lies. 'But going out doesn't have anything to do with it. Even if I stay at home every night for the rest of my life, that doesn't mean I have nothing better to do than have children. Maybe I'll want to split to Argentina for a few years.'

'You won't,' says Danny with a knowing expression.

'Anyhow, it's all bullshit,' continues Alexander. 'Why should I inflict life on some poor additional soul just to ... assuage my own loneliness.'

'Which is exactly why I want to borrow two and a half grand.'

'Did I just say "loneliness"? I meant "existential isolation". If I confessed to loneliness, I'd have to kill myself, or you, or both of us. Fifteen hundred. I can't do more than that, and even that much pains me greatly.'

'Eighteen hundred and we have a deal. It's for a good cause.'

'Last time I checked, abortions weren't that expensive.'

'You'd be surprised, when you take flights and everything into account.'

'Well, you should fly Ryanair.'

'What do you want? A detailed fucking itinerary? I'll give you a refund if there's any change.'

'Fifteen hundred.'

'Seventeen.'

'No,' says Alexander, shaking his head.

'You won't get much house for the difference between fifteen and seventeen,' says Danny, in pique.

'Well, since Dublin is out of the question, I'm focusing my efforts on Bangladesh. You'd be surprised what you can get in Bangladesh for a couple of hundred euro.' Alexander changes tack. He sips from his drink, wincing at the sickly taste of it. He really ought to have had a beer, just the one. 'OK. We can hit the bank after lunch. When do you want to go to London?'

'In the next few days.'

'What about Jasper? I suppose he's old enough now not to need a minder.'

'Jasper will be delighted to get a few days to himself. He'll mitch from school and spend the time gaming and jerking off.'

Jasper is Aoife's son from a previous relationship. He's practically an adult, a sullen sixteen-year-old with longish hair, whose standard demeanour is hostile. Alexander sees him a few times a year, whenever he is over at their house, but has long since given up attempting to establish a rapport. When Jasper was six or seven, he snapped in two a pair of designer shades that Alexander had bought a few days earlier. Alexander was sleeping off a drunken night on the couch.

'Look,' Jasper said, shaking Alexander to wake him, 'somebody broke your new glasses.'

Alexander drives down to Ashdale House in his white 1990 Honda Concerto saloon. In many ways he likes this car. It has performed honestly for him and Julia over the previous five years. Although the body is large, the 1.6 engine gives reasonable acceleration, relative to what he has experienced. The interior is spacious. He enjoys driving the car. It feels safe. He has never had any complaints about the steering, road-holding, cornering, braking. Not that he is a connoisseur of these things. He knows the difference between an exhaust pipe and a battery, but would never be able to point to a carburettor, for example, or explain what it does. On the one hand, then, he is privately satisfied, even pleased, with this car and has no requirement for a different car. On the other hand, the Honda is a source of shame, in particular the 90 D reg.

Recently, out in Malahide, parked near the seaside, a guy he was at school with drove by, a perfectly likeable type with two kids in the back seat of his 02 BMW 3 Series. The guy gave him a friendly nod from behind the wheel of his car, and his very next glance was low to the front of Alexander's car to read the reg. number, which, together with the marque and model, provided him with an instant reading of Alexander's status in life.

Alexander is a loser, he read. He was one of the cleverest in our year at school, but now I drive a 02 BMW 3 Series and he only has a 1990 Honda, the sad fuck. It goes to show that I was always a more worthy human being, a better man. Vespucci was a jumped-up prick, a cocky nerd, and now he's had his comeuppance.

Alexander knows there are other ways to read 90 D. He has sufficient imagination and intellect to recognise that there are better perspectives on the world, but he is nevertheless unable to rise above the dominant perspective of the day. He looks at himself through the eyes of the observer and finds himself wanting.

He has fully internalised the prevailing value system. Before he knew how to drive, he often dreamt of driving, of being in the back seat, which meant not being in control. In these dreams, the characteristics of the car itself were irrelevant. When he became a driver, when he passed the test, on his third attempt, those particular dreams ceased. Instead, his focus switched to the cars themselves, with the hitherto unnoticed details of make, model and year beginning to assume enormous importance. He began to distinguish very carefully, to watch and evaluate in a similar way to how he watches and evaluates women, obsessively. Of objects, only a car can turn his head the way a woman can.

The hotel is situated off the N11, the main road from Dublin to Wexford. Alexander enjoys the topography of the drive, how the road runs – must run – on the narrow strip of flatland between the Wicklow Mountains and the Irish Sea. He loves the bare shapely Sugar Loaf, the forested Glen of the Downs, and speeding through the ugly little villages along the way.

He arrives shortly after four. The drive from the city centre has taken him about an hour, which is pretty good. He turns smartly off the main road (left, toward the sea) onto the tree-lined avenue that leads to the house. There are only a half a dozen or so cars in the car park at the front (including two Mercedes, a BMW, and a long narrow Volvo), but he nevertheless drives around to the side to protect himself and the Honda from comparison. By the time all the Council members have arrived, the car park will be brimming like a box of chocolates with plush high-powered vehicles. In these conditions, the Honda likes to keep a low profile, tucked away beside the servants' entrance and the fire escape.

Ashdale House is a medium-sized Georgian country residence. The decor is sumptuous, eclectic. The entrance hall, the finest space in the house, is dominated by a huge chandelier, incorporating hundreds of pieces of grimy yellow glass. There are numerous doors and passages off the hall, including a grand wooden staircase, which Alexander doesn't usually ascend because it leads to the best bedrooms, which are reserved on these occasions for the Council bigwigs.

His favourite feature of the hall is the large fireplace (dormant in the summer season), with sofas and armchairs around it, where one can sit in an idle moment (for example between the end of the first session and dinner) and study the gilt-framed paintings on the papered walls.

There is an oil painting of an English hunting scene which he likes: men and women in red coats on well-groomed horses, waiting at their meeting point, a pack of eager hounds around their feet. Alexander has done a fair bit of horse-riding himself in the last few years. He and Helena go out to a riding school in the country most Thursday evenings. His passion for the sport has waned recently, but there was a while during which this session was by far the high point of his week, an exercise undertaken with religious fervour, leaving him afterwards physically exhausted but energetically high.

He reports to the small mahogany desk inside the door and falls in love with the French girl who checks him in – the reserved brown eyes of her and the sallow bony face.

She performs the formalities with economy. There is a trace of melancholy in her well-disciplined expression, something graceful in her professional manners. He wants to run away with her to Switzerland, to untie her hair in front of a dying log-fire, drinking Glühwein, intoxicated with Eros, requiring nothing further than each other for the rest of their lives.

But she doesn't see him.

'Would you like me to call the porter?' she inquires kindly, her hand moving automatically to the antique silver bell-press.

He joins the Council Chairman, Stephen Banner, in the meeting room at the appointed time.

The room is already laid out with a U-shape of tables covered in green baize, each place set with several bottles of water, a crystal-glass tumbler, a pad of headed paper, sharpened pencils, and a dish of mints.

At the open end of the U stands a large portable projection screen, and in the middle of the space a projector to which will be connected Alexander's laptop containing the agenda and all the presentations for this evening's session and the one in the morning.

When Alexander enters, Banner is already seated in his chairman's position at the bottom end of the U, going through his papers. He is alone in the room. His jacket is off and he is picking his nose with great concentration, tunnelling deeply, searching for purchase on a bogey that is apparently just evading the nail of his little finger.

'Greetings, young man,' Banner booms as Alexander makes his way across the room. The Chairman's little finger has emerged, successful. As he continues speaking, he examines the fruit of his excavations. 'I trust you are in energetic form. There's a lot of work to do. . . . This is an excellent set of papers. Well done. But the proof of the pudding is in the eating.'

Banner is an impressive and likeable man. He is chief executive of the Irish subsidiary of a US pharmaceutical company that makes astonishing amounts of profit from a number of patented drugs. Like all the Council members, his position is a voluntary one: he receives no payment and claims no expenses. 'I do this pro bono publico,' he often remarks to Alexander, and Alexander believes this, up to a point.

By all accounts, including his own, Banner's multinational career has brought him considerable personal riches, but Alexander suspects that the job is not much fun, and probably rather isolating. By contrast, the chairmanship of the Council gives him an opportunity to play on a broad stage. He concerns himself with the important economic issues of the day. He gets his picture in the paper, sometimes appears on television news, and is quoted saying wise things about the state of the nation, about what has to be done to keep the good times rolling. In appearance at least, he is a broker in social partnership deal-making, schmoozing with trade unionists and business leaders, 'developing consensus'. And he gets to meet the big chief, the Taoiseach, which clearly excites him. He makes presentations to the cabinet, tells them what is required to facilitate business into the future. Alexander writes the words and Banner delivers them, to politicians and journalists, sounding remarkably authoritative, although his knowledge is superficial. Alexander waits always for someone to scratch the surface and find that there is nothing behind it, but this has never happened. Everyone who matters is playing the game. If the Council started saying things that caused any discomfort to anyone, the civil servants would kill it quietly through restructuring or amalgamation into some other forum. Its role is to utter pieties from a business perspective – sanded down as necessary by the trade union minders – as part of an orchestrated national debate, in which all the insiders get some of what they want. Within these constraints, the Council can attempt to make its mark. Alexander isn't sure if Banner appreciates just how irrelevant he and his Council actually are. He suspects that Banner doesn't calculate in this way. What matters is his picture in the paper.

Now, in his first moments of seeing Banner, based perhaps on nothing more than his noticing that the flesh around the man's eyes is increasingly puffy, Alexander has a piercing insight that Banner is on an accelerating downward curve: in his early sixties, hurtling toward retirement and oblivion, desperately looking for something to hold on to, already practically a doddering fool.

They sit together to go through the agenda.

'You said you wanted to deal with broadband first,' Alexander reminds him. 'The way we left it the last time, the Council asked for a survey to be conducted of availability for small businesses and private users around the country. We've done that. Black and Associates, the economic consultants, undertook it on our behalf. I'll be making a short presentation on the findings. Basically, availability is about the same as in Afghanistan. And the situation isn't improving very quickly. The question now for the Council is what to do next. We can present the problem as a problem, or we could put forward some solutions. But—'

'Grace Sharkey is the one who's pushing this, isn't she?' Banner asks thoughtfully.

Alexander flushes, feeling found-out.

'Yes.'

'Tell me: does she have a personal financial interest in this?'

'I don't think so,' Alexander responds unconvincingly, blushing more deeply, feeling an idiot, since this possibility has never occurred to him.

'Don't let your mickey do your thinking for you,' Banner advises paternally. He punches Alexander on the shoulder, leans back in his chair and laughs.

'I think she might have a point,' Alexander continues tentatively. 'Maybe this is an issue on which the Council can make an important contribution; you know, take a leading role.' He is regaining his feet after the wobble and is able to eye Banner directly again. 'But to come up with solutions, we would have to do further consultancy work, see what kinds of interventions might be made by the state, which state body would do it, how much it would cost, et cetera.'

'There'll be resistance to any idea suggesting that the government should splash out a load of money on broadband.'

'Yes,' Alexander agrees, entirely regretting his earlier internal flash of condescension.

'You do your presentation. Don't say anything about next steps. I'll open it to the floor for discussion and see where it goes from there. But I may come back to you at the end. . . . OK, what's next?'

Alexander's presentation goes well. Though mentally calm, he is physically anxious to begin with, particularly in the seconds before he speaks; but by the end he is enjoying himself, showing off.

Relaxing then, once the Chairman has opened the matter for discussion, Alexander's focus drifts. The Council has its high points, but usually the proceedings are tedious. George Lucey is supposed to do the minutes, but George doesn't like to do any work, so he has long since delegated this task to Alexander. Alexander finds that he can do a good set of minutes on the basis of listening about ten per cent of the time. In the same way that he can now speed-read a hundred-page document in about half an hour, skimming over everything but the important bits, he has developed a facility for meetings which enables him to operate on automatic pilot, switching on only when somebody starts to say something with genuine content, which isn't often.

He wonders what he should do with his life. As a teenager and in college he planned great adventures. He would travel the world, go to places like Mozambique and Nepal. Nothing concrete has ever stopped him from pursuing these dreams, but he never has pursued them. From London after college, he went back to Dublin and joined ConsultEcon, where he stayed too long, before moving to the Council. At the time he got the job offer from the Council, he had a week of sleep-poor nights when he shifted restlessly in bed, increasingly frustrated, wondering why his life was taking such a boring course. At two in the morning he would decide boldly to emigrate to Africa, but when the alarm went off at seven, he would realise immediately, in his exhaustion, that this was never going to happen. He was able to decide to go to Africa, but he wasn't able to go to Africa.

'I want to emigrate to Africa,' he would say to Julia.

'Off you pop,' she would respond calmly from over the rim of her magazine.

'But what would it mean for us?'

'Don't use me as an excuse for not going to Africa.'

'Do you want to come?'

'Where to?'

'Africa.'

'Africa is a big place. You're asking me to travel to an unspecified location in Africa to live by unspecified means for an unspecified duration, and then presumably to return to Ireland to pick up the no-life we have now, except we'd be older and would have no money and no jobs and nowhere to live.'

'Doesn't that prospect fill you with excitement?'

'You need to come up for air, honey.'

He realises now that the reason his life is taking such a boring course is because he is a deeply boring and mediocre human being. There is no other explanation for it. Even in his daydreams these days, he has chickened out of Africa and is planning instead to go to Argentina, where he reckons there is less random violence, less fatal disease, plus a large population of sallow-skinned, ample-breasted young women. But Danny is no doubt right. He is never going to go to Argentina. He should settle down with Julia and have a baby. That must be why people have babies, because they have given up on going to Africa.

But having a baby means buying a house and organising a wedding. He doesn't mind marriage. They are as good as married already, but the idea of a wedding is hideous. Maybe they could do a spur-of-the-moment thing in Amsterdam? No way. Julia would want her parents and brothers, all her cousins and pals to come down from Belfast for the weekend (or maybe she would want to do it *in* Belfast, which might actually be a bit easier), and he would have to rummage together a plausible posse of friends and relations. There would have to be stag and hen nights. Vomit. There'd be a Brown Thomas wedding list of household appliances. Bridesmaids in peach dresses frolicking outside the church. Women in hats. Staged photographs. The hotel, the speeches, the crappy band. The afters (he'd have trouble enough getting people for the wedding itself). A honeymoon in some sort of half-decent location (Buenos Aires, maybe). And where on earth would they get a house? 'Vigilantes' View' in Dolphin's Barn. And what about carpets, fridges, cookers? A three-piece suite? He hates three-piece suites; but once you get into that territory, you have to have a good one or you're a waste of space.

'What we require here, Chairman, is some old-fashioned state intervention. The state should build or fund the building of

broadband infrastructure to link up small towns around the co
We need to look . . . .' This is Grace Sharkey speaking. Although there
is nothing particularly remarkable in what she is saying, she has a cap-
tivating effect on the Council. She uses her hands expressively, like an
actress rather than a businesswoman. Her nails are long and painted.
She rubs her fingers together and purses her lips as she searches for
the right word; and this pause, maintained with such confidence and
with a slight edge of sensual pleasure, draws in the listeners. 'We need
to look for imaginative solutions.'

'If I could interject here, Chairman,' says Declan Dunne, a
senior official from the Department of Finance. (Declan is not the
first punter Alexander would call on for imaginative solutions. He
is a plain-speaking, podgy-cheeked Northsider who always seems
pleased with himself that he has landed so comfortably in such
august company. Alexander thinks of him as a mammy's boy. Not
that he is effeminate; but that his mammy always fed him well, serving him while he sat at the kitchen table right into his thirties, up
until his wedding night, thinking that there was nothing better than
to be a civil servant, thrilled by her son's rapid promotions. Would
you like some more gravy with your mash, dear? I did you an extra
pork chop. Would you like another glass of milk with your dinner?)
'I think we should be careful about the Council's role here. From my
Department's point of view, we certainly can't agree to any recommendations that have financial implications—'

'All recommendations have financial implications,' says Grace,
exasperated, appealing to the Chairman. 'If we're not going to have
any recommendations with financial implications, we might as well
close shop and start singing hymns on Grafton Street.'

'Through the Chair,' says Conor Burke, chief executive of Irish
Paper plc, 'I think Declan is right in saying we should be cautious. The
state had a telecom company and decided to sell it. That means we
took the view as a country that the market could meet the demands
for telecom services. Having made that decision, we shouldn't be so
quick to leap back in again with more money. It would make the decision to sell look stupid—'

'Maybe it was stupid,' says Joe Walsh, president of the largest trade union in the country, representing almost a quarter of a million public and private sector workers.

'One at a time please,' says the Chairman. 'Joe, you'll have the floor next.'

'I think this is premature,' continues Burke. 'If there is economic demand for broadband, then the market will supply it. We shouldn't be so quick to assume there's a problem.'

'I don't believe the market will supply it,' says Joe Walsh. Unlike most people on the Council, who speak in wealthy tones, Joe has a strong working-class Dublin accent, which Alexander enjoys because it is such a different idiom, blunt and expressive. 'There's great faith these days that the market can do this and that. I've never seen much evidence of it. There are a lot of things that the market won't do. And I'll tell you this: it was a grave Thatcherite mistake for this country to sell Irish Telecom. If we still had a national telecom provider, the government could simply instruct them to lay the cable, or whatever is required in this case.'

'Let's have some vision here,' Grace begins, when it is her turn again to speak. 'The market isn't supplying and won't supply because the telecom operators don't want to invest. All across Europe, they're already over-extended from the bidding contests for 3G licences. Now they're looking to squeeze as much return as possible out of the existing assets.... Broadband is something new. It's like laying railway track in the nineteenth century: maybe the first investors got screwed, to put it frankly; but look at the benefit to the economy. Think of the competitiveness we are already losing to the countries that are moving more quickly on this than we are, and everybody is moving more quickly on this than we are, as we saw from Alexander's presentation.'

This is an effective contribution. She is passionate, but controlled. She appeals both rhetorically and intellectually. Alexander senses that the Council is moved.

He finds Grace Sharkey gorgeous. She has small brown eyes like pennies, a snubbed nose, full lips. Her jaws are ape-like: large, widely positioned, dominating her face. He realises suddenly that she *is* in fact an ape. He looks around the U-shaped table and everywhere sees apes: self-important, clothed, some of them with glasses perched on their noses, some hairier than others, some prettier than others, all more or less intelligent, in their high foreheads, blathering on seriously, comically, in some unknown gibberish. Except that he too speaks the gibberish, and his knowledge of it draws him inexorably into their meaning, away from his momentary insight into the nature of the gathering and the proceedings.

'I think we should inform ourselves further before we can make any policy recommendation on this matter,' says Banner in presidential style. 'Alexander, I believe there are some research options you can tell the Council about.'

Alexander sits forward in his chair to give himself some leverage on the question.

'We could employ consultants, Chairman, to examine the forms of action government might take, what the costs and benefits would be, how to fund it, et cetera. We could look for policy recommendations also, based on the analysis. It's a big job. The tender procedure alone would take a couple of months, the work itself a further two to three months—'

'Meanwhile Rome is burning,' interjects Grace.

'—I would estimate having a final output by December, not before.'

'And what would it cost?'

'It's difficult to quantify at this stage. In the region of two hundred thousand. However, we can accommodate that from the consultancy budget.'

At the mention of the consultancy budget, George Lucey, nicely shaven, dressed in fresh shirt and tie, sitting at the Chairman's right hand, perks up from the glazed stupor which has characterised his demeanour up to this point.

'I can agree with that, Chairman. I'm quite concerned at the under-spend to date. Something like this is ideal. We need to burn a lot more cash.'

There are one or two titters among the members.

'Well that settles it then,' concludes the Chairman. 'If George wants us to spend the money, we had better spend the money.... The waiters should be coming around now with your pre-dinner drinks. Those of you who arrived late and missed the list will have to fend for yourselves at the free bar.... Meeting adjourned. See you all at eight for dinner.'

Dinner takes place in a small sumptuous dining room overlooking the hotel's eighteen-hole golf course. On the far side of the fairway rises a linear range of sand dunes, covered sparsely with long, coarse grass. An old wooden fence is visible, running up the contour of one of the dunes, standing tall at the crest, then suddenly interrupted: mangled, dangling wires, fallen stakes.

Alexander has the opportunity to stand gazing out the window because he is the first into the room. There are no place-names and he is reluctant to commit himself for fear that no one will choose to sit beside him until all the other places are taken. He prefers to arrive late to these things so he can slip discreetly into an appropriate slot, away from the Council's stars, whose company is too taxing, if possible next to someone with whom he can have an enjoyable conversation.

Conor Burke enters. Burke is not one of the Council's bright lights. Neither does he fall into the category of people with whom Alexander would wish to share dinner. He is a boorish man with a large nose and red face, who works hard to grind out a profit in a low-margin business with increasing overseas competition.

'I see you're admiring the golf course,' he says to Alexander in a gruff friendly tone. 'We should be so lucky, huh.'

Alexander is not a golfer. Whenever he has to confess to this, inwardly he feels wholly inadequate, ashamed even, which is certainly an overreaction, but one he is apparently unable to control. Golf is totemic for him, representing something bigger than the game itself, something from which he is excluded as a consequence of his fundamental flaw, whatever that may be. He has actually considered taking up the game, in order *not* to be excluded, but he has no desire to play it. In fact, he finds it repugnant. Nevertheless, it is out of the question for him to intimate to Burke that he is watching the long grass in the sand dunes, rather than contemplating a round. The breeze blows and the grass runs with it. Enter there, says the miniature Zen master inside his head; but Alexander pulls away from that too.

'Yeah,' he answers lamely. 'No rest for the wicked.'

Other members are starting to drift in.

The chief executive of the IBA (Irish Business Association) takes a seat near the window, nodding to Burke, who opts for the place beside him. Alexander would rather be looking out the window than have his back to it, but he feels that politeness now requires that he sit next to Burke.

Having sat with them, Alexander finds that Burke and the IBA guy will engage in a huddled conversation that is closed to him. He wants to bolt, to leave the room for a pretend visit to the toilet and then return to take up another option. He denies the impulse: he has committed himself and will stay put. Soon the table will be fully populated, the dinner will begin, he'll have some wine, his uneasiness will pass, or at least he'll be anaesthetised sufficiently not to feel the pain too keenly. In the meantime, he adjusts the positioning of his napkin, which is arranged like a fan at the centre of the array of heavy silver cutlery in front of him. He wishes that he had not already finished his pint, or that he had ordered a second one from the bar to bring in with him.

A civil servant from the Department of Industry smiles at him sympathetically across the table as she takes her seat. He returns the compliment.

Banner arrives, talking as he enters with the after-dinner guest speaker, a white-haired former scientist, now a proselytiser for science in education. They take seats at the far end of the table.

Alexander jolts in shock: from a strong squeeze on his left upper arm. He turns to see Grace Sharkey seat herself beside him. She has changed for dinner into a figure-hugging, shiny emerald dress with spaghetti shoulder straps. Her copper hair, which was up in a hair-slide at the meeting, hangs freshly brushed around her neck, just touching her slim shoulders. She is dazzling, over-dressed. There is nothing immodest in the cut of what she is wearing, but he finds her explicitly sexual now. He feels a natural impetus to reach across and kiss her, to take possession of her lips and mouth, to find her hot wet tongue with his.

He straightens himself primly in the chair.

'I didn't see you come in,' he says.

'You don't mind my sitting here?'

'No, of course not.'

Big Joe Walsh sits on her left and immediately draws her in. Alexander finds himself alone between two happily chatting couples. He is unduly uncomfortable in this isolation, doesn't know what to do with himself. In case his distress is being witnessed, he tries to avoid catching anyone's eye. To have his social discomfort observed is a hundred times worse than the simple discomfort in itself. So if anyone *is* watching, he would rather not know. He removes his napkin from the table, opens it cautiously and places it on his lap. As he cuts into his bread roll, he regrets that the nearest plate of butter will have to be handed to him by Burke.

Thirty-five minutes later, Alexander is still the only one at the table uninvolved in any of the many conversations that are taking place.

He presses on manfully with dinner, fortifying himself with fine wine. As he wades through the gourmet mashed potato (having quickly finished the small fillet of monkfish and the associated five green beans), he imagines himself to be crossing Antarctica, marching solo through a blizzard on his way to the South Pole. Only fifty miles to go, through dessert and coffee, but once again he is running low on wine, with no sign of the waitress this far south of Scott's last camp.

'Oh dear, we're getting drunk here,' he murmurs sub-audibly to himself.

From his newly drunken perspective, the universe is altered. The planet is his oyster. It is not inevitable that he marry into domestic drudgery in Outer Tallaght. There must be some place in Indonesia

48

or the Philippines where he can hide away for a decade on five dollars a day, living on a beach, smoking dope. One balmy evening in a village tea-hut, he will meet a beautiful young upper-class English girl with natural blonde hair and pale blue eyes. She will be on a gap year, recovering from acne, going up to Oxford to study philosophy in the autumn, though she may postpone for a couple of semesters to stay with him and explore herself. They will dress in cheap cotton from the local market and do things very slowly.

Alexander raises his wine glass to his lips to drain what remains. There is so little left that the outer rim of the glass is touching his nose before he has created sufficient downward slope for the remaining nectar to roll slowly over the inner surface and drop onto his waiting tongue.

'Ah,' he says.

On his right side he can overhear Burke and the IBA man discussing the national pay talks that will be commencing in the coming winter.

'We're getting crucified already,' says Burke. 'Never mind India and China. Never mind the Eastern Europeans copying our low corporate tax rate. If the euro strengthens, I get hammered by UK competition. That's the reality of it. These guys are living in cloud cuckoo land if they think they can get a five per cent pay deal with no consequences. We have to tighten our belts. Otherwise, we'll have priced ourselves out of it. And that'll mean lost business, lost jobs.'

To Alexander's left, Grace and Joe Walsh are gabbing away. By reputation, Walsh is one of the toughest and most effective union negotiators in the country, but to Grace he is revealing his soft side.

'I'm not kidding,' he says. 'I do. I write poetry, particularly when I've had a few beers. In the right company, beer brings out my ... lyrical nature.'

'You amaze me,' Grace responds drily. 'You're obviously a man of hidden talents.'

'You'd be surprised, I'm telling you.'

Joe Walsh is obese, at least seven or eight stone overweight, with a vast belly that achieves its full magnificence at his trouser line. Standing, he is shaped like two cones glued together at their big ends, with little feet attached to the inverted bottom cone, and a basketball of a head – plus several chins – at the tip of the top cone. When he first met Walsh, Alexander was sure that the man was facing imminent death. He is constantly breathless, even when he is sitting down, wheezing, sweating profusely. He eats like a combine harvester, shovelling the food into his open churning mouth, loudly guzzling wine, spitting and dribbling, staining and spilling, scattering debris across acres of wide-open tablecloth.

'I'd better go to the jacks,' Joe says, as he rises with astonishing deftness, and rounds the table to leave the room.

'I have some fascinating statistics about poetry,' Alexander blurts out rashly after too short a pause. Grace looks up from her dinner and forces a smile. 'A remarkably high proportion of the population—'

'I have no interest in poetry,' she interjects sharply, then softens her tone: 'But I thought your broadband presentation was good. What do you think will emerge from the study you're proposing?'

While Alexander begins to think about this, she carefully places her cutlery on the table and swivels 45 degrees in her chair to have a more frontal view of him, to present a more frontal view of herself. She produces a closed-lip smile, which surprises him. He knows it means something, but he doesn't know what.

'It's hard to say.'

'I know how these things work,' she says in a low voice. 'Surely the consultants will write whatever you tell them to write.'

Her right hand has strayed from her lap. The edges of her long nails and the tips of her fingers touch the outside of his thigh, and remain in contact. This might be accidental, but he doesn't think so. He doesn't retract his leg, nor does he move it any closer. With the fingers of her other hand – elbow propped on the table – she tugs searchingly at the sliver of gold dangling from her earlobe.

Alexander feels his penis thickening, just enough for him to sense its current shape and position. He briefly clenches his sphincter muscle in reflexive response to this sensation. He has sobered up considerably, and pauses now to assess what is going on in their immediate environment. Everyone is occupied as before. No one is paying them any attention.

'You flatter me,' he says, and his leg pushes outward in what might be a small involuntary jerk, but one that has the effect of making her hand slide onto the top of his thigh, which she allows.

'Consultants recommend as is required of them,' Grace says. 'I think it's important that the Council doesn't make a balls of this one. I supposed it would be you who would instruct the consultants, but perhaps I'm wrong in that.'

Her hand squeezes his thigh, and inches forward toward more interesting territory. He can feel the sharpness of her nails through his trouser leg. He blows out slowly, from the sensual rush.

'No, you're right. I'm the one who will select and steer the consultants.'

'And how will you steer them?'

Her fingers inch farther up his thigh. His penis is increasingly engorged. He looks around again, but is cocky now. They remain unobserved.

'The terms of reference will specify that we want an independent assessment,' he says, smirking.

'That's sweet; like there's such a thing. What sort of steering is that?'

Her hand is climbing up his thigh again. Her fingers search out his penis, probing briefly, a little clumsily, to assure themselves that he is concentrating. Then the hand is gone, all contact withdrawn. She returns to her dinner, takes up the cutlery, prods the monkfish with her knife, as though to see what it will do.

In the first instant, he is relieved, released from tension. In the second instant, he is disappointed, missing her touch, suddenly desperate to restore the physical intercourse. She has turned away from him. He scrambles to continue the conversation.

'Well, what would you wish for the consultants to recommend?'

'Now, that's a good question,' she responds brightly, once more favouring him with a full view of her fascinating face. 'I'll have to think about that one. Why don't we meet after dinner to discuss it? We could go for a stroll in the garden. Would you be available for that?'

The warm dangerous hand, with which he is now somewhat acquainted, raises her wine glass to her mouth, and she drinks and swallows with slow sensuous movements of the lips, tongue and throat.

Outside, looking west from the main door – beyond the ground lights directed back at the front of the hotel, beyond the clumpy landscape in the middle distance, above the blackness of the humps of hills that fill the near horizon – the sky is an inky blue, with broad brush strokes of grey cloud inching slowly by, coloured orange and violet on their undersides by a sun that has now disappeared.

Alexander lights a cigarette, and suddenly yearns for the West of Ireland with an almost physical pang.

Maisie has rallied. He learned this on Monday. She came out of her coma, sat up in the bed and demanded breakfast – two soft-boiled eggs, toast with butter and marmalade, tea with milk and two sugars. The doctors were astonished. Brigid stayed for a few days and was coming back to Dublin this very evening, which means she must be home by now. Alexander will meet her tomorrow when he and Julia go to Helena's for dinner.

When he went to college, he dropped his previous identity, and with it his childhood connection to the West. Years later, having re-emerged from the indolent student life of overconfidence, drink, drugs, sex, music, working holidays abroad; reacclimatising to the true nature of the universe, he discovered, to his surprise, that his love for the West had remained buried within him, like bedrock. With the thin cover of soil and weak grass scraped away, there it was: in granite, a bit smeared with muck, but gleaming also from the wetness of the fallen rain.

For the millennium New Year, he dragged Julia to a rented house on Inis Meáin, the smallest in population terms of the three Aran Islands, off the coast of Galway. They went with Helena, her husband

Derek, and their two little kids. Julia didn't get it: the sea, the wind, the remoteness, the absolute darkness of the night. For her it was a few days in a damp house on a bleak barely living rock in the ocean, with nothing to do and nowhere to go, no shops, no television.

There was a man there Alexander liked, called Máirtín, who gave them the keys to the house when they arrived. He was a shy, bleary-eyed man in his late thirties who spent ten or twelve hours every day drinking slowly at the bar in the hotel, in almost complete silence, probably drinking the rent money, or his cut of it from his brother on the mainland who owned the house. Alexander encountered him early one afternoon, paused at the corner of the road before the hotel, foot up on a rock, staring out to sea, toward the mainland. He looked to be in a trance, and it seemed to Alexander that this gazing out to sea was his daily prayer, his reorientation, before he passed through the swinging doors into the sleepy hotel and drowned his human imperfections under a weight of alcohol. Alexander saw in his pale ruined eyes a clear, far-away mysticism. The man never uttered much, never more than a few mundane words. But there was no reason that his mystical soul and his speaking personality should be connected, or even know of each other's existence. On the other hand, perhaps Alexander entirely misread the thing. Maybe Máirtín did not generally stop to gaze at the sea on his way to the pub. On that one occasion he may simply have been waiting for a painful spasm of the bowel to pass.

He sees her before she sees him. She emerges from the front door of the hotel, seeming unsteady on her feet, taking smallish steps, holding one shoulder slightly higher than the other. He is standing at a shrub by one of the windows, at an oblique angle to the entrance. She looks first the other way, thus missing him, and there is something in the tilt of her head as she seeks him out that is suggestive of anxiety. She is worried he won't show. When she turns and sees him, standing on the grass verge, unusually presented by the ground lights, silently watching her, enjoying a cigarette, a flash of pain or anger appears on her face, which she then quickly replaces with a momentary false smile.

'You're late,' she says, beckoning him over with her fingers as one might call a servant.

He concentrates on being slow in his strolling across to her, so as not to appear completely biddable; pauses on the way to take a final drag on his cigarette before flicking it onto the gravel.

'How can I be late if I was here first?'

'I was out here fifteen minutes ago. I don't like to be kept waiting. That's something you'll have to learn if we're going to work together.'

Already, at these words, his penis is stiffening. He chooses not to mention that he made a pit-stop to his room: splashes of water on key locations, quick rubs of soap, more splashes, towel. He jumped into a fresh pair of jocks, heart thumping, while his mind pondered what moves she might expect of him, how to play the opportunity, whether his performance would meet her requirements. Now that the event is running, he feels a lot better. It helps that he is still under the good influences of the beer and wine consumed over the course of the evening.

She beckons him to come in close, which seems odd until he understands that she wants to take off her shoes. She holds onto his arm for balance and removes one high-heel, then the other. She drops the shoes onto the gravel below the first step. She seems much smaller now, like a miniature version of her previous self, but her relief at having her feet flat on the smooth stone of the step is obvious, and from this she derives fresh strength.

'Fucking high-heels. They're killing my back.'

'So why do you wear them?'

'You wouldn't understand. . . . Let's walk.'

Avoiding the gravel, she steps directly onto the narrow grass verge that runs in front of the house. Between the sash windows the verge is planted with bushes, including some climbing varieties that have colonised the masonry, in some cases reaching almost as high as the first-storey windows. They walk side by side. He allows her to set the pace, which is slow to begin with, then quickens as she gains confidence in walking on her bare feet. She has left her shoes behind her. As they proceed, the tiny green leather bag hanging from her shoulder swings rhythmically, catching his attention. He finds something beautiful in the arc of its movement, and wonders why so small a bag should have such a long strap. They reach the front corner of the house and turn inward, down by the side wall toward the fire escape. The grass verge ends after a few yards with a large bush in exuberant flower (lilac-coloured in the light of the day, greyish now). Beyond the bush begins a line of parked cars, including Alexander's Honda.

'I suppose this will do,' she says, hurriedly grabbing his hand. She misses her grip and ends up with a handful of his fingers, compensating by holding on too tightly. Her hand is surprisingly sweaty. She tugs him to the far side of the bush, then pushes him forcefully – both hands on his ribs – against the pebble-dash wall, where he bangs the back of his head, producing a moment of agony.

'Owa, what the hell—'

'Shut the fuck up,' she orders in a curiously alluring whisper, and again pushes him into the wall, though with much less violence. Alexander is gently rubbing the sore spot at the back of his head, wondering if there is any blood flowing or brain damage. Two plus two equals four, he thinks to himself, to make sure that his faculties are not impaired.

'Shhssh,' she says, in a soothing voice. Her warm hands reach inside his jacket, and instantly his sexual interest is reawakened. She lays her hands on his rib cage, runs them up and down his shirted torso, right up to the top of his chest, down again, pausing at the nipples, which she searches for roughly with the sides of her thumbs, down then to his abdomen.

'Bit of flab there. You should work out more.'

He has yielded to her now, completely. She takes two fistfuls of his shirt and pulls it up out of his trousers. She finds the cloth flap across the waistband of his trousers and tears it out. He hears the button popping. She pulls down the zip with such force that it catches and the stitching rips loudly under the continued pressure she applies. Alexander is frightened, fascinated.

'Let me see your cock,' she whispers.

He doesn't have the will left to make any response. She moves in closer to him, threateningly. She reaches up and grabs his throat, tightly enough for him to find it unbearable. He is unable to breathe. He feels that the veins in his head must burst with the pressure. She squeezes further. 'Do what I tell you. I know your type. You will do what I tell you.' She spits slightly in her forced anger. 'Now, show me your cock.' She eases her grip. His hands find his trousers and jocks, and he pushes them together down over his hips. He pushes his pelvis outward, offering his erection for her inspection, conscious of the paleness of his thighs under the spilt lighting from around the front.

'Good boy,' she tells him mockingly. 'That's much better. I like what I see.'

Ensuring first, with an automatic sweeping gesture, that the strap of her bag is securely lodged on her shoulder, she takes his penis in one hand and his scrotum in the other. For a short instant she squeezes his sack with her fingers, not using her nails, but implying that danger. He gasps in shock rather than pain, arching away from her, his scalp once again grazing against the pebble-dash surface behind. She laughs. She is pumping him now. Her grip is tighter than he would choose, her hand movements rougher and quicker. But to be in her hands in this way, cock and sack, to be fully in the hands of this woman is exquisite to him. She is fucking his very personality, wanking him off, and his overwhelming response is: Yes.

She stops. Hand behind the base of his skull, she roughly draws his head down and reaches up to whisper breathily into his ear.

'Here's what we want the consultants to say on broadband: the state should invest. A hundred and fifty million, two hundred million. With that sort of money, we can pay ... contractors ... to lay optical fibre wherever it's required. All those neglected provincial towns. ... Do you understand what I'm saying?'

He understands perfectly the connection she is making, but finds the interruption rather ill-timed. Her intense little speech is an absurdity to him. He wants to laugh in her face, but doesn't dare.

'Whatever you say,' he mumbles unconvincingly.

'Say please,' she tells him in a more playful tone, apparently thinking her point has been sufficiently made, which surprises him.

'Please,' he says.

'You can do better than that.'

'Please,' he implores her, almost meaning it.

She takes him in her hands again, begins to work his erection. He regrets that the spell has been slightly broken, and tries to rebuild it, groaning lightly, thrusting himself forward.

'Aaah,' he says, in his best sex wheeze. 'Aaaah.'

She is pumping harder. He overcomes the interruption. The sensual sexual thrill once again hits a peak of painful ecstasy, which spills over naturally, quickly, voluminously, into ejaculation. But the experience is broader than this mere localised physical orgasm. Cynicism shed, his entire person is transported in these final moments. It is his magnificent pleasure to come for her, however she chooses. And how she chooses is mechanistic, humiliating. She arranges it that he comes on his own shirt, and afterward she wipes her hands on his tie.

Again she draws his head down, reaches up on the tips of her toes.

'We have a beautiful future ahead of us,' she whispers into his ear, then bites him on the lobe, which hurts sharply. She drops to her feet, turns away, disappears around the bush, and makes silent progress over the grass on the other side.

'That was ... interesting,' he says to himself quietly with a giggle.

He reaches down and lifts up his jocks and trousers in a single movement. The zip and button are destroyed, and he hasn't brought a spare suit. He'll have to improvise. He tucks in his shirt, which is stained slimy-wet, and the slimy-wetness is already cold against his belly. He calculates: with his jacket closed and his hands in his pockets, he can make it to his room; then he'll ring room service for safety pins. It'll be fine. He can hand the suit into the dry-cleaners at the weekend for a repair job and clean. Julia will never notice the shirt. He washes his own.

He reaches into his jacket pocket for his cigarettes and lighter.

By half past two the following afternoon he is driving back to Dublin with the sodden outskirting hills of the Wicklow Mountains on his left. It rained heavily during the night and throughout the morning. Now the roads are drying quickly, mist rising off the tarmac.

He is always exhausted after Council meetings, particularly the overnight ones. It is the coming down from the higher gear of preparation and performance, the hangover from the drinking, the consequence of sleeping poorly in the unfamiliar hotel bed. On this occasion, he is taxed also by his encounter with Grace Sharkey, the recollection of which is regularly surfacing to the top of his mind, occasioning mixed emotions of elation and shame.

As ever, the fun part of the Council meeting was George. Toward the end of dinner the previous evening he was already very well oiled. Alexander caught his eye at one point across the table. George was listening – but not really – to a self-loving speech from the Department of Finance drone sitting beside him. To Alexander, he raised the corner of one eyebrow, saying: Isn't this a hoot? Later, when the thin ageing after-dinner speaker had finished his ardent but curiously uninspiring speech, George was first in when the Chairman opened the discussion to questions.

'Chairman, can I suggest that we move our consideration of these excellent propositions to the bar,' George said, with real appeal in his voice, since they had stopped serving wine a good while earlier. 'Or else we could bring the bar in here.'

George – as he might have put it himself – had a goo on him. Restraint forgotten, tie off, sleeves rolled up, he was on a mission to get seriously plastered, displaying – Alexander felt – admirable vision and commitment.

As a consequence of this mission, George missed the eight-thirty start of the morning meeting by a cool two hours. Too late to be in a hurry, he entered the room in grand fashion. He was washed and properly dressed, his hair still wet from the shower. He was also clearly still drunk from the night before, his eyes bloodshot, pickled in gin. Bowing and waving his arms flamboyantly, he made a declaration through the Chair: 'Chairman, I apologise,' he said, his voice ridiculously thick and throaty. 'I abase myself before you.... My alarm clock didn't go off.... You know me of old, Chairman. You know that there is none more enthusiastic than I to get up early for the Council.... And I should say as well that those of us who soldiered on in the bar, till three or four in the morning, devoted ourselves exclusively to affairs of state, and I believe we worked out some solutions to a number of the problems that this august body, ably led by yourself, sir, has been considering. However, I cannot guarantee that we remember the solutions.... I abase myself.'

By this point the Council was delighted. In the first moments, George's late entrance and his condition were appalling, embarrassing; but as he proceeded eloquently, the members woke out of their torpor like school kids excited by an unexpected diversion. They hid their enjoyment for as long as possible, until finally they were openly grinning and laughing. It would have been impossible for Banner to be hard on him.

'You have abased yourself sufficiently, George. Take your seat.'

Alexander is stuck now behind a Land Rover towing a horsebox, with a well-groomed athletic backside sticking out the rear. The horse lifts its tail and calmly shits out several dollops of tasty-looking light brown material.

Alexander lets his speed drop off and swings across slightly into the other lane to get a view for overtaking. A rigid truck, racing bumpily along the road in the opposite direction, barely twenty yards away, looking unsteady on its wheels, gives two sharp blasts of the horn to clear him out of the way. Alexander swings back in behind the horse-box, chastened, his quickened heart skipping beats.

'Ooops.'

It's not that the Land Rover is going too slowly. He hates not being able to see what's coming on the road.

Faced again with the horse's arse, two things come to mind.

The first is that Helena will have been out riding the night before in Thorny Valley Riding School, where they take their weekly lesson. He wonders which horse she got. He himself always accepts what he is given. Helena is pickier. She used to ring in advance to lobby, but stopped when she suspected that this was becoming counter-productive. The rule is: you take the horse that is assigned to you; you read your name across from the horse's name on the neatly written list that is pinned up on the arena door; you go to the stable and fetch your horse, unless it is already in the arena with the lesson just finishing.

Alexander wonders why he is less enthusiastic now about this pursuit than he was a year ago. In fact, he knows why, but hasn't yet articulated it fully to himself. He had reached a particular point in the sport where the weekly lesson and occasional weekend excursion were no longer enough; where he would have needed to start riding a few times a week in order to satisfy his appetite, to achieve the curve of improvement that he knew was possible, that he wanted to achieve; where it would have made sense to start thinking about buying a horse, while at the same time it was also clear that owning a horse would be impossible for him, given the required commitment of time and money. And so the point he had reached turned out to be a peak, and now he is cruising downhill, running off the intensity built up in the preceding period. In all matters, motion is unceasing. This appears to be the only law.

The second thing that comes to mind is less obviously linked with the horse box in front. It is an image or stream of images, pre-verbal, not word-thoughts. The subject-matter feels important to him, weighty, coming from the dreaming place where truth is symbolic rather than logical, the submerged twisted undergrowth of personality. He cannot discern the significance of this image, but he fears it.

It is the truck full of sheep that he would sometimes see as a child on his way to school, parked in front of Tom Kearney's butcher's shop in Malahide village: the smell of sheep shit; the animals bleating, their light hooves dancing on the metallic base of the pen; horribly crowded, confused, individual sheep trying to turn around; their dirty woollen pelts and skinny black legs visible between the horizontal wooden planks; little snouts sticking out, trying to get a glimpse of what was going on.

In the afternoon on the way home, the truck would be gone, but he would be reminded of what he had witnessed by little streams of blood and water running out of the side alley, out onto the cracked uneven pavement, down the hill. Unsentimentally, carefully, he would enjoy making sure that he didn't step in the blood.

Why is it again that people have children? Why do so many people couple off and reproduce? It's remarkable really, Alexander thinks. When there are so many other possibilities in life. He corrects himself. All the other possibilities can be summed to one. You have children or you don't. That is the choice.

The youngest of *George's* three children has Down's syndrome, a boy of ten called Pádraig. Alexander doesn't know what difficulties this creates above and beyond the usual challenges of child-rearing. George himself has never mentioned the subject. It was Marilyn, their secretary, who told Alexander, in a whisper, as though it were a crime.

He is back in the office before four. There was no work reason for him to return; no one would require him to be there after the Council meeting. It would be very surprising if George turned up. Moreover, Alexander is certainly too tired to bother with anything other than checking his emails. He has returned because the prospect of going home depresses him. In his hangover from the Council meeting, he longs to chat to someone and has returned to the office for company.

Rounding his desk to sit down, he picks up three or four sealed envelopes from his in-tray. He leafs through this post, gleaning in a few glances that there is nothing here of any interest, nothing that requires immediate attention. He drops the unopened letters back into his in-tray, swivels in his chair to face the computer and hits the go button.

While the machine is booting up, working through its tedious routine of whirring and clicking, generating mysterious messages of system errors that the IT people have told him to ignore, chugging its way through the start-up of anti-viral software, Alexander checks the voicemail on his phone, on which the red light is flashing. The voicemail software has its own long-winded sequences, presented by a sing-song American female voice. She tells him he has three new messages, then forces him to listen to a comprehensive menu of available actions before letting him hear these messages. The messages do not deliver on the promise of the flashing red light. The first two are hang-ups – the sound of a phone hitting the receiver, then the beep-beep-beep. The third is Imelda, telling him that she will be late that morning. Dozy bitch. It is typical of her to forget that he was away at the Council meeting. She could have breezed in at lunchtime with impunity.

By now his PC is running. He opens his mailbox and finds that he has nine new messages, lovely little sealed yellow envelopes, with cheerful bold script explaining what they are about, who they are from, when they were sent. He scans the sender column to see if there is anything interesting, anything personal, which there isn't. He then re-scans them to see if there is any he wishes to open, which there isn't. He also has a large number of opened messages in his inbox. The emails he leaves in his inbox are the ones that require action of some sort on his part. He doesn't bother to scan through these now, but slips out the top sheet of A4 paper from the feed-tray for his printer, finds a biro from the mess in front of him on the desk, clears some space for the sheet, and writes the word *Monday* across the top. Underneath this, indented a little, he draws an asterisk and after it writes *Do emails*. This makes him feel better. It feels like the first step in re-establishing order from chaos.

He pats the pockets of his jacket for his mobile, locating it in his left inside breast pocket, next to his heart. The screen is completely dark, sleeping. If there were any messages or missed calls, there would be a little sign interrupting the darkness. So he knows already when he presses the two-button sequence that unlocks the phone that there is nothing to check, but he checks nevertheless. It is necessary for him to wake up the phone, to see its normal screen in order to verify doubly that there are no messages, that everything is functioning normally and there are no messages for him.

He slips his hand back inside his jacket and lets the mobile fall into the breast pocket. It is the perfect weight for such a fall, bouncing lightly when it hits the bottom seam.

All means of communication thus checked, and each having yielded a zero return, Alexander wonders what to do next.

Despite the fact that he ought to know better, every time he sees the flashing light on the phone, every time the PC utters the electronic sigh that signals the arrival of a new email, every time his mobile phone goes blup-blop, every time he gets a letter, his levels of cheerfulness rise a notch. And when the message turns out to be something mundane or impersonal, as it almost always does, he feels a brief disappointment and his mood drops – lower than originally – before gradually recovering. These are some of the infinitesimal psychological swings in the day. What does he expect? And why does he continue to expect it? That this new message will lead to something special, something that will change his life: an offer from a head-hunting company of a big job in South Africa; a new lover; a blossoming friendship? His expectation, though tangible, is never quite so specific.

Alexander observes himself in the isolation of his office, surrounded by technological possibility. Within seconds, he could be in touch with someone in the South Pacific. But he has no one to talk to in the South Pacific. In fact, right now, despite having a SIM card loaded to the brim, he feels he has no one to talk to in Dublin, where he has spent his entire life.

Obviously there must be something wrong with him. But what? And was it always like this? He doesn't think so, but he can't be sure.

He re-observes within his modest desperation the small hope that even a moment ago flared up in a tiny way, sufficient for its extinguishment to be perceptible. He realises that, despite what he tries to tell himself, he is not resigned to his life of drudgery interspersed with minor fleeting pleasures. He wants something more, and is prepared to exert himself to get it, if only a little, in a half-hearted way, without any belief.

He takes out his mobile phone again and calls Julia. Her phone switches directly to voicemail without ringing.

'Hello, this is Julia. I'm not available at the moment. Please leave a message after the tone.'

As he ends this call with a movement of his thumb, he has another flash from the night before, a picture, a physical memory: his back against the pebble-dash wall; his cock and scrotum in Grace Sharkey's hands. His penis thickens now with lust.

Alexander ventures out into the open-plan area between his office and George's. There, amidst the jungle of yucca plants, felt-covered desk dividers, curved fake-wooden work-stations, endless, almost-useless documents and reports, personal colouredy bits, photographs, carefully selected screen savers, dusty PCs, overweight cabinets, piles of files, fans on stands, stacks of boxes of paper, a water cooler that is dripping down onto the carpet, creating a patch of rot ... he finds his team.

Luke's work-station is the nearest, and Luke is also the friendliest on this sort of social call. When Alexander drops around just to say hello, as opposed to when he comes with specific intent, he tends to position himself at Luke's station, talking mostly to Luke, but loudly enough that the others can hear, and turning his head sometimes to peek over the dividers and include them in the conversation.

He gives a brief report of the proceedings of the Council, then asks – in as offhand a manner as possible, to guard against rejection – if anyone would fancy an early Friday-evening drink.

Luke thinks this is a terrific idea and chuckles happily. Neville plays harder to get. He says that he is working on something he wants to finish and that he'll join them later. Imelda copies this admirable affectation, saying she'll follow them down. Dympna wishes that she had the time for such frivolity. Unfortunately, she has to go home to make dinner for her family and clean the house.

'That's unfortunate for them,' Luke says under his breath.

As Luke and Alexander stroll from the building across the open courtyard, which serves in the evenings as a meeting ground for prostitutes and their clients, Alexander tries to kick a used condom from his path. He does not succeed, even with two attempts, in dislodging this previously distended, now flattened item from the paving stone to which it has adhered itself. And then it is behind him. You don't stop for these things, he narrates inwardly. You get it on the move or you leave it.

'Never underestimate the sticking power of semen,' Luke says.

'Surely the semen is on the inside.'

'The boys probably swim out overnight, desperately searching for ova as they tragically freeze to death, reflecting, collectively, in their dying moments: well, at least we can glue this condom to the ground; that will be our revenge for the fruitlessness of our existence.... Did you ever notice how none of the condoms you see around here has ribbing for extra pleasure?'

'I confess this is a detail which has escaped me up to now. Next you're going to tell me that none of them is strawberry flavoured, and I'm going to wonder: how can he know this?'

'Hey, you've got to pay attention to the details,' Luke exclaims pedagogically. 'As an economist, I'm a perpetual student of human behaviour. So I'll tell you why none of them has ribbing for extra pleasure. It's because the hookers buy them and they're not interested in extra pleasure.'

'Are you saying that the punters would be buying the ribbed variety?'

'The punters don't buy any condoms at all – well, except for private use. The hookers buy the condoms and actively shun ribbing for extra pleasure. One – they don't want the extra pleasure. Two – they're keeping their costs down.'

'I might buy a ribbed condom and plant it back there just to mess up your theory.'

'You'd have to use it of course – one way or the other.'

'I know how to use a condom,' Alexander responds quietly, as though this might have been in doubt.

A couple of minutes later they are standing at the bar in Sarsfield's with two creamy pints of Guinness in front of them. They enjoy a moment of silent contemplation. Because they left early, the pub is not yet full, as it will be by six o'clock. Alexander raises his pint to clink glasses with Luke.

'Cheers,' he says.

'Sláinte,' Luke says.

Luke is from Belfast. He always says 'Sláinte'. Alexander likes Luke's accent. Julia, also from Belfast, has a similar accent, and it was one of the reasons Alexander fell in love with her. On the few occasions when she and Luke meet, they swap news about people they have discovered they both know. There are quite a lot of them, even though they come from different parts of the city. At college, Julia used to trade a bit on being a rebel from the North, particularly when she was drunk, but in fact she never knew much about Northern politics. Luke – Alexander has gleaned gradually – is probably quite a serious republican, although one wouldn't guess it at first because he likes to make fun of everything.

'Any crack at the Council?' he asks. 'Any good jokes?'

'The whole thing is a joke,' Alexander responds sourly, too tired and undone to keep up any professional pretences.

'Here, I've got a good one. It's about this guy who loses both testicles in a tragic motorcycle accident—'

'But is otherwise left intact?'

'Yeah.'

'That's a pretty unique motorcycle accident.'

'Yeah, it was a tragic and bizarre motorcycle accident, which resulted in the loss of both testicles, but let's not labour the detail. . . .'

One long thirsty gulp and Alexander is already halfway through his pint. This is pleasant. The atmosphere in the pub is congenial, relaxed. Everything is fine, in fact. His sex life is suddenly exciting. His marriage plans are brewing nicely. It's Friday night. He'll have a couple of hours in the pub, then Julia and he will drive out to Malahide for dinner at Helena's.

He inhales deeply on his cigarette, nodding as he does so to indicate that he is listening enthusiastically.

'So, our man says to the foreman,' Luke continues. 'Before I take this job, there is something I want to tell you. I don't want this getting around, but I lost both my testicles in a bizarre and tragic motorcycle accident....'

At this point in the joke, two things happen. Luke spots Imelda and Neville coming through the door, and waves them over, while Alexander, who is facing the other way, simultaneously notices Danny farther down the bar, the upper half of his body swinging backward off the fulcrum of the barstool. Only the back half of his skull is visible to Alexander, but the shape of it and the dark hair, which is due for a cut, are immediately and unmistakeably recognisable. He hears Danny's light, forced laugh, further confirming the identification.

'Sonofabitch,' Alexander says, his jaw clenching in anger. 'Sorry, I don't mean you. I've just seen a mate of mine.'

'You're obviously very fond of him.'

'Press pause, Luke. I'll be back in a minute.'

Danny seems pleased to see him.

'Ah, the very man, me heart and soul,' he says slowly, carefully enunciating every word, and lazily embracing Alexander with his free arm. His other arm is parked on the bar, close to a three-quarters-full pint of Guinness, an unlit cigarette held limply in his hand. 'This man is solid as a rock,' he tells his overweight drinking companion on the next barstool. It is Dermot O'Hara, the journalist, Aoife's cousin. Alexander endeavours to keep his countenance clean of any flicker of recognition.

'Dermot O'Hara,' says Dermot O'Hara easily, reaching out his hand, which Alexander takes and shakes firmly, as would be fitting for a man who is solid as a rock.

'Alexander Vespucci.'

'Good name.'

'Yes, I made it up all by myself.'

'Haven't we met before?' asks O'Hara, scratching his forehead to aid recollection. 'I think I had a good chat with your girlfriend. She has long curly hair, right? What was her name again?'

'I can't recall,' says Alexander.

Danny titters. He lights his cigarette. It is a slow labour for him to accomplish.

Apart from his deliberate but nevertheless slurred diction, there are a number of clues to indicate that Danny is deeply saturated in alcohol, that he has been drinking more or less non-stop for the thirty hours since Alexander last saw him. His eyes have a glazed and wounded sardonic partially blind appearance to them. His side vision is gone, physically and metaphysically. He is also clearly working at keeping his body upright. But the most telling sign for Alexander, which he knows and loves from previous benders of Danny's, is the way Danny holds his cigarette, in his dirty shaky slow-moving fingers, with such a light grip – zero pressure – that seemingly it must fall. Friction alone is the force that keeps it in place against the pull of gravity.

Danny is in open country, windswept, war-torn. He glides over the landscape, a good-humoured ghost, lingering by whim wherever some feature catches his interest. He is faintly warm hearted; slim, as all ghosts are; dark and elegant, as some can be; and subtly arch, like Lucifer. In his alcoholic condition, the nobility in Danny which first attracted Alexander is evident, however prismatically contorted. Alexander is too in awe of him to muster any outrage – right now at least.

Danny removes his arm from around Alexander's shoulders and marshals himself to light the cigarette in his hand.

'Let me buy you a drink, Alex. What are you having?'

'I'm with some people over there.'

'Have a quick shot. I'll get you a tequila. You've always liked tequila. Let's have a round of tequilas.'

'Count me out,' says O'Hara, sighing as he shifts his heavy body off the stool to head for the toilet. He seems sober.

While Danny is looking to attract the attention of the barman, Alexander sits up on O'Hara's stool to take the weight off his feet. For a couple of moments, his buttocks squirm squeamishly at meeting the patch of intimate warmth that O'Hara's arse has left behind on the cushioned seat.

'You've spent the money.'

'Sure, it was only a drop in the ocean of my need. It was gone by yesterday evening. I'm drinking here now on my tab. I know the owner.'

'Even you can't drink sixteen hundred euro in one day. You gambled it, right?'

'I was trying to work it up. If you'd given me what I was looking for, I wouldn't have had to gamble.'

'I see.'

'I was up to three and half grand by two o'clock this morning at the blackjack table. I was on a roll, but I got greedy, got burnt.' Danny draws lightly on his cigarette. He takes his time, enjoying each tiny inflexion of movement. He exhales. The hand goes to the bar again for support. 'Went down in flames. . . . I can tell you, it's a remarkable torture.'

'You make it sound like a fine wine. I can't afford that sort of pleasure.'

'You'd be surprised how much you can afford, if you make the effort. I could get more money out of you than you could possibly imagine.'

Dermot O'Hara returns from the toilet. Alexander's anger attaches itself to this new object. He moves to vacate the stool.

'No, stay where you are. I was just leaving.'

O'Hara lifts a light yellow V-neck – probably cashmere – from the back of the stool, locates the appropriate aperture and ducks his head into it. He's vulnerable now, Alexander thinks. One good smack on the crown with the glass ashtray from the bar and he'd be banging off the furniture like a pinball.

O'Hara's head emerges from the neck-hole with his glasses awry and his hair stuck down on his forehead. He straightens his glasses.

'I always forget to take off my specs before putting on the jumper,' he observes, with the confidence and composure of one who assumes he is naturally witty and interesting. 'You'd think I'd know better by now.'

'It's not really that cold,' Alexander comments.

'I'm recovering from a summer virus,' O'Hara says. 'You know the kind you just can't shake off.'

The barman arrives back with two shot glasses full of transparent tequila. A little slice of bar lemon is perched across the top of each. The pips in the lemon are turning brown.

'I have a sensitive throat,' O'Hara says. 'I get this strep thing and I have to take antibiotics, which then wrecks the immune system and I pick up every dose that's going.'

'That's quite interesting,' says Alexander sarcastically. 'Do you take any supplements?'

O'Hara steps backward abruptly and squints at Alexander from behind his glasses, to reappraise him. Danny forces a bit of a laugh, a delayed reaction which is nevertheless tinged with genuine amusement.

'I should have mentioned that Alex doesn't always relate well to human beings,' he says.

'Which excludes journalists,' Alexander adds cheerily. 'But I hope I'm not expressing myself too freely. It's just that I have a lot of pent-up opinions. For example, my road-rage levels astonish me. You wouldn't believe the stuff I come out with. There I am, driving along, thinking I'm in a good mood, then some sonofabitch does something he shouldn't do and a frenzied stream of hateful expletives flows forth involuntarily from my mouth. I want to smash his car and mutilate him. Do you know what I mean?'

'I'll remember not to cut across you,' O'Hara responds mildly.

'Do you have any more items of clothing lying around?' Alexander asks. 'Perhaps I'm sitting on your hat and gloves.' He makes a gesture of looking under his arse.

'Fuck you,' says O'Hara, less mildly. He turns pointedly to Danny, saying, 'I might see you Sunday afternoon so.'

'If body and soul are still together.' Danny parks his cigarette in the glass ashtray. He reaches across with his infirm hand and shakes O'Hara's. 'Don't mind this young man. He's an economist. He loves your column.'

'I'm a big fan,' Alexander says.

O'Hara nods to him reluctantly, nods again to Danny and makes for the door.

'Here's the salt, Danny,' says the barman generously, as he pops an ugly little glass dispenser down beside the tequila shots.

Alexander watches O'Hara's back as he leaves. He passes Luke, Neville and Imelda, all of whom seem to be having a good time. Imelda is doing her braying laugh, then breaks into a squeal of excitement.

'That's exactly what I said to him,' she says, loudly enough for Alexander to hear her. The three of them are laughing now, and Alexander feels they are laughing at him.

'Come on, let's do it,' says Danny.

They throw the shots down their throats. It is a matter of ritual that this be done in a single movement. Danny struggles a bit. The tequila goes into his mouth, and from there is swallowed in two or three distinct gulps. Alexander, who has the considerable benefit of freshness, executes as choreographed, gasps, and bites into the lemon slice, which instantly overrides the burning sensation.

'Are we back?' Danny asks, carelessly dropping the remains of his lemon onto the floor.

'We're back,' Alexander lies, and takes a cigarette from Danny's pack on the bar. 'I'd better get a pint. Actually, I still have a pint down below.... Fuck it, I'll have a-quick-nother one here.'

As he is lighting his cigarette, he sees Aoife enter from the street, pushing the door open with force and purpose. She looks magnificent. The colours of her are elemental: the redness of her hair, wiry and wild; her long, green big-buttoned jacket with the high collar turned up; the pallor of her skin (she looks a bit ill, in fact); her tall black punk boots. She charges into the pub as though she has stepped from another dimension, like the horse that came out of the wardrobe in *Time Bandits*, sweating and steaming. She scans the assembled drinkers with intensely focused, marauding eyes, and quickly spots Danny and Alexander.

'Angry missus at three o'clock,' Alexander says to Danny.

Danny does not respond. It appears from his expression that he hasn't heard properly or doesn't understand, or perhaps the drink is delaying his reactions.

'Aoife is here and she's coming straight for you.'

'Ah,' says Danny, and his head gives a curious upward nod. He doesn't turn around to watch her approach. Calmly he reaches for his pint and throws a good portion of what remains down his throat with far more ease than he did the tequila. She is upon them now. Alexander is nervous. He coughs to distract himself from the bodily sensations of fear. He has been on sessions with Danny when Aoife has tracked them down. It hasn't been pretty.

She ignores Alexander as she grimly lays a hand on Danny's shoulder. Danny turns around to greet her.

'My darling ball and chain,' he says. 'Is it that time already? I'm sure you must be right. Haven't I had more than enough of free living these past few hours?'

'I have a taxi waiting outside, Danny,' Aoife says in a low, livid voice. 'You're going to get up, and we're going to leave quietly. The other option is that I kick the shit out of you right here and now.'

'Well, when you put it like that, dear, how can I refuse?'

Danny turns around to finish his pint, which he does in a single swallow. He gathers up his cigarettes, lighter and newspapers (*Irish Times*, *Racing Post*, folded, frayed, smudged). He lifts himself carefully to his feet, sways deeply, corrects himself, leeringly fastens his gaze on the barman, inquiring in this way as to whether or not it was he who betrayed him. The barman gives a shrug that could mean anything.

'Do you have money for the taxi?' Aoife asks Alexander.

'How much?'

'Thirty euro.'

He reaches in for the stash of cash in his thigh pocket, pulls out some notes. This lucky dip goes badly for him: a fifty and a twenty. He reaches in again but there are only coins left. He looks at her. She stares right back.

'Here,' he says, handing her the fifty.

Danny claps him feebly on the shoulder and makes to leave. Aoife nods. She is imputing no blame to Alexander on this occasion. She expresses no gratitude for the money, gives no parting word, but her nod is respectful, an acknowledgement of shared existence, experience.

She turns and leads her tottering man out the door.

Alexander returns to his colleagues and stands modestly on the outskirts of the conversation until there is an opening for him to enter. Neville is telling the story of a suicide.

'He hanged himself in the garage.'

'At a party?' Luke asks in consternation.

'A big party. A friend of his had a free house – the parents were away. At two o'clock in the morning, he goes into the garage and hangs himself.'

'Was it something somebody said to him?' Imelda asks.

'We'll never know,' says Neville. 'But maybe you're right. Maybe somebody said something to him, or maybe he overheard something, or saw something: his best friend getting off with his girlfriend; his girlfriend dumping him, laughing at him; somebody revealing to everyone that he was gay.'

In stating this last option, Neville looks pointedly at Alexander, or at least Alexander feels that he is looking pointedly at him. Either way, Alexander experiences a moment of discomfort.

'It's an epidemic,' he says to deflect the attention. 'People are topping themselves left, right and centre. I can't understand it. If I wanted to kill myself, I'd go to Buenos Aires and drink myself to death ... have a bit of fun on the way.'

'I'd do a Hungerford,' says Luke with a laugh. 'I'd take a few bastards with me – go out in style.'

'What's a Hungerford?' Imelda asks.

'Columbine,' says Neville.

'It's a small town in the countryside outside London,' Alexander explains. 'A few years ... a long time ago now, a guy went bonkers with a rifle, killed more than a dozen people, then shot himself in the head.'

'I'd drink weed killer,' says Neville with a smirk. 'I'd pour it into a Coke bottle, put it in the fridge like it was real Coke, then drink it some day after work, if I was bored, just for kicks.'

'With slight modification, that could be a murder plan,' Alexander observes.

Neville continues to smirk.

In the car on the way out to Malahide, Alexander and Julia barely speak.

She drives. To begin with, her handling of the car is staccato, angular. She is unfeeling with the gears. She slaps the indicator arm as though she wishes to damage it. She over-accelerates, then brakes. But the evening is so lovely, warm and bright, it is impossible for her to persist with this brutality for long.

The traffic is easing off. They cruise easily down Camden Street ... Wexford Street ... Aungier Street. In these minutes, he feels a great fondness for Dublin, these bustling, downbeat stretches, the tilt and curve of the terraces, how the straight lines of human construction bend and sink into the ground with age. Julia swings the car smoothly onto Dame Street. It seems to Alexander that everyone on the streets is in good form, looking forward to the night ahead and the weekend. There are fewer hurrying commuters now, more young people: freshly washed, in their best gear, boys with gel in their hair, girls with glittery eyeshadow. He feels at one with them.

Alexander has his window rolled down, elbow out. His perception has been heightened by the beer and tequila. The physical texture of the city appears different to him: the pavements, the buildings;

these surfaces seem yielding, as if one could bounce off them. He experiences the sky as an interior ceiling, beneath which all is seamlessly integrated. Alexander finds himself on intimate terms with everything under the sun. He is superhuman, bulletproof.

At the corner of College Green, he studies with fresh attention the square-shouldered façade of Trinity College. It is the face of home. And the old parliament building, with its tall columns and scooped-out in-filled windows, is creamy, curvaceous. The traffic light here is green, but they nevertheless have to roll cautiously through the crossing flow of pedestrians, who have right of way because there are so many of them and because they jaywalk so expertly. Julia is patient in this.

When she met him earlier at the ramped mouth of the carpark under his office, she seemed unusually tense.

'Why did you ask me to meet you here?' she asked angrily, 'You knew I would look like a prostitute, standing around waiting. I don't find that amusing. And you're drunk.'

He reckons now that her mood has softened sufficiently for him to make a come-back.

'I tried to ring you this afternoon. Your phone was switched off.'

'You don't own me, Alexander,' she retorts, so ferociously that he thinks she is going crazy, until with a bolt – tinged with malicious glee – he realises she must be having her period, must be just about to get her period.

Julia doesn't speak much on the subject of menstruation. Back when they first starting screwing properly, in college, they didn't pause for that part of her cycle. He took his cue from her on this. If she didn't mind, he didn't mind. He would wake up in the morning and see the dark dried blood on his penis, some of it flaking off already, and the Catholic in him would feel like a sexual rebel, a desperado.

When they got back together again, after the split, Julia's policies changed. First it was: 'We don't have to have sex every night.' Then, a little later: 'No. I have my period.'

Over the years, which have gone by like days, sex went from being the rule to being the exception, so much so that now he discovers her period through its effect on her mood rather than the sexual disruption.

But there is another clue, apart from her mood. Sometimes he notices a tiny cloud of diluted blood – no more than the size of a twenty-cent coin – at the bottom of the toilet, far below the water-line, resting in the concavity which is the low point of the visible portion of the pipe. There is something beautiful to him about this little pinkish trace that appears always in this same location in the toilet. He doesn't know why it is there, in behavioural or scientific terms. He doesn't inquire about how she disposes of her tampons. He doesn't know if blood has a higher density than water, whether or not it is partially insoluble in water. In his teenage years, he wondered if menstrual blood was different from ordinary blood, but such questions do not trouble him now.

'You seem a bit touchy,' he says diplomatically as they turn left off the quays past Liberty Hall and head for Busáras under the heavy railway bridge.

She doesn't answer.

'Danny blew the money I gave him,' he continues.

'Of course he blew it. Being Danny. You should have given it to Aoife.'

'I couldn't have done that. He's my friend.'

On the North Strand, they pass a Chinese takeaway called Fragrant River. He remembers, during their student days, when they would get the 42 bus out to Malahide, along this same route, to make a retreat from the hectic pace of their drinking life and get properly fed by his mother.

'That's an awful name for a restaurant,' she said one evening as they passed it on the bus.

'I was just thinking that it's a good name,' he said.

They laughed about this clash of opinion, but it seems to him now to represent an early indication of a fundamental difference in perspective.

Why, again, is he planning to marry this irritable woman?

Because the time is right and he has no one else to marry. Because she is relatively good looking and intelligent. Because she is the right age, has the right education. Because she is not a bad person. Because, above all, she knows him. He couldn't bear to repeat the process of introducing and explaining himself, of working through to the point where it would be possible to marry someone else.

When and how should he raise the issue? Should he buy a ring first? That would be a waste of money if she ends up saying no. And now doesn't seem to be the right time, since they appear to have drifted into a bad patch. Some time around Christmas she mentioned it herself. They were in the bathroom: she sitting on the toilet having a pee, which she rarely does in his presence; he shaving at the mirror, reaching up carefully into one of his nostrils with the corner of the razorhead.

'So when are we going to get married, Alex? When is the day?'

'Are you teasing me?'

'You tell me.'

And he cut himself.

At the beginning, his mother took a strong dislike to Julia.

Out in Malahide, Julia was supposed to sleep in the spare room, but the first time she stayed over, she ended up spending the night in Alexander's bed, accidentally. They fell asleep in each other's arms, and remained the whole night entwined in the same position on the narrow mattress. They were very much in love in those days, and could maintain physical closeness for a long time without it becoming uncomfortable. Now, in their infrequent couplings, their bodies naturally and rapidly seek physical separation within seconds of the act concluding.

His mother woke them that morning with shocking knocks on the bedroom door, followed by a rash intrusion. Brigid in her morning glory would have scared the devil: full-length pink polyester dressing gown and matching slippers; face puffy and lined from sleep; hair sticking out as if she had spent the night sniffing solvents;

expression raw and angry. She spoke with one hand in front of her mouth to cover the absence of her false teeth.

'You, Miss, get across to the spare room, which is where you were invited to sleep, and where you would have slept if you had any manners.'

Brigid pointed across the landing and moved to one side of the doorway to give Julia room to pass. Julia rose silently and walked across the floor in a long T-shirt (one of Alexander's) and bare feet. Even in those uncomfortable moments, Alexander could not but admire the girl: the slow grace of her movement; the turn of her calves.

'You can do what you like when you have your own house,' Brigid said to her son, 'but so long as you live in mine, you'll abide by my rules.' Julia was out of sight but still within earshot as Brigid continued deliberately with a little stab of character assassination. 'And let me tell you, she's no good for you. I watched her yesterday. She drinks too much. She's dissipated.'

This was well over a decade ago. All is forgotten now. These days, Julia gets on better with his mother than Alexander does.

Helena and her family live in a housing estate on the coast road in Malahide. The estate was built in the 1970s. The gardens are full, mature – somehow dated, Alexander finds, perhaps due to all the palm trees. But the cars are invariably up-to-the-minute. And there is a great abundance of them, parked along the kerb, crammed into driveways. Some of the gardens have been paved over, typically in red and beige tiles, to make way for two, three or even four cars. Helena's front garden is one such, although they own only two vehicles: Derek's 03 BMW 3 Series and Helena's 02 Golf GTI. Their house is 'detached', separated from its neighbours by three or four feet on either side. It is a solid, square building, with a good high roof, the apex of which is directly over the front door, as it would be in a picture drawn by a child. Taking account of the house, the cars, household assets, pension rights and so on, Helena is easily a millionaire, which – when they were kids – was a fabulous thing to be. Nowadays, everyone is a millionaire. Except Alexander.

He presses the bell in three short bursts. As they wait, he is curiously nervous. An odd premonition comes to him. He turns to Julia.

'Am I a bad lover?' he asks searchingly.

His question physically knocks her. She takes a step backward, frowning. He thinks for a moment she is going to cry, but she gathers herself, steps nearer to him, reaches up with her hand on his arm, and plants a perfect kiss on his mouth, cool and dry on the outside, with a thin line of warm wetness through the centre.

'No, I wouldn't say that. But you finish poorly.'

She breaks into a loud affectionate laugh, as though she has hit upon a private joke, and is still laughing when Helena opens the door.

'You missed a good lesson last night,' Helena says to him, as she is bringing them into the sitting room.

'Who were you on?'

'Liath. We jumped quite high: four poles.'

Liath is a seven-year-old grey mare, Helena's favourite horse in the stable. For a school horse, she is sensitive in the mouth, and forward going rather than lazy. When she is walking, she wants to trot; when she is trotting, she wants to canter. But since she is so responsive, it isn't hard work to hold her back, which makes for a good ride: contained energy.

Alexander finds there is something intensely mundane – almost depressive – in the atmosphere in the big front room where Helena's husband Derek, their two kids, and Brigid are sitting around, waiting for dinner, watching *Buffy the Vampire Slayer*.

'Well, hello to you,' says Brigid with peculiar emphasis, as if this is a line she has rehearsed all evening.

She looks exceedingly relaxed, sitting on the sofa with her feet up on a pouffe and a celebrity magazine on her lap.

'Howdy,' says Derek from his armchair, with some intention to engage politely; but his eyes are repeatedly, magnetically, drawn back to the screen where Buffy is kick-boxing zombies. In a titty top and tight jeans, Buffy is indeed in mouth-watering form, as ever.

'Mammy, I'm hungry,' says skinny eight-year-old Nicky, fixedly watching Alexander. She is sitting on the sofa beside her granny, their arms cosily linked. 'Can I have a glass of milk and two biscuits?'

Brendan, aged five, is sitting on the carpet right under the television set, playing with his dinosaurs.

'Hiya, Brendan,' says Alexander, making an effort to sound upbeat.

Brendan looks back at him sceptically.

'Will you get the folks a drink?' Helena asks her husband. 'I'm just going to put the spuds in the oven.'

'Did you not have dinner in your own house?' Brendan asks, which causes Derek to chuckle.

'Don't be rude, Brendan,' says Helena, as she leaves the room.

'Our granny is a vegan,' Nicky says. 'That means she doesn't eat any meat unless she wants to. I'm a vegan too, except I usually always like to eat meat, especially chicken and burgers, but not stew. Stew is yucky.'

The sofa and armchairs are arranged around the television. Julia sits beside Nicky on the sofa. Alexander takes the free chair, while Derek is creakily rising from his. Standing, Derek fondly caresses his substantial beer belly with both hands.

'What'll you have to drink?' he asks and belches. 'Excuse me.'

Brendan launches into a big forced laugh.

Alexander asks for a lager. Julia ponders, then opts for a glass of white wine, if there's a bottle open.

'There isn't, but I'll open one for you. Do you want white?'

'Yes, that's what I said.'

'No; you said, "if there is a bottle open",' Derek continues, exercising his sense of humour, 'which there isn't—'

'You have to be careful what you say in this house,' Brigid advises Julia. 'You have to speak very accurately.'

'But I'll open a bottle for you. You're more than welcome.'

Accuracy thus satisfied, Derek departs to get the drinks.

'You should have come to Galway,' Brigid says to her son, shaking her head solemnly. 'It was just Mick and me from our side. The

Gradys were there in shifts.' Brigid, sniffing, wiggles her bum on the sofa to get more purchase for the important utterance to come. 'She might leave you something in the will if you courted her a bit. She was always fond of you.'

Alexander feigns superiority to these vulgar considerations.

'How is she doing?' he asks.

'They moved her back Wednesday to the nursing home. She's very frail. If she sneezes queerly in the night, it could push her over the edge. But there's nothing wrong with her as such, apart from a sprained ankle. And she seems to be perfectly in her senses, though she's cross. She's threatening to change her will.'

'What's in the current one?' Julia asks conversationally.

'What's her will?' Nicky butts in.

'She doesn't have a willy, stupid,' says Brendan, breaking into uproarious laughter.

'Don't be so juvenile,' says Nicky, and glances around at the adults for approval of this censure, for admiration of her vocabulary.

'Nobody is sure,' Brigid excitedly explains to Julia, laterally across the sofa, over Nicky's head, 'but I'd say she has divided it equally between her nieces and nephews. There are eight in all. You've met the four on my side. There were six Gradys in the same generation, but two of them are dead now. Cancer. Tommy Óg is the ringmaster. He's the youngest and the meanest – a butcher by trade, and a brute by nature.'

'Is Auntie Maisie D.Y.I.N.G?' asks Nicky.

'Stop spelling stuff,' Brendan says. 'That's not fair. Just because I can't understand.'

'Well then learn how to spell. Anyway, you're too young for certain things. You shouldn't listen to older people talking.'

'Fuck off. I can listen if I want.'

'Ooooh,' says Nicky with a long audible intake of breath, hand to her mouth, an expression of deep shock on her face.

'You guys are in fine fettle,' Julia observes.

'I'm going to tell Mammy on you,' says Nicky, slipping off the sofa.

'Sit down,' Brigid orders her, with surprising authority. 'Don't tell tales. It isn't nice.' She addresses her grandson equally sternly in turn: 'Brendan, don't use language like that. It's very bold.'

'I will if I like,' says Brendan, staring at her defiantly, and reminding Alexander of Helena as a child, bravely striking an attitude against their mother.

Alexander sees the same old anger flare up in Brigid's eyes.

'You say anything like that in my presence again, young man,' she says, 'and I'll whip you to within an inch of your life.'

Her forcefulness and the threat of violence shock everyone in the room. Brendan drops his head meekly and busies himself with his dinosaurs. Nicky edges away a little on the sofa, watching her grandmother with new fear. Alexander finds that his mouth is agape, while Julia is seeing the funny side.

'Brigid, I'm really impressed by your ruthlessness,' she says.

'The older I get, the clearer I see things,' Brigid responds, still infused with righteous indignation.

Derek reappears with a glass of white wine in one hand and a pint of lager in the other. He dispenses the drinks without comment, then moves back to his armchair and lets his body fall into its habitual slouch. The cushion oompfs and hisses under the weight of his arse. He picks up the remote control from the floor and switches off the television. Helena's instructions, Alexander guesses.

'Hey, I was watching that,' says Brendan, rebounding, but unheard.

Julia once again seems ill at ease, shifting around on the sofa, leaning back, then forward again. She opens the big book of wildlife photos which is parked on the coffee table in front of her and begins turning the pages, though she has no known interest in wildlife.

Helena enters, her face glazed lightly with sweat from her efforts in the hot kitchen. This sheen, together with the brightness of her eyes, creates an impression of luminosity, of happiness. She is dressed simply in a white T-shirt, chinos and flip-flops. Her waist has thickened over the course of the years (and the birth of two children), but has retained its form well. Her thighs and buttocks are trim thirty-something. There is no embarrassment in her figure. With one foot she moves the bean bag from the centre of the floor to over by the fireplace, then sits deftly.

'The duck is done, but we'll let it breathe while the potatoes are roasting. It's really juicy, even if I say so myself.'

'I can't stay for dinner,' Julia blurts out suddenly.

She is sitting now on the very edge of the sofa, her right hand tugging at the fingers of her left hand, which is her habit when she is anxious.

Alexander trips into one of his fits. They are almost unnotice-able externally, but from the inside he falls into confusion: the walls lose their orientation in space; the room contracts; the people seem smaller or farther away, and somehow absurd, alien even. The situation feels keenly unstable, unsustainable, as though reality were being crushed from outside by an irresistible force or logic. Only his famil-iarity with these episodes makes them bearable. He knows it will pass in a second if he can just hold on. In other circumstances, he would move to the nearest external door, hand on his head to keep it together, and try to get outside for some fresh perspective and a blast of air. In this moment, he does no more than touch two fingers to his temple, and rub slightly.

Julia energetically snaps the wildlife book shut.

He guesses – discerns – that she does not have her period after all.

'Alexander and I are splitting up,' she says, speaking to Helena to begin with, then Brigid, then finally facing Alexander, although ostensibly the words are not addressed to him.

'That's a pity,' says Brigid, sounding surprisingly unconcerned. 'Are you sure you won't stay for dinner, since you've come the whole way out?'

'You stupid prick!' Helena snaps at Alexander, angry to the point of almost shouting, rising from the bean bag to her hunkers.

Julia jumps to her feet, evidently intending to depart immediately, hastened no doubt by the prospect of a messy family scene. Nicky gig-gles. Brigid sniffs in slow puzzlement. Brendan watches voraciously. Derek sips his beer and leers, delighted with the free entertainment.

Alexander feels like a man shot but still on his feet, deathly pale but as yet no wound showing, no blood spilling from his mouth. Helena's attack – the implicit judgement, the viciousness of the timing, the disloyalty – is what he finds most piercing. Julia's revelation that she is ending their relationship is stunning, perhaps in time devastating, but for now he can take it with curious lightness. Helena's reaction has slaughtered him.

'Tonight, when we were coming through the village,' he says to his sister, 'I noticed that there aren't any butchers any more. When we were growing up, there must have been three or four at least. Do you remember Tom Kearney's, where they had the abattoir round the back?'

'What's that got to do with anything?' Brigid asks.

'That's exactly the kind of shit I'm talking about,' says Helena, standing now, vehemently shaking her finger at him, 'that sort of non-sequitur nonsense. That's why she's leaving you.'

'The reasons are between Alexander and myself,' Julia says, but no one is listening to her.

'What's non-sequitur nonsense?' Nicky asks her father.

Derek shrugs like a teenager.

'It's not a non-sequitur to me,' Alexander says.

He has a history of finishing poorly.

All the boys on their road had bikes. For a while, one summer, it was a bike culture. You had to have a bike to be in it, and you had to have a cool bike, ideally a Chopper, if you wanted to be a respected figure.

Alexander's first bike was a thing for a toddler with plastic wheels. When he grew out of that, he would have been ready for a Chipper, the Chopper's little brother, but this was so out of the question financially that the possibility didn't even enter his head.

His father announced one evening that they would get the old Raleigh repaired, which they had received second hand as a gift a few years earlier for Helena, although she had rarely used it. If he saw that bike now, Alexander might find it charming, but back then it was an appalling prospect: a dull dark-blue colour; oil-stained, scratched, and rusty from years of use; with old-fashioned handle-bars, an ugly chain guard, and a braking system based on steel rods. Worse, it was a girl's bike, with a V-shaped frame rather than a manly crossbar.

Alexander can recall the day when he and his father drove – in their banger of a car – to collect the bike from the repair-shop. It was a joyless occasion for all concerned, including the repairman. On the way back, Jim Vespucci stopped the car at the top of the long road on which they then lived, took the bike out of the boot, and told his son to cycle it home. This was a daunting task. Alexander knew how to ride at this point, but the old Raleigh was still a big step for him. He objected briefly, but his relationship with his father was not one in which there was any negotiation or toleration of differences of opinion. His father left him stranded; paused briefly a few yards down the road to observe through the rear-view mirror, then drove off.

Alexander walked the bike for a while, but the road was so long that he was forced to have a go at cycling the thing, which he just about managed, nervously, with a few wobbles. It was his first experi-ence of pneumatic tyres, and the bike, for all its inadequacy as a fashion accessory, had large narrow wheels which covered the con-crete ground with surprising speed. By the time he reached home, he was full of his own success as a grown-up rider and conscious enough of the possibilities of this new machine to give an impres-sion of enthusiasm which was almost genuine.

The boys on the road organised a bicycle race. The arrangements were complex. A course was agreed: they would start in the cul-de-sac, turn up the hill, do a circuit of the park, return down the hill, then race back into the cul-de-sac, where the first person to touch the wall would be the winner. A time was agreed: the race would begin at half past two.

The contestants spent the morning preparing their racing machines. One kid fastened a narrow strip of cereal-box cardboard to the rear fork with a clothes peg, in such a way that the cardboard flapped rapidly through the spokes of the back wheel as the wheel turned, producing an engine noise. Then all the boys did the same, and some had two or three flaps. One taped a coloured number plate to the front of the handlebars; and again they all did variations of the same thing. Helena helped Alexander make a name plate, although unfortunately it was in crayon rather than marker. Thunderbolt, his bike was called, with a streak of jagged yellow lightning across the top of the word.

A big gang of riders and supporters assembled after lunch. They waited for prestigious individuals to be released by their parents, clarified the rules repeatedly, had a few false starts, then suddenly the race was on.

Alexander was slow to realise what was happening, hesitant in getting moving; but once the task was clear, he began to undertake it with diligence. He was an agile and physically fit child, who spent his days running around the fields behind the houses, or playing football on the road. His Raleigh, with its big wheels, was faster than the Choppers and the Chippers. Coming off the circuit of the park, he found himself in third place. He was cautious down the hill, but quickly overtook the final two riders on the home straight. With thirty yards to go, he and Thunderbolt were winning.

The spectators at the finishing line cheered him on. He was filled with excitement, overpowered by emotion, and lost sight of his task. The flapping of the cardboard in the spokes assumed in the moment huge proportions. The world tipped strangely. The road came up to meet him. His hands, elbows, knees scraped at high speed over the gritty concrete, and his head did a double smack against the kerb, with the bike wheeling off by itself toward the crowd, arching away, falling over. Even after the bike had crashed to a halt, the back wheel continued to spin, the cardboard flapping loudly in the spokes.

Cut and bloodied, concussed, unsuccessful, heroic, Alexander and his bike were led gently back to his home by a group of his street mates, who explained to his mother what had happened and hung around to gossip.

Young Brigid washed the grime out of his cuts. She did not do this as prettily or as tenderly as other mothers he knew. She didn't have cotton wool balls with which to apply the disinfectant, nor a first-aid box with plasters and such, nor a little scissors for cutting bandages to size. And no jar of sweets to provide consolation to the wounded.

II

December

Alexander Vespucci has found that one of the many advantages of living alone is that there is no pressure to do anything on a Saturday morning. Unfortunately, his constitution is no longer such that he can take full advantage of this freedom. In his teens and twenties he used to sleep on Saturday mornings. On a good morning, he would sleep past midday. On a special occasion, he might sleep into the late afternoon. And if this happened in winter, it could already be dark again by the time he was surfacing. Such extremes were rare, certainly, but they were possible. These days, however late he hits the mattress, whatever his state of inebriation at that point, it is a struggle to sleep past ten.

On this particular Saturday, Alexander lies alone in the double bed in the back bedroom of the Rathmines flat, trying to read a book on evolution, but unable, even though he finds the subject fascinating, to make any progress. His mind is projecting a depressing mosaic of worries and negative observations on the state of his life and personality. And each old thing that is thrown up – from who knows where – his attention slavishly follows like a dog fetching a stone for the umpteenth time. There must be some pleasure in this. Otherwise, why would he do it?

He can smell Julia. Maybe that is why he has stayed in the flat when he knows it would be best to find a different place to live. She is gone now, but her smell lingers, like a spectral presence in a ruined house, at times remarkably tangible but ultimately elusive.

On first getting the keys to the flat, before they moved in, when there was still the thrill of owning access to this new private space, the sense of possibility, of unformed identity, he discovered an odour he didn't like. He walked around the flat for a good half hour, sniffing the surfaces, the corners, investigating as an animal might investigate. It was a smell of cat. Just inside the front door particularly, there was a shrill metallic smell of cat's piss. Julia didn't notice it so much, or wasn't bothered by it, but she had grown up with cats and was fond of them, while Alexander always professed to hate them.

He discussed it with the landlord.

'Well, you're right,' the well-nourished, softly spoken man confessed with a grin, 'although I don't see how you could still get it. There was an old dear here a few years ago who had a cat. It got locked in one time for a couple of days and went to the toilet there at the door. But I changed the carpet and scrubbed the concrete with industrial cleaner. I can't see how the smell would still be there.'

Years later, that smell is long gone, or faded beyond notice. Now it is the smell of Julia that his sense detects, that endures in his consciousness. And for *this* smell, it is early days yet, even though she – to his knowledge – never pissed on the floor, and all her stuff is gone, her clothes and possessions, whatever she wanted of the things they bought together, and the bedding has been washed (twice at this stage).

In this flat, in this very bed, he discovered that it is not possible in a relationship to return to how things were at an earlier time.

It is a tale of two embraces.

When they were in fourth year in college, Julia had a room on the campus where Alexander often stayed, so much so that they tripped into an almost domestic situation, which was full of unexpected delights. Simple things were infused with magic by their love: laughing over cornflakes and cold milk for lunch; a Chinese take away in front of the TV in the evening. In their best moments, they were easily as besotted with each other as any Romeo and Juliet. Not that they compared themselves with anything else in the universe. There was no need.

Julia liked to go to sleep early. Even on nights when she was supposed to be studying hard, or had an essay to work on, by nine thirty her dedication would begin to wilt. She would then quietly intimate, with a guilty smirk, that she was going to get into her pyjamas and continue reading in bed. For Alexander this meant sex, so he always encouraged her. There was nothing so intoxicating for him, nothing so steeply erotically charged, as when she – kneeling astride his body – slowly unbuttoned her pyjamas (put on only minutes previously), revealing the pale skin of her upper torso, her beautifully narrow shoulders, her superb plenteous sweet-nippled breasts.

Afterward she would sleep, curled up like a child, the profile of her little face angelic, her dark curls profound and archetypal against the pillow. Alexander would lie on the bed beside her, reading until after midnight, pausing every now and again to admire her, to monitor her breathing.

She woke one night in shock, perhaps from a bad dream, and, seeing an apparently strange man beside her in the bed, was filled with fear. She recoiled from him with a whimper, her face contorting into deep-wrinkled horror, then realised in the next moment that it was Alexander, her very own lover, and the fear flowed instantly to earth, leaving behind it a sleepy smile and a melting body, which then launched itself forward for a hug, arms reaching up to him, before drooping back again into the warm indentation on the pillow, the hollow of cosiness under the quilt.

In the morning she didn't recall the episode, and possibly had never really woken.

Four years later, after the betrayals on both sides, big and little, the split, the long period of anger and coolness, having found each other again, they moved in together – earnestly this time.

A few months into the new arrangement, Alexander returned very late one night, at three or four o'clock, thirty quid richer in heavy coin from a game of poker. He was sober. He hadn't been drinking that night. It was unusual for him to be up so late and not be drunk. He moved quietly through the flat in order not to wake her, was especially careful in opening the bedroom door, but it squeaked, and a board creaked under his foot, under the brown-sauce carpet. Julia awoke. She lifted herself up in the bed. From the light he had left on in the passageway, he could see her face, her peering expression, which flared in alarm at the sight of this tall, unknown man approaching her.

'It's OK, it's me.'

She frowned in apparent irritation, her torso shuddering, then slumped back wearily. He sat on the edge of the bed and stroked her hair, said soothing words as she settled herself to sleep again. She didn't resist these attentions, but neither did they move her.

From where he is now lying, it is less than ten feet to the French windows that look out onto the back garden he shares with the other tenants. Julia always thought it was odd to have a bed next to such windows, and probably the room did not originally serve as a bedroom. She liked to keep the curtains drawn. The windows are not closely overlooked by any of the neighbouring houses, but it was always possible, she argued, that one of their housemates would come down into the garden and peep in. Within a week of her departure, Alexander opened the curtains and hasn't closed them since. The condition of the flat may have deteriorated somewhat, but every morning the light comes spilling through the back windows into the bedroom. On clear days, he wakes with pure sunshine on his face.

He likes to look out. The back garden is another of the things that is keeping him in the flat. Her smell. This view. The fact that he doesn't have to move in order to live here.

The garden is dreary enough to the unpractised eye: the concrete yard, the untidy lawn, the ageing orange clothesline in its drooping arcs (on which the country girls from upstairs hang out their washing), the ivy-covered perimeter walls, the wooden door to the lane at the back. From his lying position on the bed, he can see over a side wall into the neighbouring garden where there are tall bushes and big deciduous trees, wiry and interesting now in their winter bareness. And out past the bottom wall, if he sits up, he can study the back of the next row of redbrick houses, all the misshapen kitchen and bathroom extensions, the ugly windows, the spinal drainpipes and settled slate roofs.

It is precisely the ordinariness of the garden that he appreciates: the microcosm jungle of the lawn, with weeds and grasses living peacefully side by side in the quiet winter months, the sodden muck, the shiny moss, stalks of dead wild flowers, voyaging snails, lost worms, birds on the lookout for a decent bite. And the concrete yard looks well after a downpour. Even the big City Council bins are redeemed in their rain-splashed condition. Behind them, a stack of planks forgotten by the landlord continues to rot happily, a feeding ground for creepy crawlies that hide away, out of sight of predators.

On the clothesline, a solitary red-breasted robin is sitting alert, body and eye movements bright and rapid.

Enter a cat stage left, moving in a low crouch along the top of the side wall. It jumps down onto the lawn, which causes the robin to spring into the air, twittering, and flap its way neatly to the nearest branch of the nearest tree, which is a beech, where grey doves live, dozens of them.

Alexander is becoming familiar with this cat. He has seen it a number of times in these last months. He doesn't know if it is male or female. He thinks it is not young in cat terms.

The cat is black, with white patches on its paws and from its throat down onto its breast. It trots purposefully across the wet grass to the couple of steps that drop from the lawn into the yard. Pausing here, it glances at the area around the bins, including the planks, continues its progress down the steps, and pauses again for a more general survey of the environment: listening with its pointy ears, raising its delicate nose and whiskers, angling its head to catch whiffs on the air. The little skull, the green slit-pupil eyes perform a scanning motion. It spots Alexander. Through one of the squares in the window, which frames its face, the cat stares in at him lying full length in the bed.

Unintentionally, Alexander finds himself in a staring contest, which he is unprepared for and quickly loses. He shakes his head to throw off the humiliation, then laughs at himself and confronts the cat again with more and comical resolve.

'Get lost. I don't like cats.'

But the cat appears to take this as an invitation. It walks with great precision across the yard, advancing directly to the window, its tail snaking up into the air behind it in a question mark. It stops right in front of the window, front paws parked side by side. Head and shoulder reaching upward, it looks intently at Alexander in a demeanour that he finds surprisingly engaging. In these moments he experiences the cat as inquisitive, cheerful, even sociable.

'Hey, you're a cool dude,' he says, admiring the line of its body from the throat to the little paws, the claws of which are slightly splayed. The cat begins to lick the white fur on its breast, brushing it down and outward with its pink tongue. The furry breastplate seems to Alexander like a decoration, like ruffles on a dress shirt.

All his life, unconsciously following his mother's training, Alexander has claimed to dislike cats, indeed has actually disliked them. But now, in these instants, he is set free from this prejudice.

'Maybe I like cats after all,' he says to the cat, and this realisation releases in him a little shot of the chemicals of love, which lifts him above his anxieties. His head drops gratefully to the pillow.

When he turns to face the window again, the cat is gone.

His hand gropes on the floor for his mobile. He finds it and sees that he has left it on all night, which is bad because the micro-waves might be frying his brain while he sleeps, but good because he doesn't have to go through the tedious routine of switching it on, entering his PIN, waiting for it to find the network and get the con-tacts up and running. He seeks out *Grace S M* and rings her, feeling fear in his stomach.

'Yes,' she answers coldly.

'Are you at your place? I was thinking of calling around to see you.'

'Why?'

'We need to discuss our project.'

'You mean you want to lick my cunt.'

'That too. . . . I'm having a good morning here. There's a cat in the back garden who is my new friend.'

'He's not your friend. He's just looking for milk.'

Having spoken to her, he needs to get out of bed.

Naked except for the ripped old T-shirt he likes to sleep in, scratching his balls, yawning nervously, he moves through the flat, looking for his cigarettes.

It surprises him that they are not in the sitting room, on the floor in front of the sofa in the ever-expanding space that functions as a platform for all the stuff that one requires or has finished with when one is lying full stretch on the sofa watching television, head propped on a cushion on the armrest, flicking endlessly with the remote control from one piece of shit to the next.

It surprises him less that his cigarettes are not in the kitchen, since he wouldn't normally leave them there. As he passes through on his way to the toilet, he automatically lifts the kettle to determine by its weight if there is sufficient water in it, and finding that there is, hits the button. There is enough water, but not much, so he hears immediately the hiss of the electric element beginning its work as he moves on.

His cigarettes and lighter are sitting on top of the toilet cistern. He lights one while he is having a piss, and worries about his low piss pressure. His piss pressure has really deteriorated in the past few years. Back in the good old days, with a few pints in him he could have pissed over a ten-foot wall. With ease he could rip apart cigarette butts in urinals within a couple of seconds of targeted shooting. He could also drink all night before going to the toilet, whereas now he is going already after the first pint. Perhaps this is the root of the issue. Reduced storage capability means reduced pressure. This is a new thought. Up to now he has regarded piss pressure and storage capability as separate characteristics, but perhaps they are linked, one the cause of the other. In any case, his pissing nowadays is notable only for inglorious reasons: frequency, limpness, bizarre coloration. He was deeply alarmed recently when he noticed that his urine was bright green, neon-light green. This was where the true magnificence of the internet became apparent. He has only begun to draw on it these past eighteen months or so, particularly since Evil Neville had recommended to him a search engine called Google. He used it to check out his condition – *bright green urine* – and got a good supply of links, the first few of which were sufficient to inform him that the symptom was due to the vitamin B in the supplements he had started taking.

Alexander stands there, dick in hand, and draws on his cigarette, hoping that he isn't dying of prostate cancer. He worries about his health these days, a lot more than he used to. He is noticing in his body all sorts of tics and throbbings, pains, sensations, quiverings. In his mind he has catalogued three possible explanations for this: (i) his health has deteriorated rapidly since Julia left; (ii) his health was always poor, but he didn't have the mental space to notice it; (iii) his health is fine but he is going bonkers.

His mobile phone rings, very faintly because the sound has to travel from the bedroom. He decides not to run for it. He is not in the mood for rushing, and anyhow it will surely have rung out by the time he gets there.

Back in the kitchen, he empties last weekend's coffee sludge from the cafetière onto a dirty plate.

He finds that no one really cleans the flat now that Julia has left. This leads to an accumulation of dirt and mess, which may be disgusting for the outsider, but which he can experience as perfectly natural. The conditions occur organically, and he works around them. It is possible to wash out the cafetière without disturbing the complex mound of dirty dishes in the sink. There is no difficulty in finding the coffee because it is just where he left it a week ago, beside the kettle – a great place to leave the coffee, if you think about it. From the stale loaf of batch bread beside the toaster, he can easily pull out two slices, pinch off the blue mould at the edges, pop in the bread. Actually the toaster is a little too small for batch, but the dial is at max and he can turn the slices around mid-cycle to do the other ends. And the advantage of never putting the butter back in the fridge is that it always spreads beautifully.

I'm a poet, he thinks. A poet is someone who enjoys the ballet of breakfast. There was never any ballet with Julia, just a never-ending supply of domestic chores.

In the waiting period for the toast (having flipped it over at roughly half-time) he makes the long trek to the bedroom and picks up his mobile phone to review the action. There is one missed call from Danny, one text from Danny: *Boy sprog dropped this morning. Pints with Paul tonight. Meet holles street hospital at 7.30. Ask for ward.*

Alexander finds himself uninterested by this addition to the global population.

On Pearse Street, standing on the pavement outside Grace Sharkey's apartment block, waiting for her to buzz open the external door, he catches the eye of a smack-head chick, a pale pimply girl of seventeen or eighteen with reddish hair and light brown eyes of almost orange tinge. She has no coat on. Her ribcage is high, her waist thin. She is a lovely wasp of a thing; in the early phases of her heroin career, blooming in it; deeply switched on at this very moment, luxuriating in her oozy low.

She lingers in the eye contact with him as she walks by. Her lips make a tiny pouting motion. I would do you, she is saying. Or perhaps she is mocking him, his dreary life, she who has the very truth running through her veins.

The girl is accompanied by two others, following loosely behind her — a tall physically powerful young man and another girl, smaller, prepubescent and obese. The man is saying something humorous that is intended to be heard by both his companions. His eyes laugh with ego evil. He moves in a mannered macho gait, the promise of violence in every gesture, in the rings on his fingers, in the tattoo at the side of his thick neck. Alexander loathes and fears this type of animal, finds his existence itself a promiscuity, a superfluity.

'What the fuck are you lookin' at? Do you wanna dig in the head?'

He has taken a stride out of his way to confront Alexander, who is now cornered, his back to the apartment block entrance, threatening male to one side of him, enticing chemically accentuated female to the other. She has stopped to watch. Her eyelids slip down halfway for an instant, as though temporarily too heavy for her to carry.

Alexander holds up his palms in a gesture of peace.

The youth's head and torso spring forward and he growls at Alexander, exactly as a dog would, his mouth stretched open, several inches of his wet tongue visible, as well as the accumulated plaque on his teeth. Alexander falls backward, banging against the heavy glass door, then bolts along the wall in the direction his attackers have come from. He doesn't dare look back, but can hear laughing and shouting behind him.

'Faggot,' the voice calls.

Alexander is sorry to have disappointed the girl, to have behaved in such an unmanly fashion. Heart beating fast, hands sweating, he keeps walking for a couple of minutes, back in the direction of Ringsend, before turning around and returning to Grace's apartment.

Earlier, he pressed the button once and waited politely while she ignored him for several minutes. Now he presses it three times, two long insistent pushes followed by a third, which he holds for a good fifteen seconds and is still holding when she interrupts through the intercom.

'What the hell is wrong with you? I'm in the bath. Come back in half an hour.'

'Open the fucking door, Grace. I just got accosted by the natives, some of your neighbours.'

'Did they beat you up?' she asks, a new, hopeful tone in her voice.

'They mauled me psychologically,' he replies, more lightly.

'But isn't that what you like, dear?'

She buzzes him in.

He takes the lift to the top floor, and tries to recall how many times he has already made this journey. This is his fourth visit, or his fifth perhaps, spread out irregularly over the months since their first encounter.

Grace has the penthouse apartment, with expansive views over Dublin: Trinity College and the Central Bank, Wood Quay, Christ Church and St Patrick's, the tower in Smithfield, Phoenix Park – these familiar central landmarks; and scores of church spires and cranes, thousands of city rooftops, running west toward the Midlands and south to the Wicklow Mountains, which seem within a stone's throw when the day is clear.

On his previous visits, after the sex, he has liked to lounge around in one of the twin window couches, enjoying the views, smoking cigarettes, drinking coffee, weathering Grace's efforts to get rid of him.

'Can you go now please?'

Or: 'OK, that's enough. Get out of my sight. You irritate me.'

The door is open, which isn't usually the case. He finds himself exercising caution as he enters, as though he anticipates a trap: a bucket of pig's blood balanced over the door; or, more likely, a new-generation anti-personnel mine that will blow off his legs without damaging the decor. But he discerns no threat as he proceeds over the rich cream carpet into her inner territory. Once inside, he turns and carefully closes the door, making a momentary childish game of doing this soundlessly.

Along the corridor, the bathroom door is open, with a thin cloud of steam rising out into the hall, floating up to the ceiling. He can hear the bath running, the throaty noise of the water pushing through the pipes, out through the taps, the heavy splash and commotion as the rushing stream collides continuously with the churning body of water beneath.

On the floor against the skirting board on the near side of the bathroom door is a fat dark-wood Buddha with several bellies and a very round head. It is the only object of any sort in the entire silk-upholstered corridor. It captures his attention every time; and each time he studies it, he has the feeling that it is laughing at him.

Still elevated on adrenaline from the encounter outside, wanting to express himself physically to exorcise his cowardice, perverted by a wave of self-revulsion, and conscious also of the silence of his entrance and of her immediate vulnerability (if she is indeed in the bath), the thought occurs to him that he could murder her now, indeed that he *should* murder her. He indulges this whimsical fantasy. He could quietly lift up the laughing Buddha, carry it into the bathroom and smash her head with it. The Buddha is certainly heavy enough for the job and would be a pleasing weapon, though probably too unwieldy. It would be better for him to find something else. Not a knife or a cleaver: he's not that type of murderer. But he could certainly strangle her with his leather belt. That would be appropriate.

He wants to *do* something. He drops to his hunkers and takes hold of the Buddha, one hand on the smooth roundness of the skull, the other on the base, which he tilts up. The object is heavier than expected. He is careful in lifting it, making sure that his knees and thighs do the work, rather than his back.

Carrying the statue with his hands and lower arms, he crosses the threshold into the bathroom. The bath is filled with an uneven landscape of foam, like the surface of an exotic planet. Above the glistening foamy mountains, which are rising perceptibly with the waterline as the gushing taps continue to fill the bath, the upper portion of Grace's body is visible: her simian head, the bare neck and upper torso, the faint twin swells which just begin to define her breasts and the interesting space between them. He pauses at the end of the bath, where the taps are, seeking to disguise the fact that his breathing is slightly laboured under the weight of the statue.

She faces him calmly from the far end. Her penny eyes are brighter than usual. Her tied-up hair is damp from the steam, with loose wet strands sticking to her forehead and hanging prettily about her ears. Her skin glows pinkly in the humid heat.

'That's an expensive piece,' she says.

99

He feels foolish now. What is he going to do with the thing? What's his punchline? The Buddha is so heavy, he finds it impossible to maintain a smooth composure. The physical strain expresses itself in his face. He doesn't want to bring the thing back to the hallway, nor to bow down and place it on the floor. And he can't hold it for much longer.

'You look like a gobshite,' she says, with more pleasure and complacency than is wise at this moment.

'You're right,' he concedes, and with a little impulsion releases the Buddha into the bath, just below where he imagines her feet to be. His execution is clumsy. He slips backward as the thing is leaving his arms and misses his aim. The Buddha crashes off the edge of the bath, crunching the tiles, losing some of its momentum, then tumbles with a heavy splash into the water.

Grace reacts with surprising speed. She pulls up her legs, her shiny knees erupting through the foam like the crystalline beams in Superman's palace, her torso shooting forward into a more upright position, which partially, increasingly, reveals her small sexy breasts as the watery foam slides downward away from them.

'I thought it would look better in here,' he says with a smile, though his heart is thumping.

'You fucking idiot!' Her lips are tight with anger. 'You could have broken my feet.'

'It was just a joke. Don't take it so seriously.' He finds that these words are insufficient, so he adds more, realising as he does so that he is contradicting himself. 'If you were a little bit kinder, or more polite, there wouldn't be any call for such gestures.'

'What?' she asks incredulously.

During this exchange, he observes with clarity for the first time that her breasts are not the breasts of a young woman. In each case the main wad of flesh has stretched downward and lost its shapeliness. The nipples point in different directions, one down, one out, like loose cannon.

She takes hold of the handrail on the wall and carefully, impressively, raises herself to stand. Water runs off the sallow planes of her body, leaving chunks of foam stranded like glacial erratics. He admires her pubic area: the narrowing rectangle of auburn-coloured hair, matted with wetness; the bikini bottom of pale skin; the leanness of her thighs.

She steps out onto the porcelain-tiled floor, which is splashed wet from the tsunami created by the Buddha's impact with the bathwater. Her shins are gleaming and bristly, her toenails crimson. She removes a thick-pile white towel from the rail, wraps herself in it as a woman does: beneath the armpits, around and around again, tucking in the top corner.

She steps forward and punches him on the jaw. It is a straighter punch than a man would deliver, direct and strong. He staggers backward until he reaches the wall by the door, then allows himself to slide down into a sitting position on the wet floor. For a second he thinks he is going to faint, but the fuzziness passes and he is left in a condition of transported awareness.

'Wow, I feel good,' he says, surprised, speaking as much to himself as to her, touching his jaw where she hit him. 'I ought to get punched more often.'

'I can arrange that,' she says humourlessly, not looking at him, focused on the damaged tiles at the edge of the bath, which she fingers exploratively.

'Sit down for a minute,' he suggests. 'Let's talk about broadband.'

'Fuckwit,' she snaps, but her anger is diminishing. 'You're going to have to pay for this. And for Buddha Bud, if he's damaged.'

'You can deduct it from my bonus,' he offers generously, speaking from the position of authority in which he appears to have landed. 'That's one of the things I want to talk to you about. Why don't you sit down on the toilet? Such a handsome toilet. Let's make ourselves comfortable.'

Amazingly, or perhaps not so amazingly, she does as he asks. Wrapped in her towel, she steps barefoot across the wet tiles, a movement he finds arousing, all the more so for her being momentarily compliant. She sits on the wooden lid, loosening the towel as she does so, crossing her legs, folding her arms across her breast.

'I'm all ears.'

'Blackmore and Associates have nearly finished the report.'

'Is he going to say what we want him to say?'

'That depends. He's a businessman. He'll be guided by me. That's why I selected him. And he's coming to see me next week to discuss the recommendations, to find out which way the wind is blowing. He won't put it like that, since it's an independent report.'

'Of course not.... This is good news.' She licks her lips, uncrosses her legs and slides her feet apart, opening – under the towel – a new territory of dark invitation. She places her open palms on her towelled thighs. 'I get horny when we start to talk money.'

These simple moves melt him, the solid thing in him that turns to liquid when he is suddenly aroused, when he experiences an erotic shock. It is an immediate shut-down of one part of his brain, an instantaneous change in the ways the neurological traffic is flowing. It precedes erection, though that physical transformation follows immediately.

She spreads her legs wider and slides her body down and out into a more horizontal position, her back pressed against the cistern, the tips of her buttocks leaving the seat. She slowly draws the towel up to the tops of her thighs, presenting her vagina to him. Her fingers feel for the labia, pulling back to reveal the pinkness of her clitoris and the sloping entrance beneath.

'Come on over,' she tells him in the silly whispery voice with which he is now well acquainted. 'Let's get your face wet.... But take off your clothes first.'

Alexander removes his coat. He pulls his fleece and T-shirt over his head in one go, carefully unzips his jeans, which are completely wet, front and back, lifts up his arse to push them and his jocks down to his ankles.

'Stop,' she tells him as he is bending forward to take off his boots. 'Sit back. Let me see your cock.'

He sits back against the wall. His penis is hard, hardening further with every move she makes, every utterance. The angle of the erection is high, but it leans to one side in a way that seems faintly comical to him.

'Hand,' she tells him.

He slowly pumps his erection a few times, watching closely. With each upward stroke, the lower part of the knob disappears into the foreskin, leaving visible the engorged purple slit and the angry globular surface around it. He finds this view too anatomical, and eases his focus. He rubs his palm down over his penis, cups his tightening scrotum in his fingers, groans lightly with pleasure because he knows she likes that.

'That's good, let me hear you. Get your tongue out.'

Meanwhile, with her expert middle finger she has begun to work the underside of her clitoris, dipping down to fetch some moisture, then pressing upward, squeezing the top of her clitoris into the apex of the labia.

'Tell me about the broadband recommendations.'

Alexander snorts into laughter, which also causes a surge of gas to rasp out of his anus, making him laugh even more.

'What's so fucking funny?'

The delightfully poisonous odour of his fart has risen to his nostrils, and he sniffs discreetly to get a good whiff of it, continuing to cackle in pure unforced enjoyment. In reaction to this mirth, Grace crossly closes her legs, pretty and almost prim in the manner she brings her knees together. She pulls the towel back down over her thighs.

'You can't talk about broadband in the middle of sex,' he says. 'I thought we'd already established that.'

'Men are so lame. You've no ability to multitask.'

Later – Alexander dressed again, Grace still in her bathrobe, sitting together on the leather couches, looking out over the grey cloud-covered city, smoking her Camel filterless, which are too strong for him, sipping espressos he made under her fussy supervision – he finds that his jaw is sore and his energy level is dropping. The coffee will help him.

'I can work Blackmore. At this stage, he can go either way. He can come back and say that the cost of state intervention outweighs the benefits. Or he can come back and recommend state investment. Then there's the issue of the form of intervention: a single contract awarded nationally; or the local authorities funded to make the purchase at local level, which would mean multiple contracts.'

'The money must go to the local authorities. I've told you that before.'

Grace is uneasy, made more so by Alexander's air of relaxation, of not being in a hurry to leave. She wants the conversation to be ended quickly. She smokes her cigarette too hard, and keeps turning her head over her shoulder to look out of the window. Beyond the heavy entombing glass it is drizzling. A fat seagull flies by within fifty feet or so, opening its mouth for a squawk which Alexander hears only faintly. He's very far inland, Alexander thinks; but then remembers that in fact the sea is quite near, particularly as a seagull would fly it.

'What's your business plan, Grace? That's the piece I don't understand.'

'Don't go there. There is no business plan.'

He drinks from his coffee, savouring the sharp bitterness on his tongue, preparing himself for his next gambit, which he delivers more convincingly than expected.

'Well that's a shame, because you need my assistance, and it's going to cost you more than a flash of your tits and a few hand-jobs.'

She smiles thinly.

'What have you got in mind? Instrumental anal penetration?'

'I want to buy a house.'

Grace laughs drily, but with genuine surprise.

'I can get you your recommendation that the money should be spent at local level,' he continues. 'And more than that: I can make sure that the recommendation lands. We have to get the Chairman behind it. He'll support it if there's publicity in it for him, a bit of national profile. So we make a big thing of it, maybe arrange for the Minister or the Taoiseach to do the launch. I know guys in their offices. I can do that.... It's important as well to have the trade unions and the employers involved, make it a Social Partnership gig. We can organise that through the Council.... And we'll round up all the regional types, west-of-the-Shannon et cetera. Everybody loves Regional Development. We'll create a big photo opportunity outside Government Buildings. The Chairman will cream himself. And then maybe we'll have a special feature on him in one of the Sunday papers: picture of him chatting with the Taoiseach; in-depth profile of top businessman doing his bit for the country. I have the contacts to set that up.'

'Everyone has the contacts to set that up,' she says, but she is thoughtful rather than dismissive. 'You're better than I imagined. But don't think anyone is going to buy you a house.'

'I don't want anyone to buy me a house. I want a decent deposit, eighty grand. Then I'll get a mortgage like everybody else.'

'Eighty grand is out of the question, and you know it. I can buy a politician for ten grand in fifty euro notes – even a good one. You're a fucking nobody, an insect on the street.... But I tell you what, because I like you: let's talk again when you've had your meeting with Blackmore.'

'I think, deep down, Irish people aren't really comfortable with abortion,' Danny comments to Alexander.

The sentiment is fitting to their current location. They are standing on the steps at the entrance to the National Maternity Hospital on Holles Street. Alexander has not yet been in to pay his respects to the mother and child. He bumped into Danny in the hospital foyer and they went outside for a cigarette. 'Even modern enlightened types such as myself,' Danny continues in an ironic tone. 'Leave aside your raving feminists and your loony lefters, people who positively enjoy the destruction of foetuses on principle, and leave aside genuine hard-luck cases and so on; when it comes to discretionary family-planning-type abortions, Joe Irish-Punter really doesn't have the stomach for it. We're too Catholic, and I say that as someone who isn't even a Catholic.'

Danny is Church of Ireland.

'Let's go in,' Alexander says, more because he is feeling the cold than because of any urgent desire to see Aoife and the new spawn. He also wants to get rid of the flowers and chocolates he is carrying.

'I never told you,' Danny continues in a confessional tone, 'we went to London for an abortion.'

Alexander experiences a moment of mental disorientation in which the fabric of existence appears to make an impossible turn, as in an Escher painting.

'Think again and you'll recall that you blew the money that you borrowed from me to go to London for an abortion.'

'Oh yes, *that* money,' Danny recalls, squinting in shame for a second, but recovering quickly. 'No, I borrowed different money from Hugo to go to London. I didn't tell him why. We flew across, stayed with Vladimir Foster—'

'How's Vlad?'

'Full of shit, as ever. We took the tube in the morning to the clinic, but couldn't go through with it. It was Aoife's call. I didn't – you know – want to influence her one way or the other, but I was relieved when she said she'd changed her mind.'

'Oh,' says Aoife with low-energy exclamation, seeing that he has brought her gifts, 'aren't you very good?'

Sitting up in the bed in a private room, she looks exhausted, but seems to be in positive humour. As Alexander lays his offerings on the rolling table at the bottom of the bed, he senses that she is making fun of him, though he doesn't know exactly why. Is it very square of him to bring flowers and chocolates? What else would you bring?

'What about a helium balloon?' she asks. 'Didn't they have any of those in the shop?'

'Evidently not.'

Swaddled in a white sheet and a standard-issue blue blanket, the baby lies quietly in a small iron-bar cot on wheels, parked within Aoife's reach. Alexander approaches cautiously to investigate.

He finds it repellent: pink and shrivelled, blind and useless, with obscene greasy black hair glued to its oblong skull.

'What are you going to call it?' he asks, for want of anything better to say.

'Merlin,' Aoife replies, evidently expecting enthusiasm.

'Nice one,' Alexander says, with a glance at Danny, who is standing uneasily between the end of the bed and the window, desperately wishing to get away, to commence with the drinking. 'But would you not go for something unusual? To give it a head start in life.'

'Did Danny tell you that my mother threatened to beat him up?' Aoife asks with pleasure.

'No, he didn't mention that.'

'I have to admit I feel like a bit of a cad,' Danny says with a shrug. 'I was out on the town, getting plastered—'

'With your mobile switched off,' Aoife interjects.

'With my mobile mysteriously malfunctioning. But how was I to know the baby was going to be born? It was three or four days early. I can tell you: coming home to your mother in that form – that was a punishment far worse than the crime.'

'She threatened to hit him about the head with a lump hammer,' Aoife explains with a beaming smile.

'I wouldn't have guessed that you guys owned a lump hammer. Not that I doubt your DIY capabilities, Danny.'

'We don't. Her mother carries one in her handbag.'

Julia arrives.

It is a physical shock to Alexander to see her. She looks changed. She looks great: fresh-faced; her hair cut to the shoulder in a new shorter, fuller arrangement. There is something more feminine about her, more grown-up, and she has lost weight.

She too has brought flowers, but better ones: white lilies, wrapped in transparent cellophane, the roots enclosed in a bulb of water. The lilies are young. Most of the pale-green lozenge pods are still closed, but a few are opening at the point where the seams meet, as though for kisses. She places them on the table next to Alexander's already wilting multicoloured offering, which lies flat, wrapped in garish pink paper, the flowers gasping silently from neglect. Beside the lilies she sets down a large crisp brown paper bag containing magazines.

'I got you a couple of mags,' she says to Aoife as she takes off her coat, 'in case you'd nothing to read.'

'Thanks,' says Aoife, this time without irony.

Julia kisses Aoife on each cheek, almost fiercely. Aoife seems a little taken aback by this show of affection, and Alexander is also surprised, since the two women have never been that close.

With her coat off, Julia's figure is available for Alexander's admiration. She is dressed in a long denim skirt and an ivory-coloured scoop-neck pullover, clothes he has never seen before, which seem to belong to a more refined wardrobe than the one he knew when they were together.

His mind knows that the probability of sex with Julia is zero right now and depressingly low in the future, but his body innocently displays a Pavlovian reaction to her presence. It associates her with sex, and wants immediately to slip its arms around her waist, to invade her mouth, to rip off her fine new clothes, to suck her breasts, to lick her skin – to penetrate her. His penis is poising itself for action, and the organ which is his skin has perked up, the individual cells eagerly anticipating her touch, greedy for it.

'Oh the baby is beautiful,' Julia squeals, which brings Alexander's ardour down a couple of points.

He raises an eyebrow at Danny, who responds with an echoing facial manoeuvre, though his heart doesn't seem to be in it. Danny is ever more strained, which is not surprising given that he is tired and hung over, and embarking afresh on a project of parenthood with a woman he would rather have much less to do with.

'What are you going to call him?' Julia asks.

'Merlin,' Alexander says.

'You can't call him Merlin,' Julia shrieks. 'Are you joking?'

Aoife gives her throaty laugh, which breaks into a cough.

'We're trying to think outside the box here,' Danny says, somewhat defensively.

'Well think again, folks,' Julia replies, but then appears to feel that she is being overassertive and changes direction. 'Of course, it's none of my business. I don't want to intrude. If it's Merlin, then. . . .'

'Then Merlin's a lovely name,' Alexander offers.

'I saw you on TV, Danny,' Julia gushes, changing the subject.

Alexander also witnessed this event. He finds that there is little more depressing in life than seeing your best friend from college appear on television while you wallow in filth and loneliness. The show in question was a particularly disgusting specimen: an Irish imitation of the dimly lit, intellectual, late-night talk show, where a panel of overly articulate, self-regarding beauties attempted to outdo each other with ever-increasing levels of honesty, insight, subtlety.

'They did a great overhead shot of your bald spot,' Alexander recalls.

'Ouch,' says Danny, his hand rising reflexively to the crown of his head to survey the extent of the damage.

'Don't mind him,' Julia counters quickly. 'He's just bitter and twisted because you're on television and he isn't.'

'You know me so well,' Alexander confesses.

Danny shrugs in feigned nonchalance, placing himself above all the bickering.

'I loved the way your title came up when you were speaking,' Julia continues. 'Danny Carter, Journalist and Broadcaster.'

'They forgot Renowned Pisshead,' says Aoife.

'I thought you were very good,' Julia continues.

'Does your man really have a stammer, or does he just put it on in the make-up room to be endearingly brave?' Alexander asks.

There is a knock on the door and a group of medical professionals enters briskly: an old guy with a moustache in a white coat; a young guy in green scrubs; a midwife in blue. The visitors are invited to wait in the corridor for a few minutes. Danny makes to leave with them, but Aoife instructs him to stay.

Outside, the two stand opposite each other. Julia looks up and down the busy corridor, which flows between them, avoiding eye contact with Alexander.

A weary woman in a nightgown shuffles through with a nod to Julia. At the same time, a young man, who gives the appearance of being an elated new father, rushes by in the opposite direction.

'You're looking great,' Alexander ventures.

Julia gazes at him crossly without response.

'Why the hostility?'

'You tell me.'

Alexander feels himself going off on a tangent. He knows it's not a good idea, but he can't resist the impulse.

'I've been thinking a lot about housework,' he says. 'You always said that I didn't pull my weight, that you did so much more. I agree that people living together should share the housework, all other things being equal. But the question is: who decides how much housework there is? Who decides the precise level of cleanliness and tidiness that is required? That should also be a democratic decision, a compromise. Now that I have come out from under the yoke, I realise that you were a fascist about how clean things had to be.'

Julia ruefully shakes her head.

'You need to get yourself a life,' she says.

'I know.'

He also senses, though he cannot be sure about this, that if you want a woman to marry you, you shouldn't tell her she is a fascist the first time you see her in several months, particularly if you don't know when you are going to see her again.

'When I said fascist, I didn't mean it in a bad way.'

Danny and Alexander meet Paul in The Ginger Man for pints.

'I have no cash resources, gentlemen,' Danny announces. 'You'll have to carry me. I do have an American Express card, which is almost certainly maxed out, but you can be lucky with these things. I'll try it later on when my courage is up. Give me a twenty, Paulie. I'll get the first shout in.'

'That is typical,' Paul says, when Danny has gone to the bar. 'His missus is inside in a private room and he can't afford a round. I bet they don't pay the bill.'

'What bill?'

'Any bill, but I meant the hospital bill. It's a couple of grand for a private room.... He's gone around the bend with the booze. My sister saw him in Renards nightclub during the week, two o'clock in the morning and he was literally banging his head off the wall, with a bottle of whiskey in his hand. She said he was incoherent, didn't even recognise her.... When he rings me now to go out, I'm searching for excuses: have to clean the windows; have to mow the lawn; have to cut my toenails; whatever I can come up with. Because it's not going to be three or four or five pints, it'll be ten, and we'll end up licking alcohol off the streets. I'm just not interested any more.'

First pint:

'I was just saying you're a scabby bastard,' says Paul.

'Fuck you too,' says Danny.

Second pint:

'Did you hear that Philip O'Brien is living on the streets in Liverpool with a big homeless-guy beard on him?'

'Why doesn't he just move into a squat?'

'Can't keep it together. It's not as easy as it used to be.'

Philip was a dealer in college. He and Vladimir Foster were partners in crime. Alexander always thought that Philip was the brains behind the operation, with Vlad doing the donkey work of bringing the dope back from London on the Holyhead ferry. But now Vlad is obese and prosperous, a software engineer living in Islington, while Philip will probably die of intestinal bleeding in a public toilet.

'We see the whole spectrum,' Danny says. 'Philip O'Brien at one end, Hugo Strongboy at the other. By the way, I want to tell you lads: we're going to christen the baby next weekend, and I'm going to ask Hugo to be godfather. You guys are my flesh and blood, but—'

'Hugo is a multimillionaire,' Alexander says.

'Don't flatter yourself that we're bothered whom you ask to be godparents,' Paul says. 'Anyhow, we know you're a closet homosexual and Hugo's giving it to you up the ass.'

'Or you want him to give it to you up the ass.'

'Yeah, yeah. What I want is to give my son a godfather who might be able to do something for him in the future.'

'With a name like Merlin,' Paul observes, 'his future is already irretrievable.'

'You've no imagination,' Danny responds angrily, rising for the first time in reaction to Paul's persistent provocation.

'But why would you have a christening a week after the baby's birth?' Alexander asks. 'That's not the usual way, is it?'

'It's my stepson's plan... Jasper. He was never christened, and now he wants to be, the two of them together. He wants to do it in a hurry for some reason.'

'What religion are you going for?'

'Catholic or Protestant,' Danny says, enjoying himself again. 'It'll depend on who can book us in for next Sunday.'

Fourth pint:

'Are you going to tell Alex about your bit on the side?' Danny asks Paul with a wink.

'It was supposed to be a secret affair,' Paul says to Danny, frowning.

Alexander knows they have an inner-circle conversation that excludes him. This has ceased to be a source of pain in itself, but he finds it humiliating that they parade it.

'Karina had some gals over a few months ago,' Paul begins with an expression of discomfort on his face. 'I think they were going to start a book club, but instead they just got plastered.'

'Women love to bitch and talk about periods,' Danny says, speaking as though he were a world expert in an obscure field.

'I was out at a jazz gig,' Paul continues. 'I got home after twelve, and the thing was breaking up. I sat down for a glass of wine. Most of them were leaving. Karina was hammered and went off to bed: she always falls asleep when she drinks. At the end, I was left alone on the sofa with one of them, and she just starts laying into me.'

'Do I know her?' Alexander asks.

'No,' Paul says, without a flicker of hesitation. 'She's a friend of Karina's.'

'What's her name?'

'Let's not get into it.... Next thing I know she's leading me up the stairs to the spare bedroom. I know that Karina is out for the count, but still I'm fairly shitting myself. At the same time though, you know, it's hard not to go with the flow.'

'Look at him, all bashful and it's-nothing-to-do-with-me,' exclaims Danny with delight. 'He had the best sex life of anybody in college. He's been fighting them off probably since he was twelve.'

'We had this amazing high-risk bonk in the spare room; then she says she's going to sleep over, to tell Karina that she was too drunk to go home. The next morning the three of us are having breakfast, blah de blah, talking about property prices, and she is playing footsie with me under the table.'

'Sounds exciting,' says Alexander, but what he feels is weariness.

'It *is* exciting – the best sex I've had in a long time – but my nerves are shot to bits.'

As the information lands fully, the moment turns ugly for Alexander. He has no moral objection to the sex, or the deceit, but the telling of the tale, the opening of that which should remain private, smashes something in his mood, like a piece of crockery.

He likes Karina.

'You're watching stuff the whole time,' Paul is explaining to Danny, 'looking for clues that might give you away, sniffing your clothes, deleting texts. I should quit while I'm ahead.'

Alexander drinks from his Guinness, drifts away from the conversation. He wonders about marriage, about the possibility of a marriage in which you really mean it.

He remembers – without immediately spotting the association – a night in a club on the quays, years previously, in the immediate post-college period, when Danny, Paul and he ended up drinking at a big table with a group of people they had known only obliquely in Trinity. He got talking to a few arty types, students of literature and drama, one of them the grandson of a famous painter.

'I don't give a shit about Christian mythology,' the grandson argued passionately in an intense passage of conversation, which Alexander recalls clearly: 'A guy crucified to the floor of Abrakebabra on Westmoreland Street – that is the kind of mythology that interests me, that moves me.'

Alexander thinks: Why couldn't I have spent more time with people like that?

'Don't you guys find that life is really difficult?' he says suddenly in a moment of reckless honesty, of madness. 'I sometimes feel like I'm drowning, you know? I'm up to my throat in water, turning my face to the sky so that it won't flood into my mouth.'

He feels his eyes scrunching up, not that he is getting teary, but he is filled with a rush of emotion that concentrates itself in this part of his face.

Paul looks at him blankly, glances at Danny, drinks from his pint.

Danny is stern. 'In fairness, we don't talk about that kind of thing,' he says.

Alexander nods, accepts the admonition. His emotion flees, and, in fleeing, becomes as strange to him as it is to the others. He drinks, reaches for his cigarettes.

He recalls often the year they spent in London together, dwells in it.

They lived for free in a house in the East End. It wasn't exactly a squat, although that was how they liked to think of it. The house was owned or managed by a mild-mannered Pakistani estate agent called Roger Singh. Their occupancy in some way suited his dodgy business, or he liked them, or he wasn't very good at insisting on the rent, or all these things. In any case, after the first month, they never paid him.

Sometimes Roger would arrive over in the evening with a bottle of whiskey and they would all get drunk. He had the eyes of a saint, but would moan about his wife in his sing-song English and smoke all the dope he could get if the lads had any.

They all had different jobs. Alexander worked as an insurance clerk in the City. Danny was a barman in a students' pub near

Regent's Park. Paul got a gig in the advertising department of a trade magazine.

Alexander was the first up on weekdays. He would stagger out of bed into the shower. There was a plumbing problem. Every shower or bath led to a minor flood, which then conveniently disappeared between the bare floorboards: problem solved; but, out of sight, things were rotting.

For breakfast he would buy two jammy doughnuts and a bottle of Lucozade in the local corner shop. He would also buy a *Daily Mirror* to read on the tube. He was a *Daily Mirror* reader that year, and it was nice. He rarely thought about anything. In the evenings, they'd go out on the tear or else get mellow with a few spliffs and a couple of beers in front of the TV. His brain clouded over, and he didn't miss it.

But it was all too much for the bathroom floor. One day the ceiling in the corner of the kitchen, the part directly under the bathroom, cracked wide open, in three distinct moves, with a lot of creaking and groaning. And the bath slid through, like a divine revelation, travelling with a wave of dirty sudsy water; it flew through the air and landed smack on the television set.

That was the beginning of the end of the year in London.

Sally Barnes works in the Personnel Division of the Department of Finance and has responsibility for matters relating to the National Economic Advisory Council. She is a big cheerful girl who suffers from clogged sinuses and lapses in concentration.

The recruitment of Imelda was a case in point. Imelda was interviewed by Alexander, Sally, and Fat Barry from Special Projects. Barry was more interested in his own performance than in that of the candidate. 'How did I do?' he asked Sally at the end. Alexander himself isn't much better in these things. He blushes when he is asking the questions, finds it impossible to pay attention to the answers, and dreads the part at the end where candidates get to ask their own questions. This is a crap job, he wants to blurt out. There is no proper work, the pay isn't very good, and the prospects for advancement are practically nil. The only advantage is that you don't have to work hard. In fact, with a little talent and determination, you could get away with doing nothing at all. For the love of God, do something else with your life.

But however poor the standard of the interview board, Imelda was worse. She failed by a wide margin, even though there were no other candidates (labour market shortages – too many jobs, not enough people). The board scored it up, signed it off, and that afternoon Sally sent Imelda a pro forma letter offering her the job.

'Tell her it was a mistake,' Alexander suggested.

'I did, but she has already handed in her notice where she's working.'

'What are you talking about? She told us she is working part-time in a coffee shop until she finds a proper job.'

'Yeah, but she's given in her notice. Plus she's told her parents. They're very pleased.'

'I bet they are.'

In the recruitment of Evil Neville, Sally's error was less grievous, but has created a difficulty that Alexander now faces this Monday morning.

During the interview, Sally got carried away (labour market shortages – trying to attract the candidate) telling Neville about the possibilities for further education, including that the Council could fund him to do a master's degree. Unfortunately, it turns out that was not true. As a graduate trainee on a fixed-term contract, Neville – so Sally told Alexander on Friday – is not entitled to have *any* fees paid.

'But you told him in the interview that we would pay his fees.'

'No I didn't! And I've checked with Barry and he agrees with me.'

Fat Barry from Special Projects had again been the third man on the panel.

'I remember it well, Sally,' Alexander corrects her. 'And so does Neville.'

'You're mistaken. How could I have said it if it isn't the policy?'

'Neville,' Alexander exclaims generously as the man in question enters his office. 'Come in. Take a seat. Tell me about your plans for Christmas.'

'I don't really have any plans,' Neville responds contemptuously as he sits down at the meeting table rather than in the chair in front of Alexander's desk, which Alexander indicated.

'Good,' says Alexander. 'I'm glad to hear it.' He decides that he will not move from behind his desk to join Neville at the table. He wants to keep distance and authority. 'I hate Christmas myself, although it sounds very Scrooge to say so.'

This is true. Alexander experiences Christmas like a difficult obstacle in a show-jumping round. It's a big effort. There is no avoiding it. All you can do is line it up, try to get into a decent canter, a good rhythm, and give it plenty of leg at take-off.

Neville isn't interested.

'I have checked with Personnel,' Alexander continues. 'It is as you described. Sally says there is no entitlement to have your fees refunded. She also denies that she made any commitments during your interview.'

'But you told her she was wrong in that,' Neville states with a level of assertiveness that is threatening.

'I didn't say she was right or wrong. I told her what I recalled, just as I related it to you.'

Alexander's legs feel uncomfortable, jittery from too much coffee. He pushes back his chair and lifts his feet onto the corner of the desk, crossing them. As he is doing so, he takes a peek through the window over his left shoulder, down into the courtyard, where the terracotta-coloured paving stones are washed with rain. There is a bronze statue in the courtyard which he likes: a naked man walking on a beam, as in gymnastics, although the image is melancholy rather than sporty. Alexander glances at the man's bare buttocks, always in movement, never making progress.

'Do you remember we had that problem earlier in the year with the premium-line calls?' he asks Neville.

'Oh yeah – whatever happened to those?'

'You stopped making them.'

Neville coughs into his fist with apparent nervousness, then looks up and smiles, his small eyes shining poisonously.

'You can't say that. You don't have any evidence. I'll sue your arse for saying that. I'll sue you at the same time that I'm suing the Council for breach of promise over the fees.'

Alexander emits an oafish snort of embarrassment and amusement, accompanied by a spray of spittle, some of which flies as far as one of his shoes, a black brogue that could do with a decent polish. Both shoes could do with a decent polish. He often notices that other guys in suits have much shinier shoes than he. Where do they find the time for shining their shoes? Or where do they get the money to buy new shoes so often? It's a mystery. The only certainty is that this is one of the many aspects of his life where he could do better. Must concentrate, he thinks.

'You don't have to take such an uncompromising stance on everything,' he says. 'What's your goal here? Are you looking to get offered a permanent contract? Are you looking for advancement within the Council?'

'Pah.'

'Threatening to sue everybody isn't necessarily the best route to get you what you want.'

'It is if what you want is to sue everybody.'

Alexander pulls his feet down. He sits forward, leaning his elbows on the desk.

'But that isn't what you want. You want the Council to pay your fees. Let's get back to talking about that.'

'What about Fat Barry? What does he say?'

'He doesn't recall any discussion about funding for your master's.'

'He's lying. Or else he wasn't listening. Or he has the hots for Sally because she has big tits.'

'Let's not interpret people's motivations,' Alexander suggests calmly. 'Let's stick to the surface of things.'

'The surface of things is that she said they would pay my fees. That's one of the reasons I took the job. It's why I shelled out three grand to do the course. I thought I was going to get it back.'

'And that's why I have a certain sympathy with you in this. On the other hand, you're a nasty little fuck who wasted a load of money ringing sex lines and tried to incriminate an innocent colleague.'

Neville jolts angrily into a standing position, the chair tumbling onto the floor behind him.

'So let's call it quits,' Alexander concludes sweetly.

'Fuck you.... You've no evidence. Plus....' Neville searches for content. 'I object to your lewd suggestions.'

'What are you talking about?' Alexander asks, already alarmed.

'That's a disgusting proposition,' Neville continues quietly with a growing smile.

'Are you mad? What are you talking about?'

Neville picks up the fallen chair, neatly tucks it under the meeting table.

'You haven't heard the last of this,' he says with theatrical dignity, all the while grinning to himself, and leaves the room, gently closing the door behind him.

Alexander's next appointment of the morning is with Bernard Blackmore.

For a change of scenery, to avoid interruption, and to lend himself a bit of gravitas, Alexander takes the meeting in the formal conference room, which is expensively furnished with an oval wooden table and large chairs upholstered in black leather.

Blackmore is a big man, well over six feet tall and wide at the shoulders. He is in his fifties now, and has recently suffered a minor heart attack. His doctors have advised him to cut down on sugar and fatty foods and to go walking every day. He undertakes this programme fearfully rather than enthusiastically. This is all supposedly to be kept secret from his clients, but Alexander knows the story because he was at college with one of the economists on Blackmore's team and they meet for lunch occasionally.

Blackmore has a wave of oiled grey hair across the top of his skull. His skin is sallow and taut, like a face mask. He always behaves affably, but seems tense to Alexander.

'Remarkably well,' Blackmore says in response to Alexander's inquiry as to his well-being. 'No doubt in the next life the gods will arrange that I get my just desserts, but for the time being I am keeping several steps ahead of the devil.'

'How's work? Are you busy?'

'To be honest with you, I'm turning work away. We're like a small restaurant that the connoisseurs love. We're booked out every night of the week.'

'So if I had some more work in the pipeline, you mightn't be able to take it on,' Alexander says, smiling playfully.

'We always try to accommodate our best customers,' Blackmore replies, allowing no trace of humour to enter his expression. 'What have you got in mind?'

The catering people have, as requested, left a tray of coffee and biscuits. Alexander pours two coffees. He removes the cellophane cover from the plate of biscuits.

'Pretty good selection,' he says in genuine admiration, observing the high concentration of quality, including Hobnobs, Jaffa Cakes and Mikado. 'We usually get a lot of Nice, but I can't see a single one here. You're getting the celebrity treatment, Bernard.'

He pushes the plate across. Blackmore declines with a small wave of the hand.

'It's a piece of work on entrepreneurship,' Alexander explains. 'But the Council wouldn't move on to it until the current work on broadband is completed.'

'I understand,' says Blackmore, with just a hint of a glint.

'A European benchmarking study on levels of entrepreneurship has recently come to the Council's attention. It suggests that the level of entrepreneurship in Ireland is only medium. The Council wants to know why we're not best-in-class. Some of the members suspect there is negative sentiment toward entrepreneurs in our national psyche. So the idea is to explore attitudes in new and innovative ways.'

Blackmore nods intelligently.

'Interesting project,' he says, though they both know it's a piece of horseshit.

'Let's come back to it. Tell me about broadband.'

' ... The big towns are catered for, the small ones are not. That's the basic story. If I'm a big user setting up in or near a town that's unconnected, one of the telecom players will lay a cable for me at a fairly competitive rate. If I'm a small company or a small residential user in the same town, it's completely uneconomical for broadband to be made available to me. I couldn't pay for the line myself and there isn't enough immediate demand to justify the investment by the telecom company.'

'So what should we do?'

'Well ... ,' says Blackmore with a cautious smile, 'as we discussed on the phone, it is possible to take different views on this matter. I understood that you would be speaking to the Chairman and some Council members to get a sense of where they are coming from. It's useful to consider the context for the recommendations.'

'Do you mind if I dunk?' Alexander asks, and proceeds, without waiting for a response, to submerge a Hobnob in his coffee. 'Since my girlfriend left me, I'm regressing,' he adds, almost involuntarily. On a different day he would never stray into such territory in a meeting like this, but the encounter with Neville has wearied him into honesty.

'From the Chairman's point of view,' Alexander continues, 'indeed from the point of view of a majority of the Council, this exercise will have been a waste of time if you conclude against state intervention.'

'I don't think we'll be concluding against state intervention.'

'There is market failure here. We have to spend money. It's up to you to tell us how much. And let's not think small here. If we're going to do it, let's do it properly. Anyhow, it's easier these days to get large sums of money out of cabinet. Go for ten million and they'll quibble over the details. Go for two hundred million, and they'll ask if it's enough.'

'It won't be ten million.'

'The next question is: how will the money be dispensed? I think the Council will welcome a view that the money should be funnelled through the local authorities.'

'The local authorities haven't got a clue,' Blackmore says, but flatly, as a statement of fact rather than as an objection. 'They can barely tie their shoelaces. In fact, they *can't* tie their shoelaces. You'd be better off having one national institute for funding and decision-making. That would give you consistency of standards and economies of scale. You could do the whole thing in one contract.'

'I'd give two sides of the argument,' Alexander agrees in a balanced and open tone, 'but I wouldn't make the centralised option my recommendation. We want to empower the local authorities. We want them to learn. It's dangerous to assume that the centre knows local requirements better than the locals themselves. Anyhow, suggesting a national institute would be politically naïve. It sounds too much like a national telecom company, when it's not long since we sold our national telecom company. But by all means let's say that the local authorities should be resourced properly to … develop adequate expertise. It costs money to spend money. Everybody loves additional resources; and the state has got so much wonga now, it doesn't know what to do with it.'

'And who is going to run the infrastructure? Would you make every local authority into a telecom company?'

'No. You'll have to advise us on that. I'm sure they could award contracts covering the design, build and operation of the infrastructure, in which case the local authorities would just have to pass over the cash.'

'Which the Department of Finance would provide.'

'I think that's the sort of guidance the Council would welcome,' Alexander concludes with a nod. 'You know, the Council is developing a very good working relationship with Blackmore and Associates. I would even say that they may come to rely on your judgement.'

Alexander meets Dympna in the corridor. She is so dynamic that one sometimes misses how neat and handsome she is. Her large brown eyes seek him out with serious intent. Her dry hair is brushed straight.

She is wearing her bright orange jacket-and-skirt suit, white blouse, black tights, simple black shoes with a low heel.

'There you are,' she says urgently. 'I'm really glad to catch up with you before you slip out to lunch.'

She is remarkably slim. The bulge below the waistline of her skirt could belong to a nineteen-year-old virgin, rather than a woman who has given birth within the last couple of years. Alexander finds that he would like to slip his hand inside her jacket and gently cup in it this slight bulge.

'What makes you think I'm slipping out for lunch?' he asks.

'Listen, I just want to warn you that something ridiculous is happening. Neville Lewis seems to be going mad. He has rung three different people in Personnel in the last half hour, very audibly ... complaining about you.'

She frowns when uttering her final words, indicating regret, sympathy.

'What is he complaining about?' Alexander asks with a sigh.

They are standing by the stainless-steel double doors of the lift. He automatically presses the down arrow on the button panel, but the intention is a vague one at this stage.

Dympna looks over her shoulders, like a driver changing lanes on a motorway, to check if anyone is coming up on her. They are perfectly alone in the square-shaped lift lobby, sealed off from the rest of the world by the fire doors at either end, but she nevertheless addresses him in a dramatic stage whisper, flinching a little on some of the crucial words.

'He is saying that you offered Council funding for his fees in return for oral sex.... I'm sorry, but I thought you would rather know.'

'Yes, thank you.'

Dympna looks at him queerly.

'Should I say any more?'

'Please do.'

Dympna swallows loudly to steady herself.

'He said to Personnel that you wanted him to perform fellatio on you there and then.'

Alexander nods.

'And the rest of you heard this?'

'Most of the floor heard it. It's probably around the whole building by now.'

'Good. That's very good.' It occurs to Alexander that he should probably reject the allegation, but he finds it impossible to muster the right tone of voice. 'I don't even control funding for fees,' he manages to say after a longish pause.

Dympna leans forward to encourage greater revelation on his part.

'Sally Barnes would be the person,' he adds.

'He didn't mention Sally.' Dympna seems disappointed in Alexander's attitude. 'What are you going to do?'

'I'm meeting my sister for lunch.... I suppose life must go on, fellatio or no fellatio.'

Dympna scowls. 'You must take this seriously,' she says with maternal concern and warmth. 'You must defend yourself.'

Alexander is moved by this implicit expression of trust. He doesn't even trust himself that much, and experiences Dympna's faith as an act of friendship.

'Thanks, Dympna,' he says and presses the lift button again. This time the bell goes bing-bing and the steel doors clunkily slide open to admit him to the smooth chamber within. 'Let's talk again after lunch. Where's Neville now?'

'I don't know. He disappeared.'

Once safely enclosed in the lift, Alexander lets out a long, medium-volume, nicely moist fart that has been pressing on him. There is some pleasure in this until he quickly recalls, with mounting alarm, that it's a serious mistake to fart in an empty lift, that anyone getting on at the next stop will instantly sniff him out. There will be no hiding place. He resolves to rush out of the lift – face down – as soon as it stops, wherever it stops, which turns out to be the very next floor, where his boss, George Lucey, is waiting to embark.

'Ah, Alexander,' George says, transfixing him on the spot before the doors are even fully open. 'I'm glad I bumped into you. There's something I want to talk to you about.' George marches forward, right into Alexander's face, then jerks his nose in different directions, with absurdly flared nostrils, to discern the source of the odour he is now picking up. 'That's a very soupy smell. Somebody must have been transporting soup in this lift. Seems a bit odd, doesn't it?'

'Maybe Catering are doing a lunch somewhere,' Alexander suggests.

'Did you have soup for lunch?' George demands in an interrogating, militaristic tone, staring straight into Alexander's eyes from no more than a few inches away.

'Not yet,' Alexander tells him, continuing immediately to a different subject. 'You know this business with Neville Lewis and the fees. He's insisting that Sally – in the interview – offered to pay his fees. I have to confess that I had some sympathy—'

'He's a little pup,' George says. 'In my day we were happy enough to have a job; now it's all me-me-me. He can go whistle for it.'

'I never mentioned it to you, but he was the one who was making the astrology calls on the phone that time.'

'The obscene phone calls, eh? I always knew he was a deviant.'

Alexander feels George's hot breath on his face as the lift drops slowly through the dark narrow shaft. He resists the muscular impulse to laugh by contorting his face into a grimace.

'It was Imelda who saw him,' Alexander continues for want of something better to say. 'She came back late one evening to get something she had forgotten—'

'What had she forgotten?' George asks piercingly, as though this were an important detail.

'I don't know. She didn't say.'

'I see,' says George, still in his investigative vein.

'The point is that she saw Neville making a call from her desk, and we were able to identify it as one of the calls in question: I got a log of them from Personnel.'

George is losing interest.

'This lift is taking a long time,' he observes suspiciously, stepping away from Alexander and turning around to examine the controls.

They are stopped now at 1, though the doors have not opened. George presses G and the lift jolts into action.

Alexander takes the opportunity of George having turned his back to slip in the subject of the alleged sexual harassment.

'Neville has accused me of making lewd propositions,' he says, recognising immediately from how George's back stiffens that he has made an error in mentioning this and in the way he has done so.

George turns around and examines him accusingly with narrowed eyes.

'Needless to say, there is no foundation in what he is saying,' Alexander continues, but George's expression does not change. His jaw seems more square than usual, with the muscle at the corner of each jawbone pulsing visibly, from the man's heart beat, or from a rhythmic clenching and unclenching of his teeth.

'I didn't proposition him,' Alexander further asserts, but senses that the situation is getting worse with every word he utters.

George turns away abruptly to face the controls again.

Alexander falters in his comprehension of reality. The steel panels of the lift chamber alter their proportions and close in on him. It seems for an instant that George and he are suspended horizontally, free from gravity, hurtling in this box through the dark outer regions of the universe. Alexander cannot breathe. His hand goes to his neck and he tugs at his shirt collar to create some space. His other hand reaches for the side wall to steady himself. He feels as though his equilibrium is gone, but he doesn't fall.

Bing-bing. They have reached G. The doors open onto the spacious foyer. George is on the move without a backward glance.

Alexander is due to meet Helena in L'Ecrivain. He arrives early and opts to wait downstairs, seating himself on the sumptuous sofa. The hostess offers him a drink, as though it were free. His first thought is to get a sparkling water, but he decides instead for a single-malt whiskey with one cube of ice.

'Hiya, kiddo,' says Helena, flopping down beside him on the sofa. 'It's a bit early for hard liquor, isn't it?'

'I'm having a difficult day. Or, rather, I *was* having a difficult day. At this very moment I am deciding to bunk off for the afternoon and get plastered, so things are looking up.'

'It's a pity I can't join you. I have a meeting with clients about a litigation.'

'Well, if you have to be there, you have to be there,' he says with mock sympathy, 'but do allow yourself a moderately boozy lunch. It'll ease your passage through the afternoon.'

'I'll have a glass of white wine, and maybe a dessert wine at the end. . . . Listen, while I think of it: I was talking to Siobhán at the weekend—'

'How could you have been talking to Siobhán at the weekend?'

Siobhán is their riding instructor.

'I bumped into her in Tesco's. They're going to have a show-jumping competition in January. I put our names down.'

Upstairs, in the bright airy space of the restaurant proper, they are shown to a table that is closer to the busy traffic from the kitchen doors than Alexander would like. It is not so much the traffic as the lack of regard that bothers him. In fairness, he forgot to book until this morning, and didn't specify any table preferences, but there are plenty of unoccupied tables in better locations.

The key in these situations is to be gracefully assertive, to have natural authority, to require a better table simply because you require a better table, without giving the thing any thought. On his better days, he can sometimes hit such heights. But today the waiter is superior to him. Alexander could allow the whiskey to bring out his brash, argumentative aspect, but that is not the tone he wants to set. So he sits where he is told.

'It's not the world's greatest table,' Helena says, after the waiter has helped her into the seat and left them to consider the menus.

'I think it's fine,' Alexander says, a little abruptly, not wanting the embarrassment of her insisting on their being moved.

'Do you remember when we were kids and we talked about our souls?' he asks, once they are well engaged with their starters.

'No,' says Helena, as she picks a mussel out of its yawning shell.

'I would say that you were eight or nine and I was six-seven. We were talking about the shape of our souls, what we imagined them to look like.'

'How do you remember this shit?'

'You must recall that they used to teach us in school that everyone has a soul, which is immortal.'

'Almost. Being Catholic is so far in the past now.'

'We talked about it. You imagined that your soul was round, "like an egg", you actually said. And I thought that was all wrong. Mine was like a spear or an arrow, which ran through my body. Isn't that amazing?'

'Not really.'

'Don't you see what it means? We were kids. Consciously we knew nothing about sex, but we were thinking in archetypal symbols of sexual identity.'

'Mmm,' says Helena, dipping her fingers in the bowl of water and lemon slices, drying them on her napkin. 'Have you seen Julia at all? Have you rung her? You were supposed to ring her. We're all worried about you, living in that grotty flat by yourself, going mad.'

'I saw her at the weekend. I met her in Holles Street by coincidence, visiting Aoife and the new baby. We didn't really get a chance to talk, but I'll see her again at the weekend, at the christening. I'll try to talk to her then.'

'And what are you going to say?'

'What do you want me to say?' he snaps, not liking the space into which they have moved, Helena being all big-sisterly and condescending. 'I don't know what to say. If I knew what to say, we'd be married now, living in Inner Mongolia, with two overindulged brats in the local Gaelscoil.'

Helena sits back and raises her eyebrows. I apologise for caring, her expression says. He sees this as just another aspect of her condescension, but allows himself to be manipulated.

'Sorry,' he lies. 'I appreciate your concern. And you know I'm crazy about the kids. I wasn't implying anything. Let's talk about something else.'

'Oh my God, yes, how could I have forgotten?' she blurts out warmly, relenting immediately, sitting forward in her chair to recreate their intimacy.

'What? What is it?'

They were very close in their teenage years, when they were both in Malahide Community School. Back then, Helena used to love to talk about her precocious sexual adventures. (Later, in college, something happened to her – he doesn't know what – and she turned prim, relatively, almost overnight.) He could have told her back then about his recent epiphany, his insight into the shapes of souls, how he was walking down Grafton Street and saw all these pricks and cunts. Not that they *had* pricks and cunts, but that they *were* pricks and cunts, that this was the beginning and end of their identity. How he now understood, retrospectively, the Picasso nudes which had previously puzzled him, the painter's focus on the cunt, his putting it at the centre of the picture, the centre of the anatomy.

'It's about Maisie,' Helena begins. 'She's back in hospital again, this time for an irregular heart beat. Mum says she's in great form, giving out goodo.'

'Is Mum down there?'

'She went down on Friday. She says that Maisie has been asking after you, that she wants to change her will and leave the farm to you. How about that?'

Helena is beaming. Alexander experiences no more than a light internal change of tone, like the effect of a drop of colour in a Petri dish of water. He is not excited by the prospect because he doesn't believe that such a thing can come to pass.

'When did this happen? Why didn't Mum tell me herself?'

Helena shrugs, indicating that she considers this an unimportant detail, given the significance of the news itself.

'I was talking to her on the phone on Saturday. I said I was meeting you for lunch today and that I'd tell you.'

'There'd be blue murder. Tommy Óg Grady would have my guts for garters.'

'Don't worry about Tommy Óg Grady,' says Helena impatiently. 'I thought you would be delighted. It must be worth a fortune . . . like a few million maybe.'

'It's not going to happen,' he tells her heatedly. 'Nothing good like that ever happens to me.'

'That's because you never go for anything.'

'How do you go for something like this? What do you want me to do? Do you want me to go down and sweet-talk the old dear? Do you want me to threaten her with a kitchen knife? Anyhow, she's probably not in her right mind. Who is going to let a 95-year-old dying woman write a new will?'

'Those are exactly the kind of people who do write new wills. The rest of us think we're never going to die.'

Alexander takes a swig of his wine.

'I wish I were a Buddhist monk,' he says.

'Well you could be,' Helena points out agreeably. 'You could be a fat cat Buddhist monk sitting on forty acres of prime rezoning land in County Galway.'

Alexander drinks again. His wine is getting low. It tastes watery to him now, with a cardboard flavour, where before he thought it was debonair. He looks around for a waiter so he can order more.

'We should have got a bottle,' he says.

Most years, before the kids reached their teens, the Vespucci family would drive to Galway for a fortnight's holiday in the summer. To them it was an epic journey. They made a day of it, stopping late in the morning in Kinnegad for sandwiches, 'minerals' and tea, and again in the mid-afternoon in Ballinasloe. Jim Vespucci never drove above forty miles an hour, and if the kids moved around in the back seat, or complained too much, he threatened to turn back, which shut them up immediately.

Crossing the Shannon at Athlone was the fulcrum in the journey.

'We're in the West now,' Brigid would say, as though the West were a completely different country – by understood implication, a rough windswept land where life was more real and more attractive than the suburban Dublin monotony to which the Vespuccis were accustomed.

Not long after the Shannon, the dry-stone walls appeared, lining the roadside, dividing the grassy fields into sequences of irregular rectangles. These pretty walls – their infinite idiosyncrasies, the lichen stains, the beaten weathered look, the kiss of the rocks off each other, the patchwork of fresh air between them – became for Alexander synonymous with the West and evocative of freedom and happiness.

They stayed in a caravan park in Salthill, which was excitement enough in itself. Alexander, Helena and their mother spent the day on the Salthill promenade, swimming in the sea at Blackrock, racing down the slide in Leisureland, pushing pennies and tuppences into the casino slot machines.

Jim Vespucci was not much of a man for outdoor activities, or indeed for indoor activities. He would disappear shortly after breakfast, and they would meet up in a bar or hotel in the late afternoon, where he would be drinking a pint, smoking his pipe, reading his book, all at a stately pace.

In the evenings, they had dinner in the caravan and played cards, laughing a lot. On the best days, they were so fatigued by the time they lay down to sleep that they did not notice the musty smell of the pillows or complain about the tough spongy cushions with the asthma-inducing upholstery. For a brief few minutes, before disintegrating into a deep sleep, Alexander would be conscious of the dried crystals of sea salt on his back, his sunburnt skin emitting in pulse rhythm some of the heat it had absorbed during the day, and the pepper of sand that felt like grit between his body and the bed sheet.

Two or three times during their holiday they would visit Maisie, and these were the days they loved most.

At the time, Ballyryan was deep in the countryside, though only twenty miles from the centre of Galway city. Maisie had no phone, so initially she wouldn't even know that the Vespuccis were in Galway unless Brigid had dropped her a note in the post.

The farmhouse was a stone construction, built in the second half of the nineteenth century, with a big blonde thatched roof. Adjacent to it was a bigger two-storey barn, also made of stone. The walls of the house were thickly plastered, whitewashed, giving it a skin that had an organic quality, curving slightly on its lines, bulging in places. The house and barn were on about three-quarters of an acre, fenced off from the surrounding fields; with gates in two places, a narrow one that led to the front door, and a broad one behind the house for workloads. In previous years, the fence had shielded a busy herb and vegetable garden from grazing animals. By the time the Vespucci children were old enough to pay any real attention, the garden was riotously overgrown, made interesting by the things one could discover in this growth, picking one's way through hazards of nettles and long thorny limbs of gooseberry bushes gone wild: bits of an old tractor, including a seat on which one could pretend to be driving; a rusty scythe; galvanised-iron buckets full of muck, with the grass growing out of them; a configuration of large flat rocks that might have been a man-made something from early history, collapsed now. And when their nerves wearied of such explorations, they could return to the relative order of the yard behind the barn, where – in season – they could climb and slide down the beehive-shaped haystacks, held together with rope and rocks. Panting in the August heat, the kids would pause then to drink and splash cold water from the outside tap – the only source on the farm.

When they arrived, Jim would park the car by the narrow front gate. If the folks were home, the front door would be open, to let in the light.

Auburn-breasted hens would be wandering purposefully around the lane, clucking, pecking, slipping under the closed gate, strutting in and out of the house, calmly varying speed and direction, randomly, or as required by changing circumstances – for instance, the arrival of the Vespucci's car. The droppings would be everywhere, in varying shades and states of disintegration; mistaken by Alexander for chocolate when he was very small, as Helena liked to recall.

Maisie would emerge from the house when she heard the car pull up in the lane; but not immediately. There was a waiting period, no more than a minute or two perhaps, but seemingly long to the children, a period during which they were instructed to remain politely seated in the car. When she had done whatever it was she did in this mysterious lapse, Maisie would shuffle out into the yard, putting her hands to her cheeks in her surprise at seeing them; and though not smiling exactly, she would seem to be pleased at the visit. She was a medium-sized woman with curly grey hair, a fat red-skinned face, and deep-set intelligent eyes, overlaid with thick-rimmed glasses, the standard issue from the health board. At home, she was always dressed in the same outfit: a big apron, long black skirt, manly boots. Even then, her ankles were flabby, spilling out over the tops of her boots despite her heavy beige stockings. Her clothes were so much a part of her identity as to be indistinguishable from her person in Alexander's comprehension of her.

Husband Johnny was a thin shy man who said very little. He wore a cap, and smoked a pipe with a perforated steel lid across the top to stop the tobacco from falling out when he was going about the farm. His trousers were held up with a piece of twine. The biggest thing about him was his boots, which had steel studs nailed into the soles to stop them from wearing out. When he moved across the flagstone kitchen floor, they made a great noise and gave out the odd spark, which the children loved. Johnny – their mother would tell them – had fought bravely in the War of Independence. But in another breath, without cross-reference, it would be given to understand that he was a mouse of a man, too nice by far for Maisie, that it was she who wore the trousers. By inheritance, it was Maisie's house, Maisie's farm.

The culture of these visits was unlike anything that Helena and Alexander were used to. In a standard visit back home in Dublin, you would ring the bell, go in quickly, sit down. In a visit to Maisie's, there would be what seemed like twenty minutes of conversation at the car, half an hour in the yard, half an hour at the door, twenty minutes standing in the kitchen, two hours sitting at the kitchen table, twenty minutes sitting at the kitchen table with imminent departure signalled, half an hour standing in the kitchen, twenty minutes standing at the door, another long while in the yard, then at the car, then in the car but with the windows rolled down. And all the time Brigid and Maisie would be yapping, yapping, yapping, laughing, while Jim and Uncle Johnny would offer occasional comments to the general discussion or have their own sparse manly interchanges about the weather or sport or politics, never anything too contentious or even interesting, just enough to signal friendliness, affection. The children mostly ignored these conversations, wanting just to run off down the lanes, in search perhaps of neighbour Michael Phaddy, who might let them sit up on his old horse and go for a bit of a stroll, bareback. Sometimes they would wander off on arrival and wouldn't cross Maisie's threshold until a couple of hours into the visit, when they were getting tired and hungry. Or, if it was later in the afternoon when they called, near milking time, Uncle Johnny would take them down to the field to collect the cows.

The two huge Friesians would be waiting at the gate, and Uncle Johnny would walk behind them up the path, carrying a stick he never used on them, saying: 'Wooooe na beh-hee, wooooe na beh-hee,' which Alexander guessed years later to be a remnant from the Irish language: na beithígh – the beasts, the beings.

Up to the Famine, this area had been Irish-speaking. But following those years of great hurt, the people who had lived that life were almost all dead or departed. And what remained of the language was soon rooted out. When she went to school – barefoot, with a lump of turf in her hand for the fire – Maisie's mother had to stick out her tongue so that the teacher could judge if she had been talking Irish at home. Speaking Irish put black spots on your tongue, and these were rewarded with the cane.

'Wooooe na beh-hee,' Uncle Johnny would intone, taking slow strides with his thin legs, the soles of his boots scraping musically off the dried-muck surface of the lane.

And the animals would mosey along, their hooves drumming, their tails swishing ineffectually at the flies that buzzed around them.

Sometimes, to the children's amusement, one of the cows would release – as it moved – a dripping of shit, some of which would stick to the rear shanks or hind legs, depending on how the line of its fall intersected with the swaying walking movement.

And the progress of the procession would be far too slow for the children. They were running on ahead and doubling back, getting involved in side issues, pestering Uncle Johnny with endless questions, which he benevolently ignored, or answered tersely after long pauses, as though he didn't speak the language, which he didn't in so far as it was their language.

When they finally got to the farmhouse, the animals would turn undirected up the lane and head into the yard. It delighted Alexander that such brutes could know the way.

'If they got lost, Uncle Johnny, would they be able to make it back home?' he asked, thinking of Lassie and carrier pigeons. 'Like, if somebody took them in a truck and dropped them in Athlone, would they know how to get back?'

'Sure, why would a person do that?'

Uncle Johnny milked the two Friesians by hand in the barn. Helena wasn't interested in this, but Alexander liked to watch.

The two cows were secured in their places with heavy old chains that had been mortared into the wall, probably when the building itself was erected. It surprised Alexander that this would be necessary, since the animals were apparently so docile.

Johnny used a three-legged stool to support himself. He didn't sit on it exactly. He wedged one leg of it into the uneven earthen floor, and pressed his bony backside against the seat. Leaning forward, he grabbed two of the cow's teats and began pulling on them rapidly, rhythmically. The practised speed of these movements was astonishing when first witnessed, because Johnny was so phlegmatic in everything else he did. In milking, he slipped back into the hurry of youth.

The wires of milk shot out from the teats at different angles, depending on the precise direction of the pull; made a thin ping sound off the base and sides of the galvanised-iron bucket. As the body of warm frothy milk accumulated, the pitch of the ping sound dropped; the available surface area of metal declined, till soon all the impacts were milk on milk, and Alexander had to concentrate to hear the sound at all, with the competing creaking of the stool and the animal's heavy breathing. She turned and looked back at him with her big olive eyes, examining this new feature in her environment. And the fleas circled her face like crazy electrons.

A piece of dried shit fell from the animal's hind leg into the milk. Johnny reached in and picked it out, tossed it away. Alexander noticed that tiny particles of this dingleberry had broken off and remained in the foam, floating, like a sprinkling of cinnamon powder on a mug of hot bedtime milk.

'Can I have a go milking the cow, Uncle Johnny?'

Johnny laughed.

'Get in there,' he said, staying in position on the stool, but making way for the boy to come between him and the cow. 'Grab on and pull hard.'

Alexander tentatively closed his fingers around one of the teats and pulled on it. Nothing happened, which surprised him: he expected the milk to come flowing out the way water issues from a tap that has been turned.

'You have to squeeze and pull,' said Johnny. 'Give her a good squeeze.'

But Alexander was afraid to squeeze the tit, afraid he might offend the animal and that she would kick him in retaliation.

Without further conversation, Johnny shoved him out of the way to continue the work. Alexander was not used to such gruffness from an adult. He didn't question or criticise the behaviour at the point when it occurred, but years later, from a more grown-up perspective, he thought that he ought on that occasion to have been given more time and better instruction.

The christening is already underway when Alexander arrives at the church. He deliberately arrives late for this sort of thing, and for other sorts of things, in order to minimise his exposure to free-form mingling and small talk. He would gladly visit the dentist for a filling rather than submit to ten minutes of unstructured standing around before a christening or wedding. In fact, he quite enjoys the dentist (although he almost never goes) because the attention is concentrated on him and the opportunities for chat are strictly limited.

His footsteps are loud on the church's tiled floor. He leans forward, shifting the weight from his heels to the balls of his feet, and does the crouching walk of a person arriving late for a ceremony and wishing not to disturb, or signalling a wish not to disturb. Not that anyone is looking at him. They are all facing the other way, focused vaguely on the priest, an inoffensive middle-aged man in his ritual frock, standing in front of the altar being informal and intimate, 1970s' modern.

'And it is right and important,' he says gently, 'that we welcome these new souls into our families and communities, into the Church.'

There are evidently two christenings taking place, with each group occupying a few pews on either side.

As he proceeds along the centre aisle, Alexander notices Danny's dignified profile in the front pew on the right-hand side, then Aoife's bright hair, then other familiar figures. He slips into the last occupied pew, where there is space on the outside. He finds that he is next to Vladimir Foster, whom he did not recognise at first glance because Vlad's head is entirely shaved, a new look for him.

Vlad gives him a wink.

'Good to see you, man,' Alexander whispers. Vlad is someone he is always genuinely pleased to see, although it helps that the doses he gets of Vlad's company tend to be small and well separated. Vlad is refreshingly implausible. 'Did you come across especially for this?' Alexander continues.

'No, we're back for Christmas,' Vlad replies, 'which I'm taking very seriously this year. Say hi to Mary-Lou.'

Vlad sits back in the seat, which, given his large size, in fact doesn't make much of a difference to Alexander's visibility of the young woman on Vlad's other side. Alexander leans forward to have a look at her, reaching out for a handshake.

'I'm sorry, I don't shake hands,' she says in a delicious Scottish accent.

Mary-Lou is a plum, ripe. He wants to fuck her immediately. Her skin is luminous, her hair peach-coloured, her cheeks full, her lips large and finely drawn, protruding. She is wearing ripped jeans and a couple of strapped tops, plus a black bra.

'I don't have any communicable diseases,' Alexander points out. 'At least, none that I'm aware of.'

'It's more of a religious thing,' Vlad explains with a smirk.

Alexander nods in understanding and refocuses his efforts on the proceedings, switching into church mode, which he recalls automatically from his childhood: the outward aspect of devoted attention, masking complete indifference.

The people on the other side of the church are salt-of-the-earth types, the men scrubbed and besuited, red-faced, respectful, the women all flowery and frilly. These – Alexander thinks – are the kinds of people who still go to mass every Sunday, if there remains anyone in Dublin under forty who falls into that category, excluding Poles.

It is difficult for him to generalise in a similar way about Danny's crowd, which he clearly belongs to in some sense, although it doesn't feel like that from the inside. There are fewer people Alexander recognises in this group than there would have been at a similar event five years ago. Not having seen most of them for a while, he picks them out now in their church condition and finds them altered, like variations on familiar themes: grave, vacant, dressed-up, older, different in their faces and bodies, accomplished, insecure.

He imagines them on the whole to be a more interesting lot than those across the aisle, hitting higher peaks of education, wealth, income, cultural refinement, but also lower depths of alcoholism, depression, vanity, interpersonal cruelty. If he had to go on a mission to Mars with one of the groups, which would he choose? Danny's group. Not simply because he knows them. On the contrary, that would be a negative point. Perhaps because Vlad's new girlfriend might defect to him and take his cock into her beautiful mouth.

Would that be a good enough reason? Yes. Why not? What would be a better reason? Although it must be a bit of a long shot.

The priest is calling on the parents and godparents to come forward to the dipping bowl with the relevant offspring. In the front pew, Danny and Aoife, still seated, are exchanging aggressive whispers.

Pimply, bespectacled Jasper tugs on his mother's arm. His shoulder length hair is greasy. He is wearing a crumpled suit and shirt, but no tie.

'Is Hugo not coming?' he audibly asks his mother. 'The sonofabitch. I knew he'd spoil my christening.'

'Shssh,' says Aoife. 'The best thing you can do now is shut up.'

This exchange gives rise to gasps and murmuring on both sides of the church. The priest is serenely looking the other way.

Danny glances back anxiously at the front door, then scans the rows of his supporters behind him. He rises gracefully, steps out of the pew with his back to the altar, and walks purposefully down the aisle, fiddling with his mobile as he goes. He stops next to Alexander, drops to his hunkers and leans in confidentially, one arm wrapping itself around Alexander's shoulders, the other resting on the back of the next pew. Alexander finds that he doesn't wish to be embraced in affectation right now.

'We've got a problem on the Hugo front,' Danny says in church whisper.

'I can see that. He's not here.'

'His plane was delayed in Heathrow. He's on his way in a taxi now, but we can't wait.'

Vlad leans in from the other side.

'Mary-Lou and I will do it for fifty euro, so long as there are no actual long-term duties or expenses involved.'

'Piss off, Vlad; this is serious. Alex, I need you to step into the breach here. Kitty is doing godmother in any case. Will you do godfather?'

This is unexpected. Like a suddenly wounded animal, Alexander looks around for an explanation. He spots Kitty in the front row, looking back at him with her toothy grin. Kitty is Aoife's friend. She has always been very pleasant to Alexander, although he feels he hardly knows her. She is perpetually, ridiculously cheerful. Perhaps because she has buck teeth. It occurs to him that the reason Danny has singled him out is that he is sitting in a convenient place.

'In your own time,' Danny says rather snidely.

Alexander winces in discomfort, angrily shrugs off Danny's arm. His body expresses fury, but he doesn't immediately trust the appropriateness of the reaction, which puts him in a state of confusion. In his mind an image forms of tiny kittens lifted by a human hand into a hessian sack, for dropping into the river. Alexander has malfunctioned. He stares blindly ahead, smarting with pain.

'You just have to dip their heads in the water,' Mary-Lou says kindly.

'Yeah,' adds Vlad. 'And if Jasper starts to struggle, it's time to let him up.'

'I'll take this as a yes,' Danny concludes.

The godparents and parents from both sides stand in a large semi-circle around the bowl, with the priest positioned magnanimously at the centre.

Little Merlin is howling, apparently agonised. Kitty continues to grin, as genetically predetermined, but anxiety is apparent in her eyes and in the jerky movements with which she attempts to settle the infant. She makes a high-pitched shssshing sound, which Alexander finds excruciating. He has been taught never to shsssh a horse, because it drives them crazy. One must say wooooe instead. They like that low-pitched wooooe, as did Uncle Johnny's two cows. Alexander – recovered now – thinks that one should say wooooe to the baby, but doesn't feel this is the moment to introduce the idea.

Jasper does not howl. He is composed, cool even.

In the pew, Alexander hadn't been able to see Julia, but from his position now at the front of the church, facing the congregation, he has a good perspective on her, sitting in the third row. He discreetly avoids eye contact, which allows him to study her.

'Do you reject Satan and all his evil works?' asks the priest.

'Yes,' says the congregation, half-heartedly.

Alexander moves his lips, but emits no sound. He thinks: Why pick on Satan? Why not reject something really odious, like Brown Thomas' department store or Sky Sports.

With a creak, followed by a screech as it jams against the floor tiles, the main door of the church swings open and Hugo Strongboy strides in at a good pace, coat-tails flying.

'Hold the water,' he commands, as he marches up the centre aisle. 'The godfather is here. Sorry for the delay. The traffic was outrageous.'

The priest turns quickly to the Carter group. 'This isn't a fucking barbecue,' he whispers in Danny's ear.

Danny smiles lamely, shrugging as if to say that all this has nothing to do with him.

Alexander leans across Aoife and whispers in Danny's other ear.

'If you so much as even think of replacing me with Hugo, I will personally kick your lights in right here and now in the middle of the show.'

'Why are people always threatening me with violence?' Danny asks.

'Remember that I paid for the abortion,' Alexander reminds him in a low mutter.

'So did Hugo.'

'Well, I was first.'

Hugo is almost upon them now. Danny walks toward him to intercept, his carriage ridiculously good: back straight, shoulders squared, chin upright. This is a clear sign that he is under pressure or pretending not to be drunk. He holds his two arms out to Hugo as if for a hug, but instead manfully clasps him at the upper arms.

'Hugo, I'm sorry. I thought you weren't going to make it. We had to ask Alex to stand in.'

'My word is my bond,' Hugo says. 'I told you I'd be here. I've flown in specially.'

'Can we please continue with the ceremony?' the priest calls out.

'It's scandalous,' an old dear among the Catholics complains loudly. 'I've never seen anything like it.'

'Well, if it hasn't happened yet … ,' says Hugo, signalling that he wants to switch places with Alexander.

Danny is blocking the way.

'Let's just finish what we're doing here and work it out later,' Danny suggests winningly, with the implication that the mere details of the ceremony are unimportant.

Hugo's large jockish head jerks back in shock, but he evaluates the situation quickly and nods. With an upward flourish of the arms, he indicates that he is retiring from the pitch, and moves to sit in the precise place Alexander previously occupied, beside Vlad.

Danny returns to the altar, his posture even more erect than on the outward leg of the journey.

'As I was saying,' continues the priest with fresh equanimity. 'Do you reject Satan and all his works?'

'You bet we do,' says Alexander.

In the kitchen at Danny's place, in a loose uneasy conversational group, Alexander is drinking too much red wine. He has nothing to say to anyone in these sort of setting. Usually, he falls into sullen muteness, or forces himself to become involved by making boring comments and asking searching questions. Whichever the emerging pattern, Alexander expects that the pleasure of his company will send others fleeing at the earliest opportunity. In fact, if he could, he would gladly flee his own company, which essentially is what he accomplishes through getting shitfaced.

'Pretty good grub,' says Vlad in a surprised tone, or perhaps just sounding surprised because his mouth is full of chicken and rice and he has to contort his voice to get the words out through the food. He gives Alexander a perfect view of the chewing process, the mush of crushed rice grains, the strands of chicken sticking to his darkly filled teeth, the traces of yellow curry sauce on the wet red granulated surface of his tongue.

How does Vlad do it? Alexander ponders. How does he always end up with a beautiful young woman at his side?

'It was a good idea to use paper plates,' says Hugo.

'That's only because they're too lazy to wash the dishes,' Paul interjects, nodding venomously to the far end of the kitchen where Danny and Aoife, with a group around them, are working together in remarkable harmony, ladling out the food.

Paul's comment elicits a weak laugh from the others.

'I'm not joking,' he continues, a rising tone of indignation entering his voice. 'I was out here a couple of weeks ago and the place was stinking, absolutely disgusting. Things were so bad, they were running out of places to put the dirty dishes, so they had started to put them back into the presses, still filthy.'

Alexander wonders: How filthy can dishes be? A bit of furry mould. A few crusty smears of gravy. Why does Paul get so worked up about these things? Alexander himself doesn't put dirty dishes back into the cupboards, but it strikes him as an innovative solution.

'What harm is a little congealed tomato ketchup?' he asks, but the timing and confidence of his delivery are poor, and the comment – even to himself – sounds odd rather than witty.

'That won't do,' says Vlad, clear in the mouth at this moment. 'You're part of the family now. You'll have to intervene to ensure that your godsons' living conditions meet hygiene standards.'

'Hugo's the godfather,' Alexander responds decisively, with a deferential nod to the man in question, who is maintaining a regal silence as he concentrates on his food. 'I was just standing in, in loco godparentis.'

Hugo looks at him shrewdly. 'You signed the book,' he says.

'Even if I am the godfather,' Alexander continues, 'I'm responsible only for the spiritual well-being. They can live in dirt, once their souls are clean.'

This produces half a laugh from Paul.

'You don't believe in God,' Vlad states aggressively.

'Ah Jesus, don't start that crack,' says Hugo. 'Anyway, you don't have to believe in God to be a good Catholic.'

This gets a better laugh than it's worth. Not that the laughing on the part of Alexander and the others is forced. Hugo is naturally funnier than average because he is imposing, successful and rich.

'Hey, Fitzer,' Hugo calls across the room to another rugby-type from college, who has just entered. 'What hole did you crawl from? I haven't seen you in two centuries.'

'I'm down in the salt mines, working for a living like an ordinary mortal,' Fitzer responds, although in fact he is a lawyer in one of the city's big firms. 'Did they get you yet for insider trading?'

'Shush now, don't be using bad language. I'm squeaky clean. Listen, I want to talk to you about something.'

Hugo excuses himself, sets down his unfinished curry on the nearby counter-top, and moves purposefully toward his target through the crowded room, surprisingly nimble for a man of his ego size. He even finds time to ruffle the blonde hair of a little boy he passes.

The boy is Danny's sister's son. He is seven or eight. Danny's sister Cordelia is married to an aristocratic Swiss investment banker, but her eldest child nevertheless has a long liquid snot hanging from one of his nostrils. He snuffles it up, but not with enough force to stop it from dropping down again a moment later. He is standing with Cordelia and Aoife, singing a pop song for them, shyly but competently, in a light squeaky voice. As the song proceeds, he wins the attention of one or two innocent bystanders, including Karina, and all hang on his performance, willing him on, cheering him, so that his confidence grows and he sings more loudly.

' ... I believe I can fly. I believe I can touch the sky. ...'

Alexander experiences a fleeting image of smashing the boy's head open with a hammer; not that he wants to do this, but he senses the possibility of the deed. It wouldn't require many blows. It wouldn't even have to be bloody. One well-placed hit to the temple and it's beddy-bye-bye for ever.

'I have to go for a leak,' Paul says and he too moves away.

Alexander feels certain that he has broken up the group by emanating negative energy. He half expects Vlad to vanish as well, leaving him stranded, but Vlad seems relatively settled, still shovelling chicken curry and rice into his mouth.

'Do you want to get stoned?' Vlad asks, again through the food.

Alexander's reflex reaction is to look around to see where Julia is. When they were together, she didn't like him to smoke dope, because – so she said – it made him all weird and paranoid. He spots her in the same moment that he remembers he is free of her, that he can smoke his head off if he wants without fear of reproach. She is coming into the kitchen, exchanging words with Paul on his way out. As ever, Paul is a lot taller than she is. There is something odd about them, the way they are standing there, she facing upward, he looking down.

When Paul leaves, Julia turns fully into the room, and immediately her eyes meet Alexander's. They lock into each other. Julia looks puzzled for a moment, then smiles a sweet crooked smile.

In the previous second, if he had asked himself how he was doing – in general, not in this particular instant – he would have said: Fine. But now that she has smiled at him, he feels he has been desolate for months, so much so that he has forgotten the possibility of alternative conditions. She breaks the eye contact, which requires an effort, creating a moment of clumsiness, and moves toward Aoife. Cordelia's son has finished singing. The women are finished praising him. He looks exhausted, overheated. The stringy snot is down again, glued now to his upper lip, well beyond recall. His mother pops down onto her hunkers beside him and lovingly cleans it away with a fresh paper tissue.

Alexander knows what he wants. He wants to escape with Julia. He will have to engineer a moment with her. They will dip into a groove, a happy funny mood. He'll convince her that they should run away together. They could rent a room. There must be hotels along the coast here, if they drove south past Dún Laoghaire. They could spend an hour by the sea, then go indoors, order champagne and salmon from room service, make love, fall asleep together. He would spend long silent hours with her asleep at his side.

There was a time, early in the second phase of their relationship, after they had first moved into the flat, when his desire for closeness was astonishingly intense. One winter's night, he experienced a pre-sentiment of a physical wish to climb into her womb, to exist there, enveloped within her, curled up, wrapped closely in the amniotic caul. It was a remarkable never-repeated urge, which mostly extinguished itself in becoming observable to his conscious mind. It was certainly not something that could survive being enworded.

'That is really fucked up,' Julia said, when he tried to articulate to her what he had almost felt. But even if she was right about many things, she was not right about that. It was not fucked up. It was a moment of truth.

'What did you say?' he asks Vlad.

'Do you want to get stoned? I've got an eighth of golden Moroccan hash in my pocket. It's my Christmas stock.'

Alexander knows what he wants. It would not be wise to get stoned now, because he wouldn't be able to talk to Julia properly then, wouldn't be able to win her.

'That sounds like a great idea,' he finds himself saying. 'Where'll we go?'

'We could go for a walk,' Vlad says, 'but I'm feeling a bit lazy. There must be somewhere upstairs.'

Forty minutes later, stoned out of his head, Alexander walks down the stairs, trying to keep his face straight.

Because he has been throwing back the wine, he is drunk as well as stoned – a good balance. The dope has him buzzing, while the drink gives him sufficient relief from himself to be able to function socially, approximately. Nevertheless, the prospect of returning to the party is formidable. He resolves to secure more alcohol.

He peeks into the sitting-room where the old folks – the grand-parents' generation – have clotted together. The air is thick with cigarette smoke. They're a boozy lot, drinking whiskey and gin rather than wine. They're putting a lot of energy into the conversation: tall anecdotes, generous affirmative listening. They seem to be enjoying themselves.

He moves toward the kitchen.

'Make way for a man bearing drink,' he hears Danny call from behind in a cheerful I'm-lifting-something-heavy voice.

Alexander steps aside. Danny passes quickly with three large trays of beer cans, still shrink-wrapped in polythene. Behind him is his mother, Ursula, carrying crinkly plastic shopping bags full of fizzy drinks and other colourful goodies.

She pauses to greet her son's friend. She is small and sallow-skinned, more deeply wrinkled than the last time Alexander met her.

'Hi, Alexander. I didn't get a chance to say hello to you outside the church.' She puckers her lips and reaches up to kiss him. It is clearly implied in the gesture that he should meet these lips with his, which is somewhat shocking, but he manfully complies. Her lips are more moist than he would freely have chosen. 'Thanks so much for standing in at the last minute.'

This puzzles him. His brain whirrs, searching for material: recent incidents of standing in at the last minute. But alarmingly, comically, he can find no such reference.

'As godfather,' she reminds him bluntly.

'Ah yes. No problem. Any time you want a grandchild dipped, just give me a call.'

Ursula frowns at this irreverent tone, which he meant as a joke.

Meanwhile, three screeching children have appeared, crowding around Ursula to get a look into her shopping bags.

'Did you buy any ice-cream?' one of them asks.

'But didn't you love the way Hugo came storming into the church?' Ursula continues, ignoring the children. 'If Clint Eastwood drops dead in the morning, they'll have the man to replace him.'

Doped-up Alexander experiences some difficulty at this point. A glimpse is revealed to him of the dark gleaming underside of things. On the surface, Ursula is friendly, humorous, but something dangerous has flashed briefly in her eyes, which nudges his perception infinitesimally, revealing her as a gloating hag, the skin hanging off her bones, her neck emaciated, liver-spotted, her thinning hair a perversely purple shade of brown. The faded tawny irises – which even now remind him of both Danny and Cordelia – appear as lids that

147

might be flipped off with a single movement of the right surgical instrument. And what would two such flicks of the wrist uncover? Black bottomless straw-like cavities? Maggots emerging happily into the fresh air? Or an ooze of blood and pus?

'You're looking well,' he says, inspiration dropping down on him from heaven, bringing salvation at a number of levels. 'In fact, I have rarely seen you look so well.'

'Don't be such a liar,' she says, but she cannot fully resist the flattery.

He offers to help her with her bags.

'Let's see if we can find Hugo,' he suggests unctuously. 'We'll tell him what a beacon he is to us all. I bet he doesn't get told often enough just how marvellous he is.'

A little boy has his hand down the throat of one of Ursula's plastic bags and is rooting for something he wants. Alexander decisively pushes him back, lifts the bags from Ursula's hands, and masterfully leads the way to the kitchen.

He works through the crowd to the open fridge where Danny is down on his knees looking for places to stash the cans. Alexander leaves the bags on the floor beside him and moves to the adjacent space, where Julia, Kitty and Hugo are now standing. Alexander's glass of wine is exactly where he left it on the windowsill, and this gives him an excuse to join the group.

'It's ridiculous that that guy was able to get a job in a school,' Kitty is saying. 'I mean he had past convictions.'

'Hmm,' says Hugo as he winks at Alexander in greeting. The wink could be perfectly neutral, but Alexander also reads into it that Hugo doesn't give a shit about the guy in question and is slightly amused by Kitty's earnestness, while at the same time he doesn't wish to suffer her for very long.

'Paedophiles are people too,' Alexander offers, as he raises his wine to his lips.

Julia splutters her drink in shock. Hugo laughs, though more at the outrageousness than at the witticism itself.

'I don't think that's very funny,' Kitty says.

'I just think paedophiles get a bit of a hard time,' Alexander goes on. 'I mean you can kick somebody to death on O'Connell Street and nobody minds very much. You were drunk. It was high jinks that went wrong. The guy was a loser anyway. You'll get off with a two-year suspended sentence. But paedophilia is up there with genocide. You can get two years for just looking at pictures of it.'

'This is a bit of a concern for you, is it?' Hugo asks. 'I can see now why you ditched him,' he adds to Julia.

'That was the least of it,' she says drily.

'That's all over now,' Alexander tells her. 'I threw the PC into a skip last week.'

'Did you wipe it for fingerprints?' Hugo asks.

'I transferred your fingerprints onto it. I have a special kit that you can do that with. I bought it from Mission Impossible.'

'Excuse me, I have to go to the bathroom to puke,' says Kitty, peeling away.

'I know how you feel, honey,' says Julia. 'I'll come with you.'

'Did I do that?' Alexander asks Hugo as they watch the two women cross the room, confiding in each other, presumably about what an idiot he is.

'You shouldn't have let her get away,' Hugo says seriously. 'Why didn't you marry her years ago?'

In a straight state, Alexander might have made some quick response to this, but now he pauses and genuinely searches for the answer. With his awareness distanced from his ego by drugs, he scans the landscape for explanatory features. He was too lazy to make the effort. He was too vain to make the statement. It wasn't necessary, since they were already living together.

'I couldn't rise to it,' he confesses.

Hugo says nothing, which is the right response.

'How about you and Emma?'

'Never better,' Hugo says, but without much emphasis in his voice, as a matter of politeness perhaps. 'She couldn't come across for this today, but we'll be over again next week for the Christmas.'

They are both leaning against the window now, their backs to the sill, facing into the room, watching the people as they speak, their heads tilted almost together to facilitate the conversation.

'From the outside, it seems like you have had a charmed life,' Alexander says. 'College to bank, bank to business, business to glory, smart beautiful Emma by your side, both of you so at ease with yourselves.'

'I know.'

'I bet you get on well with your father.'

'Never better,' says Hugo.

'I bet you go fishing with him.'

'We play golf.'

'Naturally. . . . When I think about you, which, to be honest, isn't often, I see that you were on a higher path from the outset. And I'm on a lower path. I don't know why. I wonder was there a point at which I could have taken a different trajectory? I suppose there must be those points of inflection.'

'Don't beat yourself up. We all have problems.'

Hugo drinks his wine. His tone and pace of delivery had dipped, but now the pitch is higher again, and the body language a little restless. He wants to depart from the soul-searching.

'Any good business projects?' Alexander asks, sounding upbeat, and turning to face Hugo to punctuate a change in mood.

Hugo's eyes brighten with enthusiasm.

'I shouldn't tell you,' he says in a whisper, 'but I have this sweet thing going. It has to do with the roll-out of broadband for small users here in Ireland. Any day now the government is going to set up a bucket of cash for local authorities to invest in a broadband network. We're going to help them spend it.'

'Maybe somebody else will help them spend it,' Alexander suggests. He finds himself surprisingly calm in gaining this new, dark intelligence. It assimilates quickly into his understanding, creating a sense of internal spaciousness.

'Maybe,' Hugo concedes, 'but we have a head start. We have a few people on the ground who've been driving around for a year, giving free advice about options, possibilities, how to get funding. We've been getting to know the local players, making some donations to good causes.' Hugo smirks on this point. 'It's small beer really, but I can't help myself. It's so easy to suck up government money. You have to do it, just for the sport.'

'So, let me see if I've got this,' Alexander says, as if puzzling over something very complicated. 'The local authorities will invite tenders and you'll win the contracts. Is that it? Won't somebody smell a rat if the same company wins all the contracts?'

Hugo's head jerks in surprise.

'Well, there is no rat,' he says pompously, and Alexander doesn't know if he is joking or not. 'Anyhow, it's not the same company. We can have a dozen companies, or two dozen, however many you want: Optimal Broadband, Alpha Telecoms, Bugs Bunny Networks – you name it. In fact, why don't you name one right now?'

'I'll think about it. How can you be so sure the government will put up the money?'

'Because we influence these things,' Hugo says, serious and definite.

'What? Have you got photographs of the Minister for Finance with his trousers down?'

Hugo laughs, as though he might have.

'It's the other way around. I'm a supporter.'

'But you have to get the issue onto his desk?'

'Yes, you're right. That makes it easier. But there are vehicles for that kind of thing. Watch out in the papers after Christmas. See if the National Economic Advisory Council makes recommendations on the issue. You probably keep an eye out for that kind of stuff, right? You still work in that consultancy firm, don't you?'

'Yes, something like that,' Alexander says. 'I have a name for one of your broadband companies: Amazing Grace.'

Hugo blinks slowly.

'What did you say?'

'I mentioned the name Grace.'

Hugo's patience is cracking. Beneath, his countenance is hard.

'You always were an odd fucker,' he says. 'And you haven't improved with age.... Excuse me, I have to go talk to somebody about something.'

These last words are enunciated carefully, coldly. Hugo sets down on the sill his unfinished glass of wine, nods to Alexander, and moves off toward the centre of the room.

'Hey, baby, how come you're such a big hit with the girls?' Alexander asks himself.

The party is humming, the different generations now intermingling easily.

In the sitting room a sing-song is underway. A few moments ago they were on *Galway Bay*. A tall fifty-something with fat hands and a forced tenor voice belted out some fragments of verse, filled in with la-la-la and plenty of smiling, his supporters coming in with the chorus at every opportunity.

In the kitchen, the temperature is high and the laughter increasingly raucous. Alexander has been knocking back the wine without interruption, and is rapidly passing through the threshold of restraint. On his last trip to the upstairs bathroom, he pissed into the sink for variety, leaning his forehead onto the mirrored surface of the bathroom cabinet.

'I'm drunk, I'm drunk, I'm a silly old skunk,' he said as he happily relieved himself. This is the rhyme that usually pops out at some point on his way to getting seriously wasted.

Standing now at the doorway between the kitchen and the hall, talking to Vlad and Mary-Lou about drug tests, he is trying to communicate telepathically with Julia, who is farther into the room, sitting on the kitchen table (which has been pushed against the wall), swinging her legs like a little girl.

She is together with Paul, Karina, Danny and smug Dermot O'Hara, who must be a new arrival, since Alexander didn't notice him before. O'Hara is mid-flow in some sardonic patter, the others encouraging him with their approving laughter. It seems a better conversation than the one Alexander is currently in.

'I couldn't believe that,' says Mary-Lou. 'You can't forget that kind of thing. He must have been sniffing coke at the weekend, and needed another couple of days for it to get through his system.'

'How long does it take for coke to get through your system?' Vlad asks.

'Look it up on the internet,' says Mary-Lou smartly.

Bimbo, Alexander thinks. High on dope, his physical desire to fuck her is greatly diminished, though he maintains a scientific interest in exploring her body and is still particularly intrigued by her gleaming cleavage.

But she is not the mission. The mission is to speak to Julia. He focuses again on shooting thoughts through the air, from his brain to Julia's: Look around. See me. Know now that I want to speak to you. He notices – to his surprise – that the thought packages appear to travel with just the same trajectory as physical items. He sends them in an arc to a landing point on the crown of her head, where, unfortunately, they bounce off and tumble – lost – down the sheer slopes of her body.

Finally, in an instant of great good-fortune, or because he is genuinely telepathic, one of his carefully flighted thought-bombs penetrates her skull. It assumes at the moment of impact precisely the physical properties and direction of momentum required to slip through the bone. She looks around and sees him. He beckons her urgently, his lips silently telling her that he needs to talk to her. Please, he mouths.

She deliberates, grimacing with irritation in the same moment that she decides to comply. She excuses herself from the group as she slips off the table, and walks across the floor to him in a carefully measured gait, eyeing him with self-assurance.

'What do you want?' she asks with affected gruffness.

'Not in front of the children,' he says, nodding at Vlad and Mary-Lou. 'Can we go out front for a minute? There's something I want to ask you.'

'He wants you to marry him,' Vlad explains conversationally.

'I wouldn't if I were you,' says Mary-Lou.

'Don't worry. I've no intention of it.'

'I'd like to get your opinion on something that is important to me,' Alexander explains with what he hopes is disarming genuineness.

'Lead the way,' Julia says and the tip of her tongue darts out from her mouth to touch her upper lip, which gesture expresses her feeling of superiority and her willingness, just in this second, to indulge him.

Out on the front driveway, on this cold early-dark December evening, removed from everybody, she is more defensive. She refuses to go for a stroll with him.

'This is far enough,' she says, a few feet beyond the front door, her arms folded across her chest, her lips quivering a little from the cold.

Alexander staggers, laughs, straightens himself.

'I'm sorry, I'm a bit drunk.'

'You should be sorry for wasting my time.'

'Vlad was speaking the truth. I thought maybe you might want to marry me.'

He smiles modestly, wobbling again, though this time under the weight of the words, which for him are earth quaking. Unfortunately, they appear to leave her untouched.

'What could possibly have given you that impression?'

'You were so angry with me last week in the hospital.'

'And from that you deduced that I might want to marry you? Is that it? Are we finished? Can I go inside again?'

'Please don't be in such a hurry,' he says, stepping closer to her, his arms stretched out slightly in appeal, his voice taking on its most tender aspect. 'Give me a few minutes. Sit down with me … take a cigarette. I won't trouble you again after this, I promise.'

'It's icy,' she says, relenting, shivering.

They sit on the low window ledge, which is comfortable enough, though the concrete isn't welcoming at first touch. From behind them, through the window, they can hear the party noise from the sitting-room: laughter, chat, the blended sounds of drunken people enjoying themselves. Alexander lights two cigarettes, giving the first to Julia. They blow their smoke into the evening air.

The road beyond the garden is narrow, tree-lined, jammed with parked cars, lit in this section by a street light, which is surrounded – from their angle – by the bare branches of one of the trees growing up through the pavement. Abstracted in this way from its supporting post, the orange light – amidst the branches – appears like a fruit, an urban winter strain.

A fat black BMW 5 Series rolls slowly and quietly into view: a fine animal, poised, powerful, immaculately finished, lit like a piece of theatre. He can see the female driver checking out the house, looking around the street. There is something familiar about her.

'She must be here for the party,' he says to Julia. 'She'll have to go well down the road to find a parking place.'

Julia does not respond.

The woman in the BMW makes a decision, and the machine shoots off at a speed that could be dangerous on such a narrow street, clogged as it is with cars, where a cat or a child might wander naïvely onto the road, coming unseen from between bumpers, offering to get knocked down.

There are many things he might speak of to Julia.

He could tell her about his problems at work: that Personnel has launched an investigation into Neville's accusations of bullying and sexual harassment; that a fat fuck from Special Projects who doesn't like Alexander is chairing the investigation; that Neville and Alexander are to continue working together in the meantime, but are to communicate only by email, which makes things in the office rather awkward.

He could let her know about the Maisie developments: that she's still alive; that there's talk of her leaving him the farm in her will; that he still hasn't visited her; that one of the reasons for his reluctance is that she mistook him for his father the last time he saw her, which confused him, left him thinking that he might in fact be his father – essentially.

155

But he doesn't want to bore Julia with these things, has himself no desire to talk about the details of his current existence in which she has no living role. He wants to recollect some high point from their shared life, something that has meaning which is relevant to them now, which speaks of the possibility of their having a future together.

Like the time they nearly crashed the car, speeding on the coast road through Monkstown on a heavy summer's day. They got caught in a sudden deluge of thundery rain. Julia was driving, going too fast on a curve. She over-braked in unfavourable circumstances: the speed, the turn, the camber of the road, the sheets of rainwater already washing over the surface. They tripped into a spin, which happened in the slow motion of acutely heightened perception. The car did a double twirl, as in a dance. It was a beautiful move, which he admired even as it was occurring. Julia darted him a look for help. Her hands were gripping the steering wheel, but she had ceased trying to exert control. And he was reaching across to her, to warn her, to protect her head from the impact with his hands.

When the car stopped spinning, it was positioned in the correct lane, pointing in the right direction, with a few cars of traffic behind, waiting patiently.

They laughed.

'You look so beautiful,' he said to her. Let's go home and make a baby, he thought. But he didn't trust the impulse.

'I was proud of you back in the church,' Julia says, breaking the long silence just as he himself is nearing speech, and her voice coming from just such a place of sobriety and honesty as he has now arrived at. 'When you stood up for yourself. You usually let those guys walk all over you.'

He has no response to this, but in parallel has reached a resolution as to what he should say to her.

'You know that line that gets used,' he begins. "You're the best thing that ever happened to me?" It's in a song as well. ... in our case ... in my case ... I would put it differently. ... You are the only thing that ever happened to me.'

He draws heavily on the cigarette, enjoying it, though his throat is starting to get sore.

A woman, whom he supposes must have come from the BMW, enters the driveway from the pavement outside. She is wrapped in a heavy woollen shawl. Her heels click-clack sexily on the concrete as she proceeds, moving between the parked cars and the lawn, swerving her body to avoid the side-view mirrors. She falters at one point, hitting a seam in the surface of the driveway.

It is Grace Sharkey.

Julia stands. She takes a final drag, tosses the cigarette out onto the lawn, still burning.

'I have to go,' she says in a low voice.

'What are *you* doing here?' Grace asks him with marked irritation.

She is paused before the front door, behind which Julia has disappeared only a couple of seconds earlier, inadvertently – or perhaps deliberately – closing it after her. Grace has rung the bell and is waiting.

He finds her diamantine. Her copper hair is slicked back over the top of her skull, gathered behind in a tight ball. The individual parts of her long dangly silver earrings swish in domino concert with the movements of her head, her angular jaws.

'I'm waiting for you to give me the keys to your car,' he says.

'And why would I do that?'

'In payment for services rendered.'

'Piss off, you little turd. The report is out. That's already everything I want from you. And by the way, you don't get keys with a car like that.'

She presses the bell again, impatiently.

Alexander draws calmly on his cigarette. He feels fluent.

'Let me guess why you're here,' he says. 'To meet Hugo Strongboy, maybe to give him a lift to wherever he is staying. Maybe he's staying with you, in fact. You guys might be fuck buddies as well as business partners. And here is why you're going to give me your ... let's just *call* it a key. If you don't, tomorrow or the next day I'll ring the

Chairman and tell him that one of the Council members, who was highly influential in forming the Council position on broadband, stands to make a significant personal financial gain if the recommendations are implemented.'

'I don't give a shit what you say. Nobody gives a shit what you say.'

'You're very right. That has been my experience to date, but I remain hopeful. I'll explain to the Chairman my role in channelling your influence through to the consultant. I'll explain also that I'm planning to find a journalist to whom I can spill this story of corruption, if the Chairman allows the recommendations to stand. The Chairman, by the way, was already suspicious of your motives months ago. I deflected him. . . . I'm not suggesting there is any threat to you here. No one has committed any crime. But there is good potential to fuck up the opportunity, now or later on. And why would we take that risk? Instead, just give me the key, and tomorrow get a change-of-ownership form and fill it out, selling me the lovely vehicle for . . . let's say a euro. How about that?'

'How about you stick your tongue up my arse?'

III

January

On a dark, windy, rain-splattered evening, Alexander is reclining on the sofa watching *LA Confidential*, sucking on a bottle of German beer, absent-mindedly fondling his dick.

He hears a board creaking in the hallway on the floor above and recalls that it is Monday, which is the day when the landlord comes on his weekly round of rent collecting. The creak in itself is not a reliable indicator of the author of the creak, even on a Monday, but Alexander's tenant's intuition tells him that this is the landlord.

The landlord starts at the top of the house and works his way downward, finally arriving at Alexander's flat. His little treble knock on the inner door irritates Alexander in being almost inaudible, but not so inaudible as to be ignorable. Probably what really irritates Alexander is the indignity of having to pay rent, and of paying it in an anachronistic fashion, with each weekly instalment recorded and initialled in a soft-covered red notebook, nearly all the pages of which, depressingly, are now filled up.

'We'll have to get a new book,' the landlord said recently, in a humorous vein.

He is a perfectly inoffensive man, but Alexander experienced a savage, primitive urge to bite out his throat.

He decides to flee. He'll leave the money in the book on top of the TV, which is their standing arrangement for the evenings when Alexander is absent.

He rings Danny on the mobile.

'Do you want to go for a spin in my new car?' he suggests. 'We could drive down to Wicklow and have a pint in one of those pubs in the mountains that overlook the city.'

'You still haven't satisfactorily explained to me where you got that car from,' Danny says.

'I didn't know I had to explain myself to you.'

'Of course you do.'

'I've been doing a bit of consultancy work on the side.'

'That's what you said the last time. It sounds like bollocks.'

'I sold my soul to the devil. How about that? How does that sound?'

'You got a good deal.'

'So, do you want to come out?'

'Not really. I'm knackered. But why don't you come over here? We'll drink some whiskey … if you bring a bottle. You can crash for the night.'

Alexander buys a bottle of whiskey in his local off-licence and drives out to Dún Laoghaire in his new BMW.

He didn't drive the car home on the night of the christening, being far too drunk. Nor was he well enough the next day to pick it up, but he didn't want to leave it parked where it was, in case she might reclaim it, so he got a taxi out to Dún Laoghaire, had the taxi man drop him a couple of hundred yards away, and approached the car surreptitiously, like a thief.

He was already feeling queasy from the taxi journey, heart racing, stomach in revolt, body queerly twisted, his pores emitting alcoholic sweat onto his sickly skin. It would have been challenging enough for him to drive his own car, which Julia left him as part of their amicable settlement. The idea of navigating the beastly Beamer through the city was horrifying.

Grace Sharkey had given him the key card, which unlocked the car automatically as he approached. He opened the door, flinching in anticipation of the alarm going off, but it didn't. The door was heavy, beautifully hung. He sat into the driver's seat, plushly upholstered in black leather. His stomach rose briefly against him, but settled. Despite the general spaciousness, he was a bit cramped, since she had the driver's seat right under the steering wheel. He felt in the usual places for likely levers, proceeded then to try the buttons in the door panel, one of which caused the seat to tilt forward. This did not improve the situation. He decided to leave things as they were, on the basis that he already had more than enough to contend with simply in getting the car to move.

He found the ignition switch and successfully pressed it, setting off all sorts of functions, with flashings, clickings, humming, beneath which, just audible, was the low luxurious turning of the engine.

He was not enjoying himself. The night before, when he had gone down to survey his new possession, all cocky, an inner voice had said to him: I deserve this. His mood then had been so ethereal that he didn't even caress the external body, perhaps also for fear that the thing might disappear under his touch. The following day, suffering from severe poisoning, sitting in the driving seat in a scruffy jumper and tracksuit bottoms, he felt overwhelmingly undeserving. He felt like a tramp. The idea that he could own such a vehicle seemed preposterous.

He shifted into Drive and nosed out into the road.

'You are going the wrong way,' a sexy robotic female voice announced. 'Turn left at the next junction.'

In front of him the dashboard, an in-built monitor was displaying the territory, a big flashing red arrow indicating his next move. His body lurched forward involuntarily, and he vomited a litre of Tropicana orange juice in four painful retches, out onto the dashboard, down onto the steering wheel, his tracksuit, the seat, his runners, the floor mat. And as his stomach was spasmodically emptying itself, the car all the while proceeded gracefully along the road, which was devoid of traffic, miraculously avoiding collision with the many parked cars.

In the weeks that followed, he spent a lot of time driving around the city, and out into the country, gradually internalising into his driver's consciousness the car's size and capabilities, but he is still far from the level of intimacy that he enjoys, he now realises, with his old Honda. He is not quick at getting to know a new car. He doesn't think of it yet as *his* car, which is probably correct, since no paperwork has been sent to him, either by Grace or by the tax authority, to confirm the change of ownership. But he has possession, and has observed in himself that this has not increased his level of happiness; has in fact reduced it slightly by introducing an additional tone of disappointment.

To begin with, he pretended to himself that he was thrilled: I can take this anywhere; this is the new me. But ultimately he could not conceal from himself that he had very few places to go, almost no one to visit. He understood why someone might drive a car off a pier at high tide; not from desperation, but from emptiness, from a complete lack of other destinations, from a realisation that the limits in life are ingrained, not circumstantial. Winning the lottery does not improve things. In fact, by not improving things, it makes them worse.

'Good man,' Danny says to him, eyeing the half-litre bottle of Jameson as Alexander enters the house.

Danny is edgy, unshaven, looks as if he hasn't washed for a few days. He is wearing house clothes: dirty cords, a T-shirt and cardigan. He goes off to the kitchen to get some glasses, having first pointed Alexander into the sitting room, which is nicely warm from the briquette fire burning in the open grate.

The room seems smaller than Alexander remembers from his last visit, when it was full of guests at the christening. It is relatively bare now, the carpet and walls dirty, the furniture fatigued. RTÉ news is running on the television. George Bush has withdrawn from Iraq a 400-man team that was searching for weapons of mass destruction. Alexander flops into one of the armchairs. At the time of the first Bush–Iraqi war, he was up for Saddam. This time round, he was up for the US. He would have liked it if they had found one or two vast underground armouries of weapons of mass destruction, just to piss off the great throng of the sanctimonious. On the other hand, he never for a second believed that there was more to be found than a couple of dozen scud missiles and a few rusty barrels of mustard gas.

'I thought Saddam looked great when they caught him,' he says when Danny returns with two cloudy glass tumblers, still dripping wet from his having just rinsed them out. 'He looked really distinguished with that beard.'

'He was living in a hole in the desert,' Danny says, clearly not liking this subject.

'That impressed me. It spoke of resilience and flexibility. Imagine you've been living in a palace with fine foods and fine wines, numerous concubines, a whole country available to you for the expression of your despotic whims. Then suddenly you've got all these American goons coming to throw you off the throne. What would you do? Wouldn't you just put a bullet in your head rather than face such a massive come-down?'

'I'm sure he didn't plan to end up in the desert like a dog.'

Danny roughly plonks the glasses onto the scuffed coffee table, gracelessly grabs the whiskey, cracks open the seal, spins off the golden top, raises the bottle to his lips, and drinks a couple of glugs with a pained but fascinated look.

'Aaah,' he says, with a growling undertone, vigorously shaking his head as the fire-water burns his throat. He brings the bottle across to Alexander and holds it out for him with both hands, so that Alexander too can drink from the bottle.

'Drink,' he says.

'I'll take it in a glass.'

'Drink,' he insists, almost shouting.

'No.'

'Are you a man or a mouse?'

'I'm a mouse,' Alexander concedes hollowly, thinking that Danny may have lost it entirely, but Danny steps back, normalises himself, takes a deep breath, and pours two large whiskeys.

'Anything strange?' Danny asks.

It took Alexander a long number of years to understand that people have different constitutions, and that these constitutions are an important factor in behaviour. As young idiots, he and his friends would criticise a guy for not being able to hold his beer, as though this was a moral error. Now he knows that alcohol is simply more poisonous for some people than for others. His own tolerance, on average, is just below medium.

Danny, though genetically lean, has the constitution of a horse. Alexander would surely have been dead many times over if he had put himself through the adventures in alcohol and drugs that Danny has enjoyed and suffered. He knows that it is risky to drink whiskey with Danny, but he needs relief from tension, release into community.

The combination of Danny and whiskey has strong curative properties, which Alexander learned indelibly on the night of an election count in college, following his campaign for student president. At a party before the count, he got ridiculously stoned, smoking a bong. Philip O'Brien, now living rough in Liverpool, led the charge that night. 'Take stock of your head,' he advised at one point, with the bong going around the room in one direction and several joints circling the other way. However vast the state of his head, Alexander was in grim form. He knew the election was lost, his reputation ruined. It was a crisis. His self-image was exploded, with the bloody remains of his vanity and cynicism splattered onto the walls around him. What had been the root of this failure? Danny – for sure – had been a poor campaign manager, exerting himself only in the evening drinking sessions. But Alexander himself had been a crap candidate, remote and arrogant. Drugs had changed him over the previous three years. The outspoken, politically minded freshman was gone. His sense of humour was arch. He had been disdainful of the electorate and had cared nothing for the so-called issues.

As they were walking up to the counting centre in the Junior Common Room, he panicked and ran back down the stairs. He couldn't face the heated crowd, the political charge, the seeming lack of oxygen, the total humiliation. Julia trotted after him, followed him to the cool dark space between the colonnade and inner façade of the Examination Hall in Front Square. He hunkered down under one of the columns, rocking anxiously, like a mad person.

'I'm a really noxious human being,' he said. 'Everybody hates me.'

She eventually calmed him enough to lead him back to the count. Julia was kind to him that night, if perhaps a little too conscious of her own maturity. She congratulated herself for coming after him and steering him back, when she could have just stayed up where all the fun was, getting drunk and maybe snogging someone who had more to offer at that moment.

She held his hand as they re-entered the JCR. He took a deep breath and led the way across the floor to where Danny and Paul and some of the others were standing around looking pissed off.

'There's Alexander Vespucci,' he heard from behind him, from within the crowd. 'I'm delighted. I never liked that cunt.'

Julia's hand squeezed his, and he achieved a tone of levity in thinking: I was right. Everybody does hate me.

Danny had a bottle of Jameson. The whiskey in it sloshed audibly as he wrapped his arms around Alexander and gave him a long hug. As Danny disengaged, he paused to whisper something. Alexander felt the hot moist breath in his ear.

'I *love* you,' Danny said with unusual determination.

Alexander was stunned by this. In his instinct for male friendship up to this moment, such a sentiment was unthinkable, but he immediately found it noble, liberating. It was an education for him that men could have such friendship, could use such words.

Five or six of them sat together at a table, ignoring the jubilation and ferment around them, drinking the whiskey, beginning to strike an attitude.

'Anything strange?' Alexander ponders now. He sips from his whiskey. 'I find everything quite strange these days, but let's not go there yet. I don't want to offend your sensibilities.'

'Good. My sensibilities are sore.'

'I'm driving to Galway tomorrow,' Alexander begins in a refreshed tone. 'My Grand-aunt Maisie is dying. I want to see her one last time.'

'I thought she was dead already,' Danny says, almost critically, as though Alexander has slipped up with his homework. 'She's been dying for a good while now, hasn't she?'

'Not that long. Less than a year, off and on. She has been *old* for a long time.'

It is always irritating to Danny that the Ballyryan townland, to which Maisie's farm belongs, is only four or five miles from Danny's parents' place, Knockboy House. Alexander himself enjoyed this coincidence when he first discovered it, but Danny was cranky.

'I wish you wouldn't go on about that,' he snapped on one occasion, when they were down in Knockboy for the weekend. Alexander had suggested an expedition to Ballyryan. Danny's response cut him, silenced him. He supposed that Danny was uncomfortable for some reason with the stark difference in the circumstances of their ancestors.

'You remember she lives near Knockboy,' Alexander continues now, quite deliberately. 'Well, in fact she's been in a nursing home in Galway for years.'

To deflect attention from this subject, Danny sits forward in the armchair, reaches for the bottle on the coffee table and pours more whiskey into his glass, which didn't yet need topping up. He offers the bottle to Alexander, who shakes his head.

'I've got a new gig,' Danny says.

'What is it?' Alexander's stomach is already sinking.

'Radio jock on TodayNews FM. A two-hour afternoon slot, three times a week, Monday, Wednesday, Friday. It's a magazine programme with in-depth sports and music.'

Danny shrugs, as if to say that the job is nothing much; but his eyes, even in their run-down state, sparkle discreetly with pleasure and pride.

'You always land on your feet,' Alexander says, taking a mouthful of whiskey for consolation.

'That sounds resentful.'

'It is resentful. There I am, plodding away nine-to-six five days a week in a job that is crushingly mundane. You're out tripping the light fantastic, sleeping till noon, swilling back the beer, blowing money left, right and centre. Then you land all these plum numbers. Resentful isn't the half of it. I'm disgusted.'

Alexander is warmed up, gesturing freely with his hands to give expression to the feeling behind the words. He has pierced the skin of his shyness and is through to a vein of truthful speaking, which he relishes, now that he's in it.

Danny smiles, picking up the tone of enjoyment. 'Let's have it all hang out then,' he says.

'Yes, let's.'

'I wouldn't for a second deny that I'm a complete waster. It was always my ambition to be a waster, and there's an art to it. Your main problem is that you're scared. You sit in your safe little job, collecting your pay cheque. The rest of us are out there taking risks, whoring ourselves. A radio show is a meagre enough return for what I've put myself through.'

'All you do is drink with the right people.'

'And you think that's easy? Let me tell you: it takes dedication and talent.' Danny points at himself to indicate the person who possesses these fine qualities. 'Drinking with the right people in college is easy as piss. Making the right connections in the real world is a completely different ball game.'

Alexander reflects honestly on these points. There is truth in what Danny says. If the two of them entered a room with a hundred people in it, Danny would gravitate naturally to the rich and powerful, the assertive, the witty, the beautiful. Alexander, meanwhile, would be drawn to the disaffected underperformers, intelligent, complex, damaged, with quirky perspectives on reality and comedy. Yet he would not be satisfied in their company. He would be looking over his shoulder all the time at the commanding figures, their presence making him uneasy because he is not one of them, not among them. He would observe them discreetly, admiring, despising, fearing.

167

'I have more to offer than you,' Alexander enunciates carefully, 'but I don't know how to offer it.'

'Well then it's not worth much.'

'It's worth a lot to me.'

'That's your other main problem. You have too high an opinion of yourself, and I speak as someone who has a high opinion of you. Plus you take yourself way too seriously.'

'I don't even know what that means.'

Aoife enters the room, tall and imperious, her red hair tied up high on the top of her head. Her face is pale, with fat waxy crescents of darkness under her eyes.

'I want a cigarette,' she says, crashing heavily onto the vacant sofa. She gives Alexander a smile, which is entirely mechanical. Danny takes Alexander's cigarettes from the coffee table, lights one and passes it across to her. She takes it without a word or a glance in Danny's direction.

'How was he?' Danny asks.

'Like you give a shit,' Aoife says.

'Now that he's asleep, I'm interested in the details.'

'He went down really well, like a little angel, not a squeak of complaint. In fact. . . .' She shakes her head slightly as she draws on her cigarette. 'He gave me this eerie little smile. Like he was . . . consoling me. . . . Anyhow. . . . Is there anything good on the box?'

They watch some TV. Aoife goes to bed. Danny and Alexander drink a lot of whiskey.

It gets to the point where Alexander can't sit up straight any more and has to lie down on the sofa, which for the first few seconds is lovely, but then he starts to feel seasick. His head spins rapidly, as it used to do in his boyhood bedroom in Malahide at the outset of his drinking career.

Up to a few moments ago he was trying to remind Danny of a summer's night in Dublin a few years previously. At the end of the evening, he and Danny and Paul decided to head back to Paul's place to smoke dope and listen to music. The city was full of tourists. They were unable to get a taxi, so instead they hired one of the horse-drawn carriages at Stephen's Green that are usually used only by Americans.

It was a warm drizzly night. The hood was up. The horse took off at a trot, clippety, clippety, clippety, and the big wheels were rolling creakily beneath them. Alexander leant out over the door, into the rain, into the breeze caused by their motion, loving the dark glistening-wet streets, the colourful wonderland lights, the shiny parked cars, the plastered young tarts in their short skirts and low tops, falling around the place, giggling and screaming at each other.

With his head stuck out into the night, he laughed loudly in perfect happiness, laughed in appreciation of the sheer gorgeousness of the moment.

'It was like something from Sherlock Holmes,' he manages to say now to Danny, 'rolling through town, the sound of shod hooves on the road.'

Paul, on the night, thought he was an eejit for this joy, an eccentric. Paul is a prick, Alexander understands suddenly.

He has ignored the mounting sickness, struggled against it, then finally he cannot but accept the inevitability of vomiting, which acceptance immediately precipitates the event. He bolts upward, staggers to his feet, falls across the room to the door, jerks it open, manages in this fashion to make it into the hallway, where the lights are off, the darkness menacing. Raggedly, with a mouth full of vomit but nothing spilt yet, he pushes through to the kitchen, in which – by the yellowish light that seeps in from outside – certain key features are visible: the table and chairs, the sink. Mercifully, the sink is empty. He lurches forward to meet it, his mouth and throat opening automatically, his stomach ejecting its heavily alcoholic contents with a force that causes pain to his upper back and the rear of his neck. His body arches itself – snake-like – to accommodate the flow.

Danny has followed him in. The 100-watt light clicks on, harshly illuminating his shame. Danny pats him encouragingly on the back between efforts.

'Good man,' he says.

Alexander retches four or five times in all, with diminishing intensity and increasing surprise. By the time he is finished, the bottom of the sink is filled with a rank mixture, including recognisable elements from his dinner.

He hangs over the sink, spent and empty, sobered up, his lower ribs still pressed hard against the heavy ceramic rim.

'Are you done, me oul segotia?' Danny asks him fondly.

Drained and shaky, Alexander nods. He wipes some drool from his lips.

Danny leads him across to the table, sits him down.

'I'll make a good strong cup of tea,' Danny says.

Danny puts on a pair of yellow rubber gloves that were lying next to the sink. They are too small for his hands. He has to pull and stretch a bit to make them fit. He sets both taps running and clears out the sink, helps the lumps down the drain with his fingers, softly singing as he works, a song from their teenage years: 'I think I'm turning Japanese; I think I'm turning Japanese; I really think so.'

Steam rises from the gushing stream of hot water. Danny gives a good few squirts with the washing-up liquid and starts to clean the sides of the sink with a green and yellow scrubbing sponge.

Consciousness arrives as a shock, like a punch to the head, presenting a reality in which he is ill, poisoned once again, depressed. He is in the spare room in Danny's house, lying under an uncovered polyester duvet, which is dirty and knobbly, still wearing his now grimy clothes and even his shoes. His body is weak, his mouth and head in a condition of familiar foulness.

'This is not going to be fun,' he mutters to himself in the same moment that an animal scream rips out in an adjacent room.

'Aaaaaaaaaaaaaaagh. Aaaaaaaaaaaaaaaaaaaaaaaaaaaagh.'

It is a human female shriek, demented, desolate, so terrible that he finds himself immediately throwing off the quilt and jumping to his feet, his hangover put aside as he rushes out the door to see what is happening. Alexander does not understand what could call forth such a noise. Aoife has had a nightmare perhaps. She has stabbed

Danny with a carving knife. She has discovered him blind drunk again and cannot take it any more.

'Aaaaaaaaaaaaaaaaaaaaaaaaaaaaaaaaagh.'

He does not hesitate to enter their bedroom, which is boxy and cluttered with mess, the atmosphere thick with the smell of sleeping humans, the curtains drawn, the overhead light on – a naked bulb. She is sitting in her nightdress at the edge of the bed, panting, hyperventilating, a bundle of blanket in her arms, the baby's basket empty on the floor next to her feet. Danny is beyond her, bare chested, half lying, propped up on his elbows. His expression says: I'm not up for this; I'm too wrecked for this shit.

As Alexander enters, Aoife's body is going limp. Her head rolls, her eyes cease to focus. A low groan emits from her pale-lipped mouth. She falls backward across Danny's legs. Danny himself collapses into a fully horizontal position and his hands reach for his ears to seal out the sound, though there is no sound now.

Alexander has leapt forward to catch the bundle as it tumbles from Aoife's arms.

The baby's little face is blue and grey. Its eyes are open, but clouded, glassy. There is no breath, nor any prospect of breath.

Alexander does not react quickly to events like this.

His father died when he was still at school, and it took him over a decade to begin to consider what this meant, what it continued to mean, if anything.

The first hours of this morning are surreal to him, and curiously pleasurable, like a strange dance. All the days, he is plodding along, labouring under his own unexceptional burdens, unable to escape himself, unable to emit light because of the heavy pull of his own gravity. And now – as with a flare – the whole thing is lit up. He sees what otherwise goes unnoticed: the fairground ride. Whoosh, here we go; around and around; up and down on the wooden horse....
And .... wow, isn't it ... yes, beautiful?

But as the flare starts to dim, which it quickly does, as the surreality, the super reality, contracts, he experiences the need to scarper.

171

In the early afternoon, after a quick stop in Rathmines for a shower and a change of clothes, he drives to Galway.

There was nothing further to be done in Danny and Aoife's except to hang around in the kitchen, keening, drinking coffee and smoking cigarettes until it was time to start on the whiskey again. When he left, there were plenty of others there. He was beginning to feel superfluous, although not so superfluous as to adequately assuage his unease about leaving.

'My grand-aunt is dying,' he explained quietly to Aoife's mother and one or two others as he made his way out. 'I have to drive down to Galway to see her. She only has a few hours.'

But even though his excuse this time was genuine, or at least plausible, it is typical of him that he withdraws, that he rations his friendship.

'If you have to go, you have to go,' Danny said in quiet anger, having initially responded with woundedness, incredulity, 'but it wouldn't surprise me if she was still dying in ten years' time.'

'She's on the way out. I have to see her.'

'Well, you might as well stay put in Galway. We'll bury Merlin in Knockboy, on Thursday probably. That's what my mother says. She's organising everything. She's still on her way down in the car, and already she has the whole thing sorted out. It's great to have people like that around you when you're in trouble.'

As he cruises past The Spa Hotel in Lucan, playing back the events of the morning, Alexander discovers an implication in these last comments of Danny's which he did not notice at the time, namely that he – Alexander – does not belong to the set of people who are great to have around when you're in trouble.

The Spa Hotel used to be out in the countryside. When he travelled to Galway as a kid, in the back seat of his father's car, alongside Helena, with his mother in the front passenger seat dispensing blue Murray Mints and good-humoured conversation, The Spa was a milestone, telling them they were out of the city, well on their way.

Dublin has now spilled out far beyond the hotel.

'Your grandfather put the central heating into that hotel,' his mother would say every time they passed it on their way west.

This was considered fresh news on the outward leg of their journey, but was never repeated on the homeward leg. They would pass The Spa on the way back to Dublin in subdued silence, knowing their holiday was over.

His grandfather was a builder, in a broad sense of the word. Brigid is disdainful of modern-day tradesmen – as she would call them – because they have such limited expertise.

'Sure, Daddy could turn his hand to anything,' she would say admiringly, although she hated the man.

The child imagined his grandfather single-handedly installing the heating in the hotel in question, down on his knees on the carpet, with a cup of tea in one hand, a hammer in the other, and a cigarette hanging from his lower lip, secured only by spittle. This was the boy's experience of how the man worked, crankily barking orders to anyone within range.

He drives the car through the ever-extending outskirts of Dublin, repeatedly rerunning his exchange with Danny. This is what he does with life. He attends obsessively to the details of past social interactions, looking for meaning, forming resolutions, flinching at ugliness, reimagining nuances. Occasionally – rarely – there is something pretty to appreciate. Now he is digging out circular patterns. If he's not great to have around, then it shouldn't really matter that much if he quits the scene. But is it the act of departing which confirms his status as not being someone who is great to have around? What conclusions can be drawn? People who are great to have around tend to be around. People who are not great to have around tend to absent themselves. Everyone should be happy with this, and no blame or credit should attach.

At the time, his inward reaction to Danny's comment was hard. He thought: Your mother is a leech. Don't you see that she'll turn this into a social whirl, a poignant drama with herself at the centre?

What he said was: 'Yeah, she's great. I'll ring you later from the car to see how things are going.'

The car is going beautifully. The driver is pumped up on adrenaline, on the energy of things being different, the routine smashed for a while, and the world seemingly full of possibilities. He is high and agitated on coffee and nicotine. His belly is full of all-day breakfast, which he himself cooked for half a dozen people at Danny's. In ordinary circumstances, his stomach would still have been refusing work, but, given the extremity of the situation, it has deferred all complaints. He is conscious of an underlying wretchedness, but right now he feels good.

He zooms effortlessly through the roundabout that begins the Kinnegad bypass.

Through the bypass and on to the narrow winding country road that runs for twenty miles or so, lined with winter-bare hedges and trees, the verge mucky. No overtaking is allowed, and usually it wouldn't be possible, but in this car, and with the traffic scant, the manoeuvre is accomplished with minimal effort, with none of the usual nervous strain, without thought almost, as easily as one swings out to avoid a cyclist on a quiet road.

When he hits the Athlone bypass, with the crossing of the Shannon imminent, his sense of pleasure at passing into the West is coloured with regret at how quickly the journey is racing by. It would suit his emotional condition better if the trip was a transcontinental one. This is always how he feels, not just today. He would love always to be driving from New York to some remote coastal corner of Oregon.

It is a journey in three movements.

In the first movement, he is up, the day is bright, but not too bright.

The second movement begins shortly after he crosses the Shannon. As he rolls smoothly through a landscape of thistly fields, flooded in places, the big yellow sun hangs low in the sky in front of him, and starts to blind him. He remembers that he remembered to bring his sunglasses. He remembers that he was clever enough to drop them into the side pocket of the door. His right hand finds them. He puts them on. And instantly everything is groovier, including himself, and he can certainly tolerate a bit of grooving up, since his good mood is faltering, his tiredness beginning to get the upper hand.

He stretches a little in the cushioned seat, leans his head back against the rest, brings refreshed focus to the external environment, darkened and grainy, freed of the everyday glare of ordinariness. He begins to give attention to the animals in the passing fields: depressed cows at their lazy work of chewing, their udders heavy, industrial; sheep with their narrow stupid skulls; fine slender horses, who even in repose seem frightened. And animals on the road: a squashed rat, pointing to Galway; a full-bodied fox, who survived long enough to make it past the broken yellow line to the hard shoulder, where it lay down to die. From his last trip, more than a year previously, in late summer, he recalls a long plentifulness of dead crows, over many miles, glued to the road's surface with their own spilt innards and juices, their jagged black wings flapping lifelessly in the wind. No crows today.

The quick and the dead. The difference between them. The baby was blue, glassy eyed. A particular class of object.

The third movement opens in busy little Loughrea. He takes off the sunglasses. It will be night soon. The early starters have their lights on already. The narrow streets of the market town are bright and colourful, more appealing, now his glasses are off. For fun, to have a target to aim at, he estimates it will take him another twenty minutes to reach Galway, but he knows that half an hour is more likely.

His body feels like wreckage. His spirit is low. He has no home to go to. He rings his mother on her mobile. He doesn't want to face her and her odious brother this evening. As he listens to the ringing tone, he tries to think of an excuse. He would like to bypass the city and drive out to Barna, book into a B&B on the ocean, have a pint with the good people of Connemara, get to bed early with the remote control, flick through the channels for an hour, sleep. In the morning, if it's a clear day, he will be able to make out the Aran Islands, three faint rocky shapes on the horizon. Just to glimpse them is a healing experience. If he is brave, if it is not too cold, he might jump into the sea before breakfast, to refresh his soul, to give him appetite.

He remembers that Maisie is dying.

'She's drifting in and out of consciousness,' his mother tells him dramatically. 'She's completely confused. Her breathing is very shallow. She could go any minute, or she could last till tomorrow, but it won't be long now.'

'What are you going to do? Are you going to wait there?'

'It's just myself and Mick now. We won't leave her alone, but there are people coming and going. We'll go back to the hotel for dinner when someone relieves us. The Gradys have been here in force all day.'

'I might stay out in Barna,' he says abruptly.

Maisie does not look well. Her eyes are dark, far back in her head. The skin of her face is yellow-grey, flaccid, anciently wrinkled. Thin flesh hangs from her jaws. Her lips are pale and shrunken, desert dry apart from a tiny crescent of dampness that is visible on the inside of the lower lip. Her breathing is erratic, laboured: the emaciated body beneath the sheet shudders and jerks with the effort of inhalation.

Alexander bends over the bed to kiss her and wants to vomit. He has been vomiting a lot recently. It's becoming habitual. He searches for the least offensive spot, and is drawn to her forehead. The tepid yellow skin feels synthetic against his lips, and he finds himself far too close to her thin dry hair and the smooth sprouting ground in which it is weakly rooted.

A low grunt-like sound issues from the dying woman's throat. She appears to be trying to say something.

'Jimmy,' translates Brigid, who is sitting in a chair beside the bed clasping Maisie's hand between her own two hands. 'Isn't that marvellous? She recognises you.'

'I'm not Jimmy,' Alexander points out, sitting down into one of the chairs by the bed, on the opposite side to his mother.

Brigid shakes her head, dismissing this objection as a mere detail, an inappropriate fussiness.

'You look like him.'

It is painful for Alexander to hear this. He desires to respond to the accusation, to refute it. He wants to say: I might look like him, but I'm not him. I'm different from him. But his anger would be wasted. Brigid wouldn't notice it. If she did notice it, she wouldn't understand.

'Where's Mick?' he asks.

'He's in the smoking room, doing his crossword.'

Brigid refers to the crossword-doing as though it were a holy rite. Mick is famed in the family for his crossword skill and his obsessive devotion to the *Irish Times'* cryptic crossword, as a consequence of which he is unable to focus properly on anything else until the day's puzzle has been solved.

Brigid thinks her older brother is a genius, that he could have been President of the Universe if he had just pushed himself a little. He was the only one of all the cousins to go to university. He studied law and became a junior solicitor in a partnership in Loughrea. Later, after a mysterious falling out with the senior partner, ostensibly on a point of professional ethics, though the details remain vague, he left the practice to join the Office of the Chief State Solicitor in Dublin, where he remained for the following thirty-five years until his retirement, without – Alexander understands – ever distinguishing himself. In the latter years of his career, he drifted into complete idleness, devoting himself increasingly to crosswords and gin. Even in this, Brigid found something noble, believing that her revered brother had become too disillusioned to bother.

Alexander has never been able to deal with Mick. When he was a child, unconsciously imitating his mother, he regarded Mick as a god. They had a love affair, man and nephew. Later, in early adulthood, having not seen his uncle for a few years owing to a family falling-out, Alexander re-experienced the man over a number of family events and was disappointed in him, found himself insulted and angered through what he regarded as the vacuity of Mick's personality and his unsettling, smart-arse wit. This disappointment was mutual, it seemed. Their interactions now are edgy and unpleasant, characteristic of soured affection. In advance of meeting him, Alexander usually intends to smooth the path between them, or at least to maintain his own internal equanimity, but Mick still has power over him.

'That was terrible what happened with the poor baby,' Brigid says. 'They must be destroyed. Do they know what it was at all? Did he suffocate?'

'It's a cot death: Sudden Infant Death Syndrome. They don't know why.'

'I read somewhere that it might have to do with cigarette smoke, but then Mick said to me that that was nonsense. It's hard to know what to believe any more.'

Brother Mick enters the room now, this wise and powerful man, who to anyone else, who didn't know him, might seem simply small and old. Under his arm he carries a neatly folded *Irish Times*, the crossword showing, beautifully completed. Mick uses expensive disposable pens with thin soft nibs. In this, his taste is good; and his writing is elegant, if affected. It is a point of honour with him that he makes no marks on the paper, that there are no corrections in his answers.

'You look a bit under the weather,' he remarks to Alexander as he sits in the chair next to his sister.

'Hello to you,' Alexander says.

'Did you get it out?' Brigid asks her brother.

'What?' he says, pretending not to know what she is talking about.

'The crossword,' she says impatiently.

'Indeed I did.'

'Hluuu hle hloor,' says Maisie, her head bobbing feebly from side to side.

'What dear?' asks Brigid ardently.

'Hluuu hle hloor,' says Maisie, admirably consistent.

'She's been very chatty this last while,' Brigid says, withdrawing her attention from Maisie's great effort to communicate. 'I think she might be telling us to close the door. When she had a bad turn before Christmas, she was seeing all these people coming through the door and crowding up the room. And sure the door was closed, and there were only a couple of us there at the time.' Brigid glances at Maisie and continues emphatically with her voice dropped to a whisper, probably more out of reverence for the subject-matter than out of any fear that Maisie will overhear. 'She was seeing the cast of characters from her life, all the people she had known, most of them stone dead for decades – may the Lord have mercy on their souls. "My people are here", she said to me, very lucidly. "They're coming to collect me, to bring me home, all the people. Look at old McLoughlin there with that hat on him and the same toothless grin."'

It is not clear to Alexander whether his mother interprets these events as hallucinations on the part of the dying or as instances of paranormal perception of actual ghostly happenings; that the dead friends and relatives did indeed turn up en masse in spiritual form to usher their loved one to the hereafter, visible to her, who already had one foot in the other world, but not to the other plain mortals gathered around.

Alexander is not one to rule out the possibility of ghosts, although he would generally be sceptical. He has noticed that people from his mother's generation often have a ready supply of ghost stories, which seem puzzlingly authentic, if one believes the details described. Brigid even has a particular voice which she employs for these stories and for discussing other weird phenomena, such as UFOs, which she occasionally reads about with passing fascination. How come he has never heard of someone from his own generation encountering a ghost? There are a few possible interpretations here. It might be that there are no ghosts and people now don't see any because they are more rational about these matters. Or one could assert that people have lost the ability to see ghosts because they are too rational.

'You remember those sessions you guys used to have,' he says now across the bed, 'late at night in somebody's kitchen, telling ghost stories. They used to scare the shit out of us kids. But we loved them as well.'

Brigid blanks. Mick stares at him with distaste, as though this comment were out of context and inappropriate, then glances sideways at

Brigid, frowning, without attempting to disguise his facial expression, which translates as: Is your son really such an idiot?

Brigid sniffs and jerks her head in embarrassment.

'Alexander is planning to spend the night in Barna,' she says with veiled accusation.

'That makes sense,' says Mick with sarcasm.

Alexander yields immediately without struggle.

'No, no, that was just a whim. I'll book a room in the same hotel that you guys are in.'

'You mightn't get a room,' Mick snaps.

'I'll take my chances.'

'You know what I'm just remembering,' Brigid says reflectively, still holding Maisie's limp bony hand in hers, caressing the back of it with gentle rotations of her fingers, which attention Alexander finds so irritating that it makes him squirm in the chair if he focuses on it. 'That time before Christmas, she told me there was money hidden behind the Sacred Heart picture in the house in Ballyryan. At the time I thought she was rambling, and then later I forgot about it. She was telling me to get it. I wonder if there really is money there.'

'We should check it out in the morning,' says Mick decisively, as if this was an urgent matter of public interest. 'We'll have breakfast, we'll call in here to see her, then we'll drive over.'

'Hluuu hloor,' says Maisie, her frail chest heaving.

In the morning, their plans require modification, since Maisie has died. She expired in the middle of the night. This information is conveyed to Brigid via her mobile phone by the ward sister, just as the three of them are sitting down to breakfast in the hotel restaurant.

'Oh my God, what will we do?' Brigid asks Mick.

'We'll have breakfast,' Mick says. 'It's what she would have wanted.'

Brigid gets up from the table and runs out the door.

'Women are emotional creatures,' Mick says.

'I suppose it's always a shock,' Alexander utters piously without thinking about it.

'It's not that much of a shock,' says Mick with a pounce. 'She was very old, has been dying for quite a while, and was completely incapacitated. In fact, I would say it was one of the least shocking deaths of my experience.'

They each order the full Irish and for Brigid scrambled eggs on brown bread, which, following her return, she insists she cannot eat.

'She was like a mother to me,' she says, her eyes red and mascara stained from weeping, her shoulders intermittently heaving with the sobs.

She holds a ball of scrunched-up pink toilet paper to her nose to capture the assortment of bodily fluids running free.

'What do we do now?' she asks again, and it seems to Alexander as much an existential question as a practical one.

'We should go to the hospital anyway,' he suggests tentatively, to fill the advice vacuum occasioned by the fact that Mick's mouth is busy with bacon and egg.

'I can't believe she's gone,' says Brigid, breaking again into a wail.

Alexander resists an impulse to laugh. There is something absurd in his mother's behaviour, he finds. But it's not only that. He often feels like laughing when he hears that someone has died, and once or twice has indeed tripped into actual laughter, before hastily correcting himself, apologising, declaring that the matter was not funny at all. It is a reaction of embarrassment.

But he had not felt any embarrassment the previous morning, even when Aoife went into denial.

'There's something wrong with my baby. Call the doctors. There must be something wrong with my baby.'

She wrapped it up quickly with another blanket from its basket and ran out of the house to take it to the hospital.

Alexander ran after her because Danny was naked and unmoving. He caught up with her on the pavement in front of the house, ran around to meet her from the front, like a rugby player bringing himself on-side, enclosed her in a loose two-arm embrace, which she first feebly tried to shrug off, but then accepted, the bundle of her dead infant between them.

'It's OK,' he said, though it was not OK. 'This happens. It's not your fault.'

'We should still go out to Ballyryan,' Mick says. 'We'll be back in the city in an hour and a half. They'll have her laid out in the hospital morgue all day. There's no hurry there. It's better to clear our heads now and drive straight out to Ballyryan. We should get in there fast, before the rush starts.'

'What rush?' Alexander asks.

'The Gradys will ransack the place,' says Brigid vaingloriously.

She appears to be sniffing her way to recovery.

'They'll clean it out like a plague of locusts,' Mick confirms. 'Get some breakfast into you, girl. There's a long day ahead of us.'

'Is this your car?' Mick asks disbelievingly, admiringly, as they arrive at the space in the half-dark multi storey concrete car park where the BMW is berthed.

Alexander does his best to maintain a demeanour of manly indifference, but his heart beats strongly with excitement. He feels a slight flush at his cheekbones, and is unable at first to speak.

'What did you do? Rob a bank?'

'Something like that.'

Although he feels a tangible – if also hollow – gratification in Mick's reaction; in the car itself, right now, Alexander takes little pleasure. It seems such a preposterous piece of engineering, an overblown hulk of metal, lustrous, but inanimate, without joy of its own and incapable of reflecting joy.

'I didn't know they paid economists so well,' says Mick, the three of them standing by the rear bumper.

'They don't,' says Brigid to Mick, then instructs Alexander: 'Tell Mick what you said to us at Christmas.'

'What?'

'You know, about not being able to buy a house. I thought it was very good.'

'Oh yeah,' recalls Alexander reluctantly, flushing.

He realises that they are standing around behind the car for no purpose. The other two have been waiting for him to lead the way. He has been waiting for them, or forgot what they were there for.

He moves around to the driver's door, but too abruptly, and has the impression of leaving them stranded.

'Sorry,' he says, looking back over his shoulder. 'Let's get in.'

His mother looks at him appraisingly, narrowing her eyes for better insight.

'You're acting strangely,' she says. 'Is there something wrong?'

He blushes deeply, uncontrollably, and half turns away from her gaze, shaking his head.

'I'm just tired,' he mutters, opening the driver's door.

'You sit in the front,' Brigid says to her brother. 'You're the man.'

Mick has already gravitated to the front passenger door, expecting no less.

Brigid is happy to observe the sexual hierarchy that prevailed in her youth. She takes a cultish enjoyment in regarding her brother as superior. There is no surprise in this, but it pains Alexander to observe it. His mother sees men in general as essentially superior, except for her own husband and son. He feels in this moment that his mother despises him.

'I thought it was a good attitude,' she says when they are all in their seats and are belting up. 'Alexander said that since he couldn't afford a house, he might as well splash out on a car. It's a very big car though. It might be too big for you.'

'It's a better car than my father ever had,' Alexander says. As it emerges, he recognises this comment to be out of order. It further disimproves the texture of the atmosphere, producing around him a depressing, ashen quality. 'That was a Freudian slip, if ever I heard one,' he adds after a silence.

'Well, I hope you're a better driver,' Mick says, as Alexander is reversing out of the space. 'Your father, God rest him, was hopeless. Forgive me for saying it, Brigid. You know I was very fond of him, but sitting beside him in the car was a painful experience. He was as slow and wooden a driver as you'll meet.'

'He never had an accident in twenty-five years of driving,' says Brigid.

'That's not the highest virtue,' Mick says.

'I disagree,' says Brigid with plenty of spunk.

'He might never have had an accident, but he might have caused a few.'

'I don't hold with that view at all,' says Brigid, speaking warmly from personal experience. 'People who drive slowly don't cause accidents. It's people who are impatient who cause accidents.'

Alexander is sweating. He is making an effort to be speedy and nimble, but the descending lane in the car park is ridiculously narrow and tightly wound. He mounts the kerb with one wheel on the inside of a turn. On the way back down, the concrete step catches the underside of the car with a screech and a scratch. He flinches, slows down.

'That was painful,' he offers meekly.

'Good driving,' says Mick.

'It takes you a bit of time to get used to a new car,' Alexander explains.

'It usually takes me about twenty minutes,' Mick retorts with the practised ease of the habitual boaster.

Alexander's driving is ruined now. In the next loop, he understeers, halts abruptly, curses under his breath as he shifts into reverse to straighten up for the turn.

'You had plenty of room,' says Mick.

'It felt too tight. I didn't want to risk it.'

'You drive like a girl.'

Alexander brakes angrily. The car lurches to a stop, the passengers bouncing forward, rebounding off their belts. He turns and faces Mick.

'Why don't you shut the fuck up,' he half shouts at the hunched old man beside him.

'There is no need to get offensive,' Mick responds, but he looks away, out through the front windscreen, rather than face Alexander's intensity.

'There is need,' Alexander insists.

'Cool it, both of you,' Brigid commands in a clear, authoritative voice from the back. 'Let's remember that Maisie has just passed away.'

A further retort to Mick forms itself in Alexander's head: If you're so smart, how come your son is a smackhead? But the words are deep down. It would require too long and too deliberate an effort to dig them up and shoot them off.

The kitchen was the pumping heart of Maisie's farm. To the visiting kids, it was more like a HQ than a room. It was a big dark flag-stone-floored space, sparsely furnished. Just inside the door, under the front window, was a small kitchen table that was the focal point for the visits. The adults would sit around in rickety wooden chairs. The children, running, would converge into this space on returning from their adventures, hang around for a while, then set off again. At some point they would be fed: soft-boiled eggs; home-made brown soda bread; a bowl of new potatoes with butter and salt. The butter was unusually soft and yellow, unrefrigerated. There were no modern appliances in the house, apart from an old valve radio with a taped-together cord linking it to a dangerous-looking electric socket. Maisie was saving for her old age. She never bought anything.

The kids sat at the table, their thin legs dangling loosely, chewing the home-produced food which they appreciated much less than their mother did, watching the hens pecking at the floor. Sometimes, one of the birds would jump onto the table and go for the crumbs. Maisie would mutter angrily and take a surprisingly brutal swipe at it, but make no contact. The hens were talented in avoiding her blows. They skipped out of the danger without giving the appearance of having noticed it.

Alexander looked for milk and was given a cupful from the bucket that Uncle Johnny had just filled.

'Can I have milk from a bottle?'

This was a source of amusement for the grown-ups.

'Sure, you can't get better than that – full cream milk, straight from the tit, still warm.'

But he found it vulgar and disgusting, undrinkable: thick and frothy and smelling of animal.

Helena looked to go to the toilet, occasioning further mirth.

'Outside, turn left and it's the second bush on the right,' Johnny said, surprisingly fluent for once – pink in the face, sniggering slightly.

In time, the children became accustomed to these features of the Ballyryan homestead, and accepted most of them as part of the fun. The joy that Brigid took in the simplicity of the couple's life prodded them along in this direction. She, for example, would always point excitedly at the iron hook protruding from the upper stone-work of the large open hearth, which – decades earlier – had been used for hanging pots and kettles over the fire. Now they had a stout black iron range, which was novel enough for the children, but which represented modernity to Brigid, relative to the farmhouse she had known in her childhood.

These then were the main features: the table and chairs, the range, the unused fireplace; at the centre of the opposite wall, a large dark dresser holding a dozen miserable paperbacks, deeply yellowed newsprint magazines, the radio; beside the dresser a rock-ing chair with some squashed cushions in it that looked as if they hadn't been moved for years; on the far wall, facing the entrance, a ghoulish wooden-framed picture of Jesus of the Sacred Heart, shrouded in cheap glass, his visage repugnantly meek and glowing, the organ in question red and sore looking, wrapped in poetic thorns, with a miniature crucifix emerging from the top where an artery might be expected, as though it had grown there through some truly bizarre mutation.

The kitchen was not the only room in the house, but they rarely even peeked into the others: a long narrow parlour, over filled with ugly stuffy furniture and ancient kitsch; two small bedrooms; a stony scullery with a deep ceramic trough in it for washing things (but with no indoor taps) and an old bleached-out wooden churn in the corner, which was no longer used. More exciting than these odd annexes was the small door in the kitchen that was halfway up the wall, above the top of the dresser, seemingly unreachable. This, they were told, was the loft, where the boys in the family used to sleep, accessed by way of a ladder.

'Can we go up there?'

'Another time maybe.'

'Where is the ladder? Is it outside in the barn? Can we see it?'

Maisie and Johnny hardly ever addressed the children directly, perhaps partly because the Dublin children sometimes didn't understand their heavy country accent. They spoke to them through the parents. And the parents themselves were by this cause moved back into a more distant perspective, seeing their children through the eyes of the old childless couple.

'I want to be a farmer when I grow up,' Alexander one day declared.

This was amusing for the adults, but charming also.

'It's hard work,' Uncle Johnny told him. 'You've to be up very early to milk the cows, in all weathers, and you can't be going off on your holidays.'

'That's fine. And I want to grow things, and have horses.'

The house is almost derelict now, the thatched roof still in one piece but sunken in the middle. The straw is dying, losing its golden colour, going grey, with open wounds in two or three places where it is rotting, congealing. The whitewash on the front wall is dirty, stained with black specks and blotches, particularly under the small front windows, the panes of which are coated in a greenish grime. And the paint on the front door is blistered and peeling, the exposed wood sodden from the rain, splintering.

The site is overgrown. The garden, in the time Alexander knew it, was always unkempt, but the front yard was relatively neat. Now it is teeming with tall, aggressive weeds. Enormous bushes crowd in from the perimeter. Only the windowless barn stands in good condition, dirty but uninjured, its corrugated-iron roofing dark and corroded, brittle looking, curled a bit in the corners, a few holes here and there, but essentially intact.

Wordlessly, the three split up, moving slowly and quietly, as though in meditation, each performing his or her own individual snoop. After a few minutes, as though by arrangement, Alexander and Brigid's paths intersect at one of the front windows and they pause together, waiting for Mick.

'I'm horrified,' says Brigid in a hushed voice, her head shaking, tears spilling lightly from the corners of her eyes. 'I can't believe it's been allowed to go to ruin like this. Why is nobody taking care of the place? It's a disgrace.'

'You can't really see too far into the kitchen,' Alexander says, his face right up against the glass. 'The window's so dirty, and it's dark inside.'

'You'd think at least that the neighbours would have trimmed the bushes.'

'But I can definitely see a bottle of Heinz ketchup on the table, underneath the window. She never used anything like that.'

'I'm surprised Michael Phaddy wouldn't have taken a hand to the place, after all Maisie did for him.'

'What did she do for him?'

'Didn't he come down to her for his dinner every day for a good ten years when his own wife went mad and took to her bed?'

'But he's an old man now, isn't he?' It shocks Brigid momentarily to hear this undeniable truth. 'I think I can even make out the tablecloth,' Alexander continues. 'Do you remember it? It had a blue flowery pattern.'

'That wasn't a tablecloth.'

'What was it?'

'It was a plastic thing,' Brigid explains. She seems irritated. 'You peeled off a skin at the back and ironed it on.'

'Oh yeah, I remember the bubbles under the surface. And the way it was scrubbed white in the places that saw the most action.'

'Those are peculiar things to remember,' says Brigid, frowning.

Mick's hunched form appears from around the corner of the house. He is sucking purposefully on a cigarette, which reminds Alexander that he could take out one of his own, although he does not do so. For some reason he has not smoked so far today. Now that he remembers, he notices the presence of the usual physical longing for nicotine in his throat, in his blood, but is happy for the moment to accept these sensations, to enjoy them even.

'We can get in around the back,' says Mick, 'through the scullery window. We can smash it with a rock.'

Alexander's phone vibrates in the back pocket of his trousers. He slips it out and spins around to consider the call in privacy. On the grey monochrome screen, the little black bell is swinging. Underneath is the letter *J*. It's a long time since he has seen that. He presses the green receiver button to take the call just as the phone would switch from vibration to ring.

'Hiya baby,' he says naturally, without thought, striding away toward the bushes. 'It's great to hear from you. I've missed you so.'

He knows from the silence at the other end that this is not what Julia had in mind, but that's fine too. There is no expectation in the attitude from which he speaks.

'I'm ringing about Aoife and Danny's baby.'

'I know.'

'It's terrible, isn't it?'

'Yes,' he agrees gravely, after a few moments of consideration. 'Maisie died, last night, at four in the morning.'

'I'm sorry to hear that.'

'It's been quite a week. . . . I haven't spoken to Danny since yesterday. The funeral is confirmed for tomorrow afternoon, right? It's just down the road from here. I'm in Ballyryan now.'

'You're at Maisie's place?'

'Yes. We're standing outside the cottage, contemplating burglary.'

'Who's we?'

'Mick, Brigid, myself. I'm always chickenshit at this kind of thing, or else too morally scrupulous, which probably amounts to the same thing.'

'I don't follow.'

'The old dear had cash stashed everywhere,' he explains, speaking slowly, searching for the words, his chest heavy with unexpected emotion, 'in mattresses, buried in buckets in the fields, hidden behind stones in the barn. . . . She didn't trust banks. . . . Mind you, it's highly unlikely that the place hasn't been raided already, many times, by people with keys.'

'Are you OK, Lexi?' she asks in a wonderfully gentle, concerned voice. It feels like a new branch of her personality, a new development, or – at least – something he hasn't experienced in her for a long time. 'You're rambling a bit.'

'I'm just saying that it's been a difficult week. And on Friday the Council is launching its broadband report. I really ought to be there. And Helena and I had planned to take part in a show-jumping competition on Friday evening. I suppose we can give that a miss. . . . I wonder when Maisie will be buried?'

'Are you sure you're OK?'

The following morning, in a dreamy tone, he decides to skip the church service for Merlin; or, rather, it happens that he does not attend.

After breakfast, he escapes easily from his relatives and goes walking through Galway in January sunshine. His body is freshly washed, but his underpants and socks are sticky, his teeth furry from two nights of no brushing, his face stubbly and dry skinned. After leaving Danny's place on Tuesday morning, he showered and dressed in Rathmines before setting off for the West, but he didn't bring a change of clothes or a toilet bag. At the time, he wanted to be spontaneous, unencumbered. He now rues this whim.

On the surface of things, it would be straightforward to buy new gear. He could duck into a department store somewhere around Eyre Square, pick up what is required, change in the jacks of one of the pubs on Shop Street, throw the old stuff into a bin. He could even shave in a pub toilet, if he is too lazy to return to the hotel. But he has no appetite for such activity. Having strolled around in circles for a few miles, meditatively, he is in the mood now for sitting in a small café, sipping cold Darjeeling, an unlit cigarette in his lips, staring out the window at the passers-by, at the physical fabric of the street, picking out the obscure features where life breaks through: in dirty pavement cracks and uneven kerbstones; in a slowly disintegrating lollipop stick caught in the gutter; in the heavy scarring of the tarred road surface, from multiple digs, filled and refilled, sunken, sinking; in the fact that the pale reflection of the street in the shop window opposite currently blocks his view of whatever it is that's on show behind the glass.

Galway has always been closer to his heart than Dublin. He likes the Bohemian thread that runs through it: the colouredy woollen scarves and hats, the German dope smokers, the organic vegetable growers, the buskers with their dreadlocks; the attractive young students with their rollie cigarettes and precious pints of Guinness, their life dramas, the things they laugh at; the busy podgy Gaeltacht mums, up from Connemara for a day's shopping, speaking rapid Irish with each other, with their sensibly dressed kids, knowing the value of money; the bookshops which seem more Irish than bookshops in Dublin, more Celtic, more literary than smart, more second hand than new, more quirky than comprehensive.

'Do you need a light?' the thin elegant Asian-American waitress inquires, proffering a little book of matches embossed with the café's logo.

Actually, he doesn't want a light. He is happy to leave the cigarette as it is, long and white, clean – rather than hot, burning, reducing. He is enjoying how his nostrils occasionally pick up the scent of the unblemished fresh tobacco. He is enjoying the absence of smoke.

'Yes, thanks,' he says, to reward her solicitude, out of politeness really, and because she is pretty, with oriental eyes like lateral commas, and a snubbed nose. She is wearing a delicate antique white cotton blouse, which – he finds himself now thinking – must have been washed hundreds of times, lovingly. She is flat chested but with wide generous hips; superior, but slightly curious about him.

He decides that he would like to live in Galway.

'Could I interest you in another pot of tea?' she asks with a lovely twinkle.

'You know, there is nothing I would rather do than hang around here for a long time, but I have to find a flower shop. Do you know if there's one nearby?'

Bouquet in hand, he passes through the gate into the small Anglican churchyard outside Knockboy.

It's a fine bouquet. The florist helped him with it. They made it up together. He didn't want a wreath. He wanted something live and charismatic, with lots of white lilies. He didn't care what it cost.

'Would you like to do a card?' the florist asked him.

He gave serious thought to this question. Why would he fill out a card? To indicate that the flowers were from him, that he had paid for them, that they arose from his impulse, his sense of duty. It seemed petty.

'No,' he said. Then instantly regretted the decision.

He has already spotted the funeral party, up in the cemetery beyond the top end of the church. He is surprised by how few people are there, no more than a couple of dozen. This is problematic, since it makes his late arrival obvious. He finds himself raw and unshaven, a solitary outlaw.

'Feel the fear and do it anyway,' he whispers, proceeding crunchingly along the gravel path by the side of the church, then onto the silence of the springy grass bank where the graves begin, through the assembly of assorted gravestones from the past two hundred years or more, some black and pristine, newly lettered, freshly flowered, some old and weathered, illegible, lichen stained, lopsided, commemorating dead people now entirely irrelevant, even those who forgot them themselves now long forgotten.

'The Lord is full of compassion and mercy,' says the prissy young rector to the silent mourners as Alexander comes within hearing. Alexander positions himself in the nearest peripheral slot, apart from the group but nevertheless clearly joined to it, just behind where Paul, Julia and Karina are standing. Paul hears the grass move, turns his head sharply, nervously, nods to Alexander, almost imperceptibly, but in a manner which deliberately conveys disapproval. Fuck you too,

Alexander thinks at Paul's skull once he has turned his back again. He removes from his imagination – borrowed from some Russian friends – a portable petrol chainsaw and tugs on the cord to get it started.

'Ruummm, rummm,' he growls quietly, but not inaudibly.

Paul turns his head again, frowning in irritation.

To disguise his indiscretion, Alexander coughs loudly into his fist. This signals his arrival to the general funeral party. Karina and Julia turn their heads. Karina winks sorrowfully. Julia gives him a tight-lipped smile. Her face is pale, and she is wearing an unusual lilac lipstick, which he finds sexy. Danny looks across, sees him, but registers no reaction. Closely shaven, gaunt and grey in his apparent anguish, Danny is dressed in a long stylish black coat that Alexander has not seen before. He stands next to the rector, on the far side of the small gaping grave. The interior walls of the grave are dense and mucky, varying gradually in composition as they descend toward the bottom. Usually, in Dublin, the grave is hidden under a wire lattice covered in green baize, with the wreaths piled up on top of it. Here in the country – evidently – they prefer to leave things more explicit.

Next to Danny, eighteen inches too far from him, Aoife, entranced, stares into the ground. Jasper holds her firmly by her elbow, as though there is a risk she might fall into the hole. Jasper appears unusually mature in this pose. He seems to have achieved a more modulated attitude, of brave defiance rather than unreasoned hostility. The wispy beard sprouting on his pimply face looks surprisingly good. It goes well with his long hair and wire-rimmed glasses, giving him a new Trotsky-ish aspect. At the christening, Alexander recalls, he wore a suit, but now he is in his usual gear: torn jeans, big boots, denim jacket. Maybe they were all too driven out of their heads to give any thought to what Jasper should wear. Or perhaps there was a row about this, which Jasper won, a victory, as he might see it, for authenticity.

Closely around the central trio stands the next layer of relations, grim and steadfast: Danny's mother, his tall angry red-faced father,

Aoife's mother, Danny's sister Cordelia, her impeccably turned-out husband, a couple of aged aunts, an uncle who has just had a stroke, or is just about to have one, or is having one at this very moment, his head twitching strangely, his complexion a little more purple than would be wished for.

'For He himself knows of what we are made,' continues the rector pompously, but also lovingly. 'He remembers that we are but dust. Our days are like the grass. We flourish like a flower of the field.'

'Goodbye, my little flower,' says Danny, an almost dandyish affectation, which nevertheless nudges his red-nosed sister into sudden, convulsive sobs.

Her husband slips his arm around her shoulders, remaining otherwise aloof, and she ends her sobs, as though they are errant, requiring correction. She dabs her nose and eyes with a small silk handkerchief. Alexander has always liked Danny's snobbish elder sister. As a student, on one particular weekend visit, he fantasised about asking her to show him her fruit-perfect breasts, imagining as he jerked off before sleeping that she would unexpectedly comply with this request, surprised by his candour, or out of charity perhaps.

The labourers have come forward, in their well-worn, dusty jackets and caps, in their dark creaseless trousers, heads dropped respectfully, shielding their eyes. They lower the tiny white coffin into the grave, using ropes, working them through their thick, mud-stained hands, though not particularly expertly: the descent of the coffin is uneven, halting.

There are no screams, no gasps, no further weeping. Just the rector's voice and the creak-thud progress into the earth of an ornate white box with gold trimmings, almost like a chocolate box, in the upholstered innards of which – it must be supposed – lies a dead little baby boy, absurdly named.

'The Lamb who is at the throne will be their shepherd, and will lead them to springs of living water, and God will wipe away all tears from their eyes.'

Alexander considers how Paul's skull might be split open with his portable chainsaw, splashing everyone around with blood, bone, brains, bits of hairy scalp. It occurs to him that it might be difficult for the blade to get good purchase on the curved surface of the skull, which of course would be moving away. The blade might slip down onto the shoulder and take that off instead. But that would be OK. It couldn't be a clean killing anyway, not with a chainsaw.

While he is thinking these pleasing thoughts, Paul's right hand – directly in Alexander's field of vision – emerges from his coat pocket and travels down to Julia's ass, reaching up under her tailored thigh-length black leather jacket, searching out her left buttock through the tweedy fabric of her skirt. As the hand squeezes with familiar intimacy, she offers herself, moves in slightly to accommodate his touch.

They sit at the oak table in the big kitchen of Knockboy House, eating smoked salmon on fresh brown soda bread, with a squeeze of lemon for tang. Alexander is already on his third or fourth portion. Danny's mother, Ursula, is expertly – generously – cutting off slices from the side of salmon, with an outward scraping motion at the bottom of each cut so that none of the precious flesh sticks to the ivory inside of the scaly silver skin. She cuts rapidly, as though in a hurry to get rid of the fish, pauses to cut off more slices of bread from one of the quarter loaves, liberally butters them with thick strokes from a pound of Kerrygold, crowning each with one or two pieces of the remarkably tender and flavourful dark-pink salmon.

'Have another,' she says to Alexander, pushing the serving plate across the table in his direction. 'Pass it along.'

Karina and Paul are next to him, also enthusiastically feasting after a hard morning of funeral. Cordelia's husband Philippe is at the far end of the table, engrossed in the day's edition of the *Financial Times*, which is a lighter shade of salmon than the salmon itself. Julia sits around from him, at the other side of the table, down from busy Ursula, who is standing.

Julia is not eating. She sips on a mug of black coffee, maintaining that she is not hungry, though Alexander is fairly sure that she is ravenous but dieting. She was never fat, but was always half watching her weight, complaining about it. When he saw her before Christmas, she was a good stone lighter than she had been at the point of her departure, and looked fabulous. Now, she seems undernourished.

'This is the best thing I have ever eaten,' Alexander says, truthfully, as he takes another slice and brusquely passes the plate along to Paul. 'I can't stop myself. This is genuinely food for the gods. I'm getting a philosophical buzz from it.'

Philippe glances up briefly from his paper to observe the speaker so effusive. In his scummy clothes, in his peasant genes, Alexander feels common and insubstantial by comparison with the dense, manicured presence of this man, who is thus far uncommunicative, a half-eaten bread-with-salmon lying neglected at his elbow.

'You're talking nonsense again, Alex,' Paul says pleasantly, as he passes the plate to Karina. 'You'll have to watch that. It's becoming a habit.'

In another context, Alexander might have scraped together some sort of a response to this. Or – more likely – would have said nothing, stunned, smarting. In the present moment, he is out of reach of anything Paul can throw. The salmon is genuinely affecting him, transmuting his pain into something at the sweet end of melancholy. Or perhaps he was simply very hungry after his wanderings through the city in the morning.

'I think Alex has a point,' Karina intercedes defensively as she too takes another slice. 'The salmon is fantastic.'

Alexander remembers Fionn MacCumhail and the Salmon of Knowledge. Perhaps the very flesh that they are eating now is imbued with wisdom, which passes then to the eater, however transiently, if the receptivity is there for it. Perhaps the fish's spirit has lived many lives, inhabited higher planes, and even at this moment might be coming into form again as a Tibetan llama.

'I get it from a woman down in Clare,' Ursula explains. 'It's the real thing: fresh wild salmon, wood smoked. You can't beat it really.'

'It's a bit pricey though, isn't it, Mum?' Cordelia says from across the kitchen floor, in another country almost, where she has many tumblers lined up on the wooden counter, half filled with black coffee, whiskey, brown sugar, waiting for the cream which she is now whisking in a big thick-lipped ceramic bowl.

'Well, it is. But she knows me, so I get a bit of bit of a deal. When she has it, that is. She often has nothing, the stocks are so depleted. Sure, they've fished them to death and are still coming back for more.'

'How is your aunt?' Karina asks Alexander.

'My grand-aunt? She's … still very ill,' he says with a glance to Julia not to betray him. He doesn't want to get into it now, doesn't want to put everybody, including himself, through another death. 'She won't last long, but then she's very old…. There's a danger she might leave me some land, so I'm told.'

Philippe looks up again. Perhaps this is a subject that spikes his interest.

'That would be nice,' says Ursula warmly. 'Where is it?'

This is a question which requires some reflection on Alexander's part. He is tempted to respond – Just down the road. But Danny and his father now simultaneously enter the kitchen, by different doors, Danny through the outside door to the backyard, his father through one of the two inside doors that link the kitchen with the remainder of the house. These arrivals alter the political environment into which any utterance would land, but also obviate the requirement for any immediate response to Ursula's question.

'How are the Irish coffees coming along?' Billy Carter asks his daughter. 'The natives are getting restless up there. I'll have to take out my elephant gun for protection if we don't get some alcohol into them soon.'

Ha ha ha, he laughs in staccato bass, his face flushing a deeper shade of red, which is stark against the lifeless grey of his hair and sideburns.

'I think I'll open a bottle of white wine,' he continues, as though this were a major policy decision. 'What do you think, Ursula?'

'Since when do you consult me about your alcohol consumption?' she answers charmingly, poisonously.

'Since the tragedy knocked me for six,' he says slowly, individually eyeing the people at the table, then resting his arrogant gaze on Paul.

Paul blanches visibly.

'Which tragedy?' he asks, panicked into stupidity, looking quickly to Danny to intercede.

Danny is not engaging. Seeing his father, he has postponed proceeding fully into the room and stands slouched against the wall beside the back door like a teenager in a snooker hall.

'The death of my grandson,' says Carter solemnly. 'Isn't that tragedy enough for you?'

'Ah,' says Paul. 'I....'

'Daddy, help me put the cream into the Irish coffees,' says Cordelia, physically taking her father by the elbow and leading him away from the table.

'Anything good in the paper?' Karina asks Philippe, who appears not to hear her.

'Alexander was just telling us that he's coming into an inheritance,' Ursula says to Danny. 'Sit down and have some salmon, love.' She points to the empty chair between herself and Julia.

'So, did your aunt die then?' Danny says in a whisper. He seems bereft of energy and vitality, advancing to the table one slow step at a time. 'Do I owe you an apology?'

'She's still hanging in there,' Julia says to Danny, though facing Alexander with a mischievous smile. 'When he gets the farm, Alex is going to chuck in his job and go back to the earth.'

'I never said that.'

'But it's what you're planning, right?'

'Obviously, you can still read my subconscious as well as ever.'

'Even though he can barely look after a cactus,' Julia says to Paul with a titter.

Danny, laboriously, sits into the chair next to Julia. His mother leans down and kisses him on the top of the head, where his hair is thinning. It is a gesture so perfectly natural that it goes almost unnoticed.

Ursula cuts more bread.

'Come on, Philippe,' coaxes Karina. 'Stop hiding behind that newspaper. Or at least tell us what's going on. There must be a morsel of gossip or scandal in there somewhere. It can't all be stocks and shares.'

Philippe lifts his face to her with an amused pout, and this time speaks:

'You'd be surprised how racy stocks and shares can be.'

'Don't get him started,' calls his wife, as she carefully pours the whipped cream into the first of the coffees, over the back of a hot silver spoon, held diligently in place by her ageing father.

Alexander encounters Aoife sitting on the steps in front of the main door of Knockboy, staring out over the dreary field that runs in a gently sloping hill down toward the public road. Above the field, above and beyond the rough border of dark gnarled trees at the bottom of the hill, the sky is filled with grey blanket cloud at medium altitude. Only a few patches of clear blue transcendent space remain. The afternoon has descended into joylessness.

'Hey there,' he says, sitting down beside her on the step.

'Hi,' she responds in a hoarse, zombified voice.

Aoife is heavily drugged, on prescription pills obtained by Alexander from the local pharmacy on the morning the baby died. The doctor who finally told her formally that her baby was dead also immediately scribbled out a prescription, so that she was not returning home entirely empty-handed. It was not Alexander who went with Aoife to the hospital. He caught up with her when she bolted, walked her home, called an ambulance, which came quickly. The two paramedics gently prised the baby from her grasp. The little bundle was held tightly to her breast, but she wasn't focused on it any more, nor screaming, just rocking gently, perched on the doorstep. She let them take it. Danny helped her up and walked her into the back of the ambulance, followed by one of the paramedics, who, perhaps out of consideration for the mother, held the wrapped-up dead baby as though it were living. Alexander stayed in the house and started to make phone calls. At that stage, there was still no sign of Jasper rising, and Alexander had no desire to wake him.

It occurs to him now, easily, darkly, dramatically, that Jasper in fact may have killed the baby, in the middle of the night, when everyone was sleeping; may have crept into his parents' room, just for the fun of creeping, then decided on a whim to smother the baby with a pillow. There is no evidence for this speculation, apart from Jasper's curious behaviour that morning, in not stirring from his bed despite the howling and commotion of the drama, and in his perplexed understated response to the news when he did finally surface.

'Jasper, I've got something terrible to tell you. The baby died in the night.'

To which Jasper said nothing, standing in the kitchen in a T-shirt, underpants and socks, looking really exhausted, as though he hadn't slept at all, scratching the side of his head.

'I have to have some cornflakes,' he finally said, turning away to look for a bowl.

'Did Cordelia send you out?' Aoife asks, pausing to clear her throat, coughing weakly into a loosely clenched fist, then laughing oddly. Her eyes gleam darkly of chemicals. Her face is covered with thickly applied make-up. Her lips are shrunken and dry. 'She thinks I'm going to top myself. The truth is: I'm too stoned to top myself. Anyhow, I'm not the type. I'm more of a murderer if anything. . . . Murderess.'

He is fascinated in this moment by how shrivelled her lips are, how pale and waxy. He imagines inflating them with a bicycle pump, smoothing out the wrinkles. You would need a really tiny pump connection, not quite nanotechnology, but something seriously miniature.

'I reckon murderer is like actor,' he observes. 'It can apply to both sexes.'

'Have you got a cigarette?'

In searching for his cigarettes, he takes out his mobile (in silent mode) and sees that he has three missed calls from his mother and two new text messages, one indicating voice mail, the other from Luke at work. He clicks open the text from Luke. *Neville gone mad.*

Distributing slanderous leaflets at front door. Personnel stopped him. Know you're at funeral. But thought should know. He quits the message, opens it again, reads it again, quits, puts the phone back in his pocket, finds his cigarettes and lighter. He takes a cigarette from the pack and instinctively puts it first into his own lips to light for her. The smoke tastes harsh to him. He doesn't want it.

'Will I tell you a funny story?' he offers as he passes the cigarette across.

'Go on,' she responds indifferently.

'You have to conceive of a really remote corner of Siberia, an ugly snowbound village, where the people are big and beefy, thick-skulled inbred peasants, uneducated, as coarse as you can imagine humans to be. The only real employment is in servicing the local nuclear power plant, which is probably poisoning the water supply.'

'This is a funny story?'

'Well, you have to have a broad understanding of funny. It's a true story by the way. I read it in a magazine at the barber's at the weekend. Actually, it's probably a load of bollocks. Plus I'm embellishing enormously. But I tell you: it really moved me. Two Russian guys get drunk. In the morning they are found with a chainsaw. One of them is missing a leg. The other appears to have cut his own head off.'

'It really moved you,' she says with interest, as a statement rather than a question.

Down at the bottom of the field, where the driveway runs, a red van has emerged from the trees and is on its way up.

'So here's the interpretation,' he continues enthusiastically. 'They skive off from their perimeter-fence security job. It's minus thirty-two degrees Celsius. They're hiding in a hut, smoking tea leaves or yak shit. They come across a few cans of paint thinner and can scarcely believe their luck. They knock back several litres, and then they get into this ridiculous dialogue about who is the toughest. Igor says: I can bang my head off the wall. Dimitri says: I can eat this rusty nail. It escalates to the point where Igor cuts off his finger with a petrol chainsaw that was lying around in the shed. Beat that, you schmuck, he says, whereupon Dimitri cuts off his own leg. Ha, shit-for-brains, I'm the toughest sonofabitch for a thousand miles. Remember they're completely deranged on industrial alcohol. Finally, Igor revs up and slices off his own head. . . .' Alexander breaks into a self-feeding snigger, which quickly becomes a self-loathing snigger. He knows he is being a prick, but cannot find the right pieties for the occasion, and surely Aoife would rather him just be a prick. 'What a hangover, huh.'

Aoife has not joined him in his laughter.

She draws on her cigarette, inhales deeply, holds the smoke in her lungs, exhales; and seems to derive strength from this.

'Julia is worried that you're deteriorating rapidly since she left you.'

'She's not the only one.'

They watch the continuing approach of the red van. It's quite a long route because the driveway loops around the bottom of the hill, cuts back in a long arc, then snakes around again to reach the forecourt, defining what Alexander believes must approximate to an S-shape.

The van speeds noisily onto the forecourt, bits of gravel flying from the wheels, slows, parks in front of the house, within a few yards of where they are sitting. It's a Toyota Hiace, 97 G reg., filthy dirty, with a screechy-looking scrape injury in the panel above the rear wheel nearest them. The driver is a short, stout man in his sixties. The comb-over component of his grey hair has been blown out of place, but he flattens it back with a practised hand as he walks around to the back of the van. He is wearing a white cotton coat, heavily stained with blood around the belly and chest.

'It's the butcher,' Aoife explains. 'They get their meat delivered here. They're too important to go to the shops like everybody else.'

Alexander recognises the man. In fact, he is very familiar. It's Tommy Óg Grady, whom he met yesterday, in passing, as he, Brigid and Mick were on the way out of the hospital morgue and Tommy Óg was on his way in.

This was the first time he was introduced to him, man to man. Previously, as a child, he had encountered Tommy Óg only at funerals, but was briefed in detail on Tommy's supposed villainy, indoctrinated with stories such as the one about how Tommy Óg had cheated poor Maisie into buying a second-hand black-and-white TV for an outrageous price, then later – repeatedly – charged more for repairs on it; or the one about how Tommy Óg stole a fifty pence piece from the mantelpiece in Uncle Mick's house in Dublin.

'You're the very spit of your father,' Tommy Óg gruffly said to him yesterday, crushing Alexander's hand in a ridiculously powerful handshake.

For the morgue visit, to pay his respects to the dead, Tommy Óg was dressed in a tight-fitting blue suit, which emphasised his barrel physique. Today he looks more like the Tommy Óg Alexander knows from family gossip.

It embarrasses Alexander to meet him here in this completely different terrain, and he deals with this embarrassment by jumping to his feet and jogging down the couple of steps to greet Tommy, who has opened the double door at the back of the van and is checking through a plastic crate filled with cuts of meat wrapped in white butcher's paper.

'Tommy Óg, how's it going?'

'What crack did you crawl from?'

This is certainly a different Tommy from the one yesterday in the hospital, who was suitably solemn and reasonably civil. He is ticking off the cuts of meat against a list on a clipboard and does not look up.

'I'm a friend of the family. There's.... A child died. Its funeral was this morning.'

'I'll be seeing you in court,' Tommy Óg says with a hiss, throwing down the clipboard with surprising violence. It clatters off the dirty metal floor of the van. He turns now to face Alexander for the first time, his eyes yellow with age and bloodshot red.

'I don't know what you mean,' Alexander says.

'And let me tell you about this family. These cunts were the landlords. They owned Ballyryan and everything around it for miles. Your great-great-grandmother peeled turnips in the back-kitchen here in the Great Hunger. And what did she get for her pay? The fucking turnip peels.'

Tommy Óg pokes Alexander in the chest with his finger, hard enough for it to hurt considerably without quite constituting physical assault. Alexander staggers backward, straightens himself. He glances up to the steps. Aoife has risen and is entering the house through the front door. Regretting her departure, he observes her back for a moment, her long full red hair stark against her green coat. He doubts she has heard anything.

Tommy Óg has stepped forward after Alexander and is under his nose again.

'In 1915, Billy Carter's uncle – Daniel Carter – knocked up a young girl from Ballyryan by the name of Mary Donovan, who was a maid here, and who happened also to be promised to your Great-uncle Martin. She threw herself off the roof of this very house, split her skull right open in the courtyard out the back, spilled her brains on the flagstones and the dogs came to lap them up. Martin confronted Carter, hit the man a few punches before they restrained him. They beat him like a savage, threw him in jail, gave him the choice of a prison sentence or the Western Front, and he died at the Somme in 1916, fighting for King and Country.'

'So what's your point, Tommy?'

Alexander is angry. The adrenaline has kicked in, and has decided him for fight rather than flight.

'You're too well educated, Vespucci. That's your problem, you and the like of you. You don't know what it means.'

'You're here selling them meat, so what are you talking about?'

'They pay top dollar. I tax them. I wouldn't sup with them. I'd sooner break bread with Lucifer himself. And you can forget your fucking will. I have it trumped. My one is the real one—'

'I have no idea what you're talking about.'

'We'll be back with the solicitor tomorrow morning. This is a sign from hell, meeting you here. I'll wring your neck before you see a blade of grass from that farm. That is my promise, so help me God.'

By two fifteen the following afternoon, the briefing room in the pala-tial Government Buildings on Upper Merrion Street is well filled with journalists, conversing loudly and talking into their mobiles: scruffy press people, among them Dermot O'Hara; business-like radio types with surprisingly cumbersome sound gear; a self-important television crew, busily checking lighting and setting up a camera position.

The seating is arranged in terraces, as in a lecture theatre. At the bottom of the room, in the area reserved for the presenters, Alexander Vespucci – once again shaved and suited up – sits with his boss George Lucey, jabbering nervously as they wait for the Taoiseach and Council Chairman Stephen Banner to arrive and com-mence the press conference.

'So let me get this straight,' George says. 'The day after the poor woman passes away – God between us and all harm – a handful of relatives descend on the solicitor and demand for the will to be read pronto.'

'Exactly. I wasn't there myself because I was at a different funeral with my phone on silent. I didn't hear about it till later. Anyhow, first the solicitor reads the formal will, which he himself witnessed five years ago. Then he goes on to explain – however – that a subsequent will was completed in the run-up to Christmas, written on a piece of ordinary paper, witnessed by a couple who live down the road from Maisie's farm and who seem simply to have been visiting Maisie in the nursing home that day.'

'And that second one leaves everything to you.'

'Pretty much. Apart from the contents of the house. So this does not go down well with the assembled crew. As I hear it, one of them practically leapt across the room to grab the bit of paper out of the solicitor's hand. He was foaming at the mouth, banging on the table, screaming that it was a forgery, that it was extracted from the old woman under duress, that she wasn't in her right mind.'

'And was she in her right mind?'

'I have no idea. Anyhow, then, out of the blue, Tommy Óg – that's the guy who was doing the leaping – says he has another will, at home in his attic, which post-dates and therefore supersedes the second one.'

'And does it?'

'Well, he hasn't produced it yet. He says it's mislaid and he'll have to find it. I imagine he's back at the ranch as we speak with a pencil and a copy book, practising his handwriting.'

'And do you think there is anything for you in this third will?'

George appears to be missing some of the subtleties.

'Somehow I doubt it.'

'So you might be a wealthy man, and then again you might not,' George concludes sagely, as though expertly summarising a complex situation. It is entirely novel for Alexander to gab so much about his private concerns, but George has adjusted well after an initial expression of surprise. 'If I might offer some advice,' he continues. 'It's better to have independent means than not. Employment income can be very unreliable.'

'That must be why we work in the public sector,' Alexander remarks, just as the panelled side door opens and a couple of civil service flunkeys lead a train of eminences into the room: Stephen Banner, in glowing condition; An Taoiseach himself, who is physically bigger than he seems on television; Grace Sharkey, whom Alexander was not expecting and who looks splendid – lean and sharp in a black trouser suit; as well as a number of senior officials, including ferrety Terry Martin, the small angular government press secretary.

The noise level drops a notch. George and Alexander stand to greet the Taoiseach. Banner performs the introductions.

'This is George Lucey, Taoiseach.'

'Sure, George and I go way back,' the Taoiseach says, shaking George's hand, and slapping him on the shoulder at the same time.

'It's hard to kill a bad thing, Taoiseach,' George jokes easily, prompting laughter.

'And this is Alexander Vespucci. He's Senior Economist with the Council, does a huge amount of great work. He has been the engine behind the Council on this one.'

Alexander is surprised and pleased at Banner's introduction. He reaches out his sweaty palm and shakes hands with the Taoiseach, who nods to him respectfully.

'Very nice to meet you, Taoiseach,' he says sincerely, momentarily star struck.

'Compliments on the report, Alexander,' says the Taoiseach. 'I hear it's very good. Of course, I don't actually read these things myself. They just give me the Ladybird version, and I can barely manage that.'

Alexander thinks: You didn't read it, mate; and I didn't write it. Probably even the consultants didn't write it. They subcontracted it out for a meagre fee to some intense solitary bespectacled grunt, who in turn cogged most of it off the internet.

'If anyone quotes me on the Ladybird book, I'll have his bollocks,' the Taoiseach declares more loudly to the general assembly, yielding a big collective guffaw. 'Excuse my language, ladies. I'm a man under pressure. . . . Let's get this show on the road. And by the way, when we come to the questions afterward, I'm not fucking answering anything on Northern Ireland. I have a pain in my bollocks with Northern Ireland. Excuse my language, ladies. So, if you came looking for quotes on the interminable fucking peace process, forget it. We're here to talk about broadband.'

He has such ravenous steely eyes, Alexander thinks. He's a steelie. Alexander doesn't remember ever before having applied such a description to a human being. The term comes from his days of playing marbles in the cul-de-sac when he was six or seven. There were standard glass marbles, beautiful objects in themselves, but worth only one point; gulliers, which were the larger glass marbles, worth three points; and steelies, which were really just ball bearings, whose point value varied depending on size, but which typically was also three. Alexander had always felt that steelies were overvalued, but they were undeniably hard.

As the celebrities are seating themselves, Banner takes up position at the lectern to deliver the presentation that Alexander spent most of the previous week working on, through various iterations. Alexander presses the return button on the laptop in front of him and the screen jolts into action, reflected electronically on the large display screen mounted on the wall behind: *Regional Broadband*

Initiative – Stephen Banner – Chairman – National Economic Advisory Council.

Grace meanwhile has lightly inserted herself in the seat next to Alexander, at the far end of the table from the lectern. This appears to be a matter of circumstance rather than choice, since the remaining seats at the table have been occupied by the Taoiseach and his senior people.

'Keep your hands to yourself,' Alexander whispers to her.

'Stay focused,' she responds, also in a whisper. 'I wouldn't want you to mess it up now.'

'There's not much scope for that. All I have to do is press the arrow button. If I faint from the pressure, you can do it for me.'

'Welcome everyone,' says Terry Martin. 'Thank you all for coming. I'm going to hand over in a moment to Stephen Banner to take us through his presentation on the Regional Broadband Initiative, which this morning was considered and approved by the Cabinet Subcommittee on Infrastructure. The Taoiseach will then give a short address about the Initiative, and finally we'll have a little time for some questions.'

'Can I get in a question at this end, Terry?' calls Dermot O'Hara.

'Why, Dermot? Can you not wait until the end like everybody else? Have you a more pressing engagement elsewhere?'

'That guy really gets on my tits,' Alexander whispers to Grace, indicating O'Hara. 'And by the way, you never sent me the paperwork for the car.'

Grace is oddly forthcoming in her response. She generously shifts toward him to address him more directly, leans forward intimately, causing him to imagine for a panicky moment that she is going to kiss him.

'It's a sort of procedural point,' Dermot O'Hara clarifies.

'He's going to be on your tits a whole lot more in the next few seconds,' she hisses hotly. 'And by the way, I'll be reporting my car stolen. I parked it outside a friend's house at a party. Somebody robbed my key card.'

'Go on, Dermot,' says Terry Martin. 'We're all intrigued.'

'I'd like to ask the Council Chairman if he can confirm that a senior member of the Council's staff has just been suspended pending inquiry into an alleged indecent assault of a younger and more junior member of staff.'

The noise level drops off entirely. There is keen interest all around.

'That strikes me as a somewhat irregular question,' the press secretary observes. 'Perhaps you would care to raise it at a different forum.'

'It's a highly irregular situation,' O'Hara presses more warmly. 'Will the Chairman confirm it or not? I'm not asking for a debate.'

Terry Martin looks to the Chairman with a shrug, indicating that it's his call. The Chairman looks to George for guidance, giving Alexander further cause for fear, since the Chairman has never in Alexander's experience sought guidance from George on any point, at any time. There has obviously been some prior exchange between them on this issue. The back of Alexander's scalp throbs furiously, hotly. George nods to the Chairman. He glances quickly at Alexander with an expression of pain on his face, then leans in too close for a confidential huddle.

'The Neville Lewis situation has gotten out of control,' he explains in a low mutter. 'I was going to tell you later.'

George leaves the huddle. He straightens himself, coughs to clear his throat for speaking, and addresses the room.

'Perhaps I might say a few words on this. A senior official has been suspended, but on full pay—'

'Well, that's all right then,' intervenes the Taoiseach grandly. 'Enough already. If I had a euro for every time I've been accused of sexual harassment, I wouldn't have to take any bribes.' The Taoiseach slaps the table on issuing this witticism and throws back his head, directing a big uproarious laugh to the ceiling. The assembled are divided in their reaction, some joining him for a bit of a giggle, or laughing at him, others stony faced, unamused. 'Here's the thing that gets me though,' he continues. 'What do you have to do in the public sector to be suspended *without* pay?' And he is off laughing again.

Alexander drives slowly up the badly potholed private road that leads from the entrance to the Thorny Valley farm buildings, far more cautious in the BMW than he ever was in the Honda, proceeding at no more than ten or fifteen miles an hour, scrupulously steering around the major cavities, which were washed out rapidly by heavy rains in the first months of winter. The car handles so satisfyingly, he finds himself preferring – on this particular surface – to drive more slowly rather than more quickly. Perhaps he is wishing also to prolong his time with the car, believing as he now does that it will not be with him much longer.

Around twenty cars are parked in rows facing the main outside wall of the stable courtyard. This is more than usual, because of the show-jumping competition. Alexander parks in the first sizeable gap.

He chooses to change into his riding gear in the car. He used to perform this operation in one of the several half-used rooms in the so-called 'office' part of the complex of linked farm buildings, but has recently been scared off by a couple of incidents. The first involved his walking in on Ben and Dodger, the cranky owner and his collie respectively, as they were eating deep-fried chicken and chips. Ben was feeding from a greasy red-and-white snackbox on the table, while Dodger engaged with another on the floor. Alexander stooped to greet Dodger with a friendly tug of the pelt at the back of his neck. The dog barked once, then bit him quickly on the finger with his dirty yellow teeth.

'Dodger is having his tea,' Ben explained flatly, without a hint of apology or defensiveness, all the while gnawing meditatively on a chicken wing.

In the same room, a few weeks later, not long before Christmas, Alexander was putting on his jockstrap, intended to prevent crushing of the rider's testicles between saddle and body, when two or three giggling girlies drifted around the door, one staying on a few seconds longer than politeness allowed, to get in a good peep, though there wasn't really any exposure to speak of, the way he managed it.

The girls – aged about ten or eleven – belong to the lesson before Alexander's. The mother of the peeper, a tall attractive woman, who rides in Alexander's hour, later commented jokingly that he should have made sure to close the door properly when he was changing. Alexander found this comment faintly threatening, and worried that she had been told an unfair account. It was true that the door had not been fully closed, but this had to do with the fact that he didn't feel he had the authority to close it, rather than that he was encouraging visitors. It was the little girl who had lingered in the room. In that sense, she was the one who had behaved inappropriately; but he felt that a repetition of the episode would further implicate him in dubious behaviour.

As he slips out of his clothes, he sees that he is governed by fear, fears.

He does as much as he can in the car seat, then steps out into the cold night and pulls up his dirty cream jodhpurs, shielding himself with the car door. Helena will give out to him for not having made an effort to look clean for the big event. She'll come with her hair all neatly plaited, riding gear immaculate. It's not a fashion show, he will say.

Next come the boots, the green polyester lining of which is ripped in both cases and has to be carefully repositioned before the foot is inserted in order to avoid tedious entanglements. T-shirt. Fleece. Back protector. Stick. He slips the stick into his boot, which makes him feel stylish, and reaches back to the passenger seat to get his black felt-covered hat, the inside rim of which is still damp with the previous week's sweat. Where are his gloves? He smiles when he remembers that he put them into the glove compartment for a joke after the last lesson. He retrieves them. He pulls them on. They didn't have the right size in the shop when he bought them and now his fingers have burst through everywhere, but there is something cool about this, making him feel like an anarchist in winter, plotting to write pamphlets. An anarchist in winter in a stolen BMW. A rare tulip.

Helena rings him on the mobile.

'You're on Comet.'

'That's my night over. I knew they'd put me on Comet, just to round off a beautiful week.'

'You're making it sound like you had a bad week. How could it be a bad week when you came into a big inheritance?'

'*Might* have come into a big inheritance. Might have lost my job also.'

'What do you mean?'

'I'll tell you later. Who are you on?'

'Liath.'

'I don't believe that that is the luck of the draw. You must have schmoozed someone.'

'Moi?'

'Toi.'

'C'est ne pas possible.'

'C'est eminently fucking possible.'

He complains about his week, but inwardly he is feeling fine, strangely at peace with the current configuration of the universe, however it may unfold. He seems to have given up smoking, without trying, and he senses that this is meaningful, that it may prefigure some important shift, though he has no idea what that shift might be. He feels himself on the verge of potentiality.

Around the yard, the mood is electric. The night sky above is luminous blue, imbued with silver tones by a prominent full moon, which affects the animals. In their boxes, the horses are doubly excited, rising above themselves. They understand that something out of the ordinary is occurring: their routine altered; more people around, in high form. Many have their noses poked out over the stable half-doors. They toss their heads to observe with their lateral vision the different proceedings, alert always to the chance of a carrot or an apple, a handful of oats, the possibility of love.

As Alexander enters this space, this atmosphere, his feet close to the ground in the thin-soled, low-heeled riding boots, he experiences a surge of exhilaration. He is enlivened by the smells: the warm body odour of the animals, the sweetness of fresh horseshit, the thin high-pitched fragrance of hay, the nuttiness of oats in water. He is wrapped around and comforted in the tapestry of sound: people calling, horses neighing, doors and bolts clattering as the animals press forward, the restless scraping of shod hooves off stone.

He meets Helena at Comet's box. She is patting his long smooth muscular neck, chatting to him.

'I'm sweet-talking him for you.'

And true enough, the ageing gelding appears to be in relatively mellow form, angling his head forward for a bit of a scratch.

Stiff and generally cranky, Comet is not a horse one would choose to ride. Alexander had him in a lesson before Christmas and became so frustrated by the horse's mute obstinacy that he overused the stick, which is uncharacteristic of him.

'Stop hitting him,' the instructor shouted helpfully from the centre of the indoor arena, which is really just a large barn with a few terraces of benches for spectators at one end. 'You're making him worse. Sit up properly. Go around again in trot, canter at the turn, then earlier into the jump.'

In the next stall along, McGyver is kicking the door, his head high in anger, ears back, lips flared to show his teeth and gums, his smoky eyes wild and frightened. He hammers the door so hard, Alexander himself is scared, thinking that the hinges must give or else that McGyver will injure himself.

'I told you he's psychotic,' he says to Helena.

'He's just jealous of Comet getting the attention,' she remarks, still whispering into the horse's ear, and now gently stroking the narrow surface that runs from the nose up between the horse's eyes. Alexander guesses that horses don't really enjoy being touched on this thin-skinned bony strip, but he says nothing.

A few boxes down, stunted Toby whinnies attractively. He has spotted his pal, the mare Stroller, being led across the yard and is greeting her. Stroller turns her head toward him and grunts crankily, pulling on her rein, but not for a moment believing she will be allowed to go across. A second later, prematurely almost, as though at the flick of a switch, she drops again into her typical groove, continuing reluctantly across the yard, unnoticing, a little depressed.

'Where's Liath?' Alexander asks.

'Someone has her in the outdoor arena. She's on first.'

This is how it works: for fifteen minutes before your allotted time in the competition you take your horse to the outdoor arena to warm up, trotting on different legs, changing into canter, popping over a few unchallenging jumps. Rhythm thus more or less established, you dismount and lead your horse back through the yard to the indoor arena, where you wait nervously at the gate, watching the rider who is before you finish his round.

In the semi-darkness of the cold wooden terraces, the spectators ooh and aah, clapping and cheering appreciatively at the action in the floodlit arena, which is transformed for the night into something that seems almost magical: the introduction of each rider and horse over the tannoy system; the formal course of a dozen or more numbered jumps – singles, combinations, some formidably high, others challengingly positioned, all in some small way individually characterised, all made pretty, the barrels and poles freshly painted, foliage added in decoration. Ben himself would be too tight and too lazy to go to this trouble, but he suffers the efforts of his more enthusiastic employees, and he knows the punters like it.

Each rider is allowed three practice jumps, then the bell goes and he must begin his round.

Comet is always heavy on his feet, a bit arthritic, but this evening feels more responsive than usual. They circle in a rising trot with Alexander tall in the seat, back straight, shoulders square. He has a nice contact with the horse's mouth.

Hitting the seat, he squeezes inward with his calves, rises earlier, pushes Comet forward into a quicker trot. Alexander's heart beats rapidly. His body is working. He is intensely focused on the first jump now, his head already turned to face it so that the animal knows early where they are headed. The spectators are invisible. There is nothing in the universe but Alexander and the horse and the first jump. At the turn, with the rider's inside heel pressing briefly behind the girth, Comet makes a perfect transition into canter. They move in unison. They spring in unison a perfect stride from the jump. They are over cleanly, easily, and focus immediately on the double ahead.

'Good lad,' Alexander says, leaning forward to slap Comet's neck.

Three strides into the double. Over the first. Bounce. Over the second. Back to trot, a little clumsily. Curve into the corner. Into canter again. A long approach into the triple, the first of which is the highest jump of the course.

'Good lad,' he whispers again into the horse's ear. 'You're doin' great.' In his own head, a small clear voice is saying to him: Wooooe na beithígh, wooooe na beithígh. And what it means in this instance is that he should hold it all together, not become over excited, not let the animal get carried away. But he takes this advice too far and almost falters, losing a little momentum in the run-up to the big jump. He can feel the animal hesitate in the second last stride. He squeezes with his lower legs, pushes forward with his seat.

'C'mon,' he calls in a loud grunt at the point of take-off, which is poor horsemanship, but effective. Comet gives extra effort, rises well, clears the jump.

A big cheer from the spectators.

They proceed through the course without incident. Comet is loosening up, his confidence rising. At the final transition into canter, he gives a little skip and a snort, saying: I can do this.

Alexander is the one who loses it. Coming into the last jump, he begins to smile inwardly, thinking forward to the clear round they are going to have. It's a tight turn. He goes in, with Comet not knowing how they are coming out. They turn late. Alexander tries to correct it, but too abruptly, too coarsely. Comet is confused and comes to a stop. Three faults for a refusal.

An aaaah of disappointment from the supporters.

They trot to the outside track to go around again. Alexander is missing his touch, his good contact. He is exhausted now. There is little strength left in his legs. Comet has fallen out of rhythm. He switches into canter again on cue, but with a frightened start, moving too quickly. Coming into the turn, Alexander already knows they are not going to make it. The horse turns later than the rider, awkwardly, unhappily. Alexander presses on hard, but Comet is arriving at the wrong angle and doesn't like the jump. He refuses again, causing

Alexander to slump forward against his neck, where he remains for a couple of seconds, unsure of what to do. Should they go round again? No. It's over. He sits up, recovers the stirrup he lost, his blind toe easily finding it. He touches a finger to the peak of his hat to indicate they are finished.

The spectators clap. Well done, Alexander. Nice one, Comet.

He dismounts. In landing from the jump, the underlying hardness of the arena floor slams painfully through his soles. He is barely able to stand on his sore jelly legs.

'Good fella,' he whispers affectionately into the horse's ear. 'You did your best. I'm very proud of you.'

He draws the reins over Comet's head and begins to lead him around to the gate, patting him on the shoulder. Alexander Vespucci is cracked right open, flooded for some reason with a big nameless love. His limbs quiver. His lips are blubbery. His eyes fill with water, which – from habit – cannot spill. Words of endearment flow from his mouth in prayers unbidden by him, drawn upward to the horse's old ears by a strange reverse gravity, and onward from there to heaven.

'Don't you mind anyone now. Aren't you the fine and handsome prince?'